Praise for

Riding the Wave

"*Riding the Wave* is a book you don't want to miss! It has it all . . . hot-as-hell hero and heroine, intense chemistry both in and out of the bedroom, and sharp, witty dialogue. Tanner and Avalon's story will enthrall you one minute, and then tug on your heartstrings the next. I loved this book, and I think you will, too."

—*New York Times* bestselling author Deirdre Martin

"A sheer delight from start to finish. Brown does a sensational job of getting to the very heart of her main couple. . . . Their chemistry is positively blistering, but what makes this romance unforgettable is the way they challenge and balance each other."

—*RT Book Reviews* (4½ stars, top pick)

"Sex scenes suffused with pulse-pounding intimacy nicely frame this escapist love story."

—*Publishers Weekly*

"[A] fast-paced read perfect for a summer escape."

—*Booklist*

Also by Lorelie Brown

The Pacific Blue Novels
One Lesson (a novella)
Riding the Wave

Ahead in the Heat

A PACIFIC BLUE NOVEL

LORELIE BROWN

A SIGNET ECLIPSE BOOK

SIGNET ECLIPSE
Published by the Penguin Group
Penguin Group (USA) LLC, 375 Hudson Street,
New York, New York 10014

USA | Canada | UK | Ireland | Australia | New Zealand | India | South Africa | China
penguin.com
A Penguin Random House Company

First published by Signet Eclipse, an imprint of New American Library,
a division of Penguin Group (USA) LLC

First Printing, January 2015

ISBN 978-0-451-46843-7

Printed in the United States of America
10   9   8   7   6   5   4   3   2   1

You went away,
but you came back.
All my love.

Chapter 1

Sean Westin had been to physical therapists before. Once, he'd sprained his knee on the North Shore of Hawaii and had to check in with a therapist near his home turf in San Sebastian for three months. But that guy had worked out of a standard, stucco-walled complex across the street from the hospital. The building Sean had just now pulled up in front of was about as far from a medical office as possible.

Sean double-checked his in-dash GPS. Right address. The California bungalow was where he was supposed to show up. The place looked more like a cottage than an office. There was a shallow porch decorated with white wicker chairs and a multitude of potted plants that bloomed green or sprouted pink and blue flowers. Cupolas peeked out of the shingle roof, hinting at a second story. Lining the front of the porch were bushes with purplish pink blossoms the size of Sean's fist.

Getting out of the car wasn't pleasant. He moved slowly, bracing himself as he reached to unbuckle the seat belt. Didn't make a difference. A dull ache of pain spiked from his collarbone and radiated down his shoulder. The black sling he wore inhibited movement. The doctors said he'd need to work on mobility if he wanted to be able to regain his spot on the surfing World Championship Tour in time to keep his place in the top half of competitors.

He wanted to regain his spot.

He wanted to badly. His entire career had been about consistency and determination. He had the skills, and he also had the means to move up.

This should have been Sean's year. The reigning champion, Tanner Wright, had retired to open a surf school and boink his supersweet girlfriend, so the rankings had all been given a sweet shake-up. If Sean didn't move into the top ten this year, he'd have to take a good long, hard look at what he was doing. Maybe he wasn't meant to be the 'CT winner.

Sean wouldn't allow that. It didn't fit his plans.

A six-inch plaque by the doorbell confirmed yet again that he was in the right place. The words SANTA BARBARA REHAB were on the first line, with ANNIE BAXTER, DPT inscribed below. But when he rang the doorbell, there was no response. He rang it again, hearing peals echo through the small house.

He wasn't completely surprised, since he didn't have an appointment. But he did have information that said Annie Baxter could always be found at her offices on Saturday mornings because she ran an unofficial drop-in program for disadvantaged teenagers.

He sighed, but damned if that didn't send another spike of pain through him as his shoulders shifted. He ground his back teeth together. He needed to talk to Baxter. It wasn't too much to expect the doctor to be where she was supposed to be.

A hollow, wooden sound caught his attention. Even though he hadn't heard the noise in person for at least five or six years, he'd have known it anywhere. Skateboard wheels rolling over wood. More particularly, over a wooden ramp.

It was coming from the back of the house. He followed the echo down the porch stairs, then down a path lined with foxtail grasses that were lush and verdant despite the barely waking spring.

The backyard was skater heaven. The Japanese wave painting Sean could never remember the name of decorated the sloping sides of an empty old-school-style pool. At the far end, a ten-foot-tall half pipe filled the only bit of spare flat area.

A kid dropped his board from the table into the vert, knees bending into the dip. He slipped effortlessly back and forth, getting higher and higher until he finally launched into the air at the other end. He kept it easy, barely touching his board as he flew. He wore a helmet and dark blue hoodie that swallowed his small frame and contrasted with his slim-cut jeans.

Sean waited as patiently as he could until the skateboarder came to earth and drew to a stop. "Hey, bro, have you seen Dr. Baxter?" The skateboarder paused for a second before pulling off the black helmet and turning around. Stubby dark ponytail. Delicate features with wide-set eyes.

Sean immediately rearranged his assumptions. "Sorry, I mean—may I have a moment of your time, Dr. Baxter?"

One finely arched eyebrow lifted even higher. "I don't deal with pros."

Being recognized wasn't anything new for Sean. The first time, he had been at the mall in Brea, eating tacos at the food court, when a couple dudes fell all over themselves talking about his first Prime tour win. And that had been before his pro career really took off, when he'd still been biking himself to the beach on the weekends and returning home to his mother's filthy house.

He hoped he never really got used to being famous. Because damn, did it still feel good. His chin lifted and he probably smiled some. The hot satisfaction lifted his mood so high that he could almost forget about the constant throb that ached through his shoulder.

"So you know who I am?"

She made a soft little *psh* sound and tucked her helmet under her arm as she started toward the back door of the house. "Everyone in California knows who you are. And everyone who knows surfing knows you were drunk and shouldn't have been on the water. Not to mention what the fallout could do to your career."

That was the downside. Everyone *did* know what a douche he'd been in Bali. He'd been drinking mai tais with a pretty waitress, and he had taken a rollicking turn toward trouble from that moment. He knew he should never have surfed, but he did it anyway because he was such a fucking sucker for a pretty face.

His fists curled, but he immediately drew a deep breath as he tried to loosen up. Tight meant pain lately. He'd learned his lesson.

"Then you know how desperate I am for help."

She slanted a gaze at him out of the corners of her eyes, dropping her board to the ground and her helmet to a folding chair. "I've heard hints."

"I have a tweaked collarbone. It's causing some shoulder impingement. There's more technical stuff, but I'd have to have the files sent over to you. I have six weeks. I can't let recovery take any longer than that."

The laugh she dropped into the air between them sounded almost bitter, and completely disbelieving. Her mouth was small but plump. She was kind of small all over. If she stood next to him, she'd come only to his sternum. "Recovery for a collarbone injury could take up to sixteen weeks. Maybe longer if you're foolish and push yourself harder than you need to."

"I can't allow that long." He moved toward her, but not too close. Women were delicately balanced creatures, and there was a fine line between charming them and being an icky kind of invasive. "Six weeks keeps me out of competition at Bells Beach and in Rio. I'm missing the Margaret River Pro this very minute. Six weeks means I'm in the water in time for Fiji. I have no choice with Margaret River and Bells Beach, and I'm going to have to choke that up. I can probably even afford zeroing August's event. Probably. But I have to get back on the 'CT by Fiji. I can't afford to drop out of the top twenty-two. Considering that I'll still be in recovery, I'll have a hard enough time requalifying for next year."

"I can give you references to three very good physical therapists. They have a practice on the other side of San Sebastian."

"I don't want very good. I want *the best*." And according to every bit of research he'd culled in the week since his injury, that was Annie Baxter.

But she didn't give a crap. She wasn't even bothering to look at him, which was like nails on a chalkboard to Sean. He thrived on attention, and he usually got it. He wasn't above admitting that.

She pulled the blue sweatshirt off, revealing a cream button-down shirt with minuscule puff sleeves. Even though the blouse was completely feminine, the way it was paired with slim, low-slung jeans emphasized her distinct lack of curves. She had little breasts and boyish hips. Exactly the opposite of Sean's type, but that didn't seem to matter when he looked at that mouth of hers. Adorably filthy. "Then you're screwed."

But Sean knew there was one thing Dr. Annie Baxter cared a whole hell of a lot about. Finding info on that had been dead easy. He tipped his head down, looking at the petite pixie, and he found himself using his silkiest tone of voice when he said, "Do you want your drop-in center funded?"

Her eyebrows flew up toward her hairline as she whipped back to face Sean. "You've got a spare three million sitting around?"

He smirked. Everyone had a price, even if they thought themselves the noble type. It was only a matter of finding it. "I do. Do you want it?"

She gave another of those laughs and stuck her hand out, palm up. "Sure. Right here. You can make the check out to the Clear Ride Foundation."

"Nothing is free."

She dropped into one of the wicker seats, hands resting on the arms. Her legs stretched out in front of her, as short as they were. She crossed them at the ankles and laced her fingers in front of her stomach. Her belt buckle was round and yellow, with a black X on it. "You mean to pay me three million for physical therapy for a collarbone injury?"

"Sure. Is that an X-Men belt buckle?"

Bright red washed across her cheeks, making her look both older and younger at the same time in a mix of innocence and chagrin. "I know, I know. I'm a total geek."

He shrugged, but instantly regretted it when pain smacked him upside the shoulder again. When he pushed too far, the hurt washed all the way through his chest and upper back. He was gonna be schooled out of shrugging right quick. Fuck, he was tired. "I recognized it. That's gotta be equally geeky."

She didn't answer for a long moment, and at first Sean wondered if he'd gone too far. He'd never been a hundred percent sure which side of the social lines he walked. It wasn't like he'd had a normal childhood, which was when most people learned normal human interactions. He'd come from shit. Literally.

"Do you know *why* I'm the best?" Her eyes narrowed, and a line knit between her straight brows. "Because I'll own you. Your diet and your exercise. How many times a week you get to surf. Whether you'll go running or do a stair stepper. How much you stretch, and *precisely* when you do it. How often you see me, or any other *anything*. Including massages."

"Deal."

"Including sex."

"Deal."

She scoffed. "You're fucking full of it. This is one of the reasons why I don't work with pros. You're too damn full of yourselves. You don't even stop to question whether you can handle it."

His impulse was to cross his arms over his chest, but of course that was out. He settled for widening his stance and tucking his hands in the pockets of his slacks. "There's one thing you don't understand. I *will* stay in the 'CT this year. The only question is whether I permanently fuck myself up in the process."

Her mouth set into a mulish knot, but she pushed out of her chair and stepped toward him. "You're an arrogant, foolish asshole."

"I am." He grinned, because he knew her body language said she was unwillingly intrigued. "But I'm an arrogant, foolish asshole who's your patient."

Chapter 2

Annie wasn't sure why she kept arguing ten minutes more. When one protested too much, it took on the distinctive *did-not, did-too* flavor of being eight and on the school yard playground all over again. Except that was the problem. Sean Westin made her feel about as self-assured as she'd been at eight. What a massive dork she'd been. Wearing blue kneesocks that were so big on her petite frame she'd had to pull them all the way up to her thighs, and a red corduroy skirt. No girls in the nineties owned corduroy. Ever.

She'd been painfully aware of her lack of coolness. In sixth grade, Elizabeth Manhein, also known as the Perfect Blonde, had teased Annie because she'd been the last one to shave her legs. The cool kids always made sure the not-cool kids knew their status. She'd thought she'd made it by the end of her senior year when she was considering her own pro surf career, but then Terry had cleared up those misapprehensions—and set her right back where she belonged.

So standing less than five feet from Sean Westin—

the Sean Westin—made the backs of her knees sweat. It made a ball of nerves twist up and take over her whole stomach. There wasn't much she could do about it, except hang on to the false bravado she'd cultivated over the past fifteen years.

But goddamn, was he cute. More than that. Gorgeous. *Beautiful* in a way that was perfectly masculine. His dark hair was the same length as his artfully scruffy beard. His eyes were so crisply blue, they reminded her of the time she'd been to Cancun for spring break. She'd spent most of the trip dreadfully sober since she remembered all too well how vulnerable alcohol made her, and she'd spent her time watching her friends make asses of themselves in bars. Hanging out at the beach during the day had brought back sharp memories of her own near miss of a pro surfing career. The water had been the same perfect blue as Sean Westin's eyes, and there was something hauntingly beautiful about them.

After another minute or two of arguing, Annie threw up her hands. "Fine. I'll take you on. You might as well come in and fill out the new-patient paperwork."

Turning on her heel, she stomped through the back door, wincing when she saw the state of her mudroom. She'd left piles of gear in the corner from the last time she'd led the kids on a hike at San Onofre—and someone had left a stack of swim fins in the giant sink. The laundry room wasn't much better. She kept donation clothes on hand for any of the drop-in kids who needed them. It was ridiculous how long one of them would wear the same sweatshirt before admitting he didn't own another one and that was the reason it stank. But that was why Annie hadn't caught up on laundry in the past nine months.

And she didn't think she was projecting, but it seemed like she could feel the weight of Sean's disapprobation like claws digging into her shoulders. He didn't like what he was seeing. Well, too damn bad, he was the one who'd come to her.

He was the one who'd called her the best. She bit back a little smile at that memory. The past four years of private practice hadn't been easy. On more than one occasion, she'd been tempted to throw her DPT degree away and run the shelter full-time. Letting someone else direct her practice would have been so much easier than trying to balance all the pieces of her life. But she'd worked damn hard for the privilege of her physical therapy career too.

If Sean didn't like how messy she kept things, he could suck eggs.

She was thankful the back section of her clinic was much tidier. She pushed open the door to a corridor between consultation rooms, then led him into the front office, which had been created out of a spacious dining room. It was a little unusual to use a residence as an office, but it'd been converted in the seventies by a general practitioner who wanted to work out of his home. Annie hadn't been able to resist the Craftsman charm. The old GP's backyard pool had been the absolute capper.

She had drained it straight away.

Fishing her key ring out of her pocket, she unlocked her secretary's filing cabinet and pulled out a new-patient packet. "Here. Most of these you can take home and fill out, but it'll be helpful if you could sign a records request from your doctor."

"Writing isn't so easy right now."

She managed not to roll her eyes. "Think around the corner, Sean."

"I'm right-handed. Exactly what do you want me to do?"

Pulling out the sheet she needed immediately, she laid it out along with a pen that she pulled from a cup on Cynthia's desk. It had a fake flower taped to it to keep patients from accidentally wandering away with it. "I need it legible, not pretty."

He opened his mouth as if to protest, but then shut those pretty lips. Wise man. He dug his phone out of the pocket of his slacks. God, even the fact that he wore slacks with an obviously tailored button-down shirt on a Saturday morning meant she shouldn't be messing with the dude.

She was probably the foolish one. This was ridiculous. She'd had a tiny taste of the pro sports world, and it had been bitter. Awful. She'd stayed away ever since, and she got enough work with regular people who had it hard getting insurance companies to pay for physical therapy. Bending her personal ethics because he was offering such an exorbitant price . . . She didn't want to think of what that said about her. It probably wasn't flattering.

Did doing awful things still count for good if she had the right motives behind them? Probably not. There was all that talk about the road to hell being paved with good intentions and the like.

Sean finished the form and pushed it back across the desk. "There. If the doc doesn't recognize my signature, I guess he can call me."

"These kinds of forms are often mostly for record keeping."

"Covering your ass. Lovely," he said with dry wit. "Isn't that exactly what I want to hear about the state of my health care?"

She took the sheet and flipped it around, scanning through the information. "The state of your health care is just fine. I know your doctor. He's good."

"Like I said, I don't want good. I want the best." He said it with a wry smile, one that said he was aware of how arrogant he sounded. He dripped attitude. He was someone who deliberated every step he took and knew how to get what he wanted precisely when he wanted it.

She was going to have a hell of a time tipping his life upside down. Everyone knew about Sean Westin. His ability to be a party boy extraordinaire as well as a championship surfer made him something of a marvel. But now he'd pushed too far. He'd been too reckless. He was going to have to do more than a few stretches to make sure he didn't lose his grip. "Tell me about the accident."

"Didn't you read Nate's account?"

Nate Coker was his Coyote surfing team comember. The guy had tweeted about Sean's busted collarbone and had posted a few photos to Instagram. Injury in the days of social media. That wasn't even counting the bloggers who'd reported on it in the following days. Sean Westin was big business as a man who'd made his face familiar on a household level. At one point, he'd even done national commercials for top-shelf vodka. Pity his career wasn't keeping up with his moneymaking. He was a midrange surfer. But, of course, being midrange on the World Championship Tour still said a lot.

She crossed her arms over her chest and leaned against the waist-high customer counter. She wasn't used to a patient being on this side of the desk. "Humor me. I ask that every patient tell me about the precipitating incident, when possible. It gives me clues about the nature of the injury and also about the nature of the person. The ways to go forward are often myriad. It helps to be able to narrow things down."

"Anyone ever told you that you're awfully smart?"

"More times than I can count."

He hitched one lean hip on the side of the desk. His thumb ran over the seam down the front of his slacks, over and over again. She wondered if he realized the nervous tell, or if he was one of those guys who thought he was perfectly put together at all times. She preferred the men who had at least some level of self-awareness. They were more manageable and didn't require her to take a baseball bat to their heads.

"I know people think I was drunk, but I wasn't." His gaze burned into hers, filled with intensity, almost as if he were willing her to believe him.

As well he might, since her belief was a little bit on short order. "Nate said you'd been drinking in a dive bar."

"Because he'd been drinking. And I'd had a drink. I'm not going to deny that."

His mouth set into a flat line. His lips weren't particularly finely shaped—he was missing much of a bow at the top of his mouth. But there was something about the way he talked. . . . It was almost as if he was considering every single word, though at such a fast clip that most people wouldn't notice. He was . . . deliberately fast. That was it, as if he were slinging the patois of a carny barker.

"You know what they say about driving. Even one is too many." She baited him deliberately, trying to see if he'd rise to the occasion. Or if he'd deal calmly.

"I had two over the course of the morning—"

"Morning?" she repeated. "Seems like that's pretty hard-core if you're drinking before noon."

He shook his head. "It was Bali. Beach life. It's normal to start drinking around ten thirty, because we'd been *up* since four and would probably crash out at dusk. It's like life on a deserted island when you're filming."

"But your island wasn't deserted. There was a pretty local girl."

"Her name was Eoun, and yeah, she *was* really pretty. But she was really nice too. When a few locals came in and started giving her shit, I stepped in."

The laugh burst out of her abruptly and awkwardly. She shoved her fingers over her mouth, smashing her lips against her teeth, but she couldn't hold the laugh in. "Did you challenge them to a surf off?"

He shot her a look from under his brows that said

he was much less than amused. "Very funny, Dr. Baxter."

"Sorry, but I just don't see the leap from a waitress getting hassled to you injuring yourself surfing."

"I have a reputation for fighting. I've been sanctioned twice."

"I know," she said, beaming a slightly obnoxious smile at him. "Trust me. It's on the mental list I'm compiling of things to address immediately."

The unimpressed look didn't go away. "I couldn't afford to get in a fight. I'm too low in the rankings this year to cope with point penalties from the ASP."

The Association of Surfing Professionals—Annie knew that one. She didn't follow the World Championship Tour devotedly anymore, but she knew the ASP still managed it. Sanctions from them would cause any competitor problems, most especially one who was in danger of not making next year's cutoff. "Fighting is a poor relief for conflict, anyhow. It usually only serves to deepen tensions."

"You've obviously never been on a boat with ten men filming a surf vid for three weeks. Fighting is practically like playing poker. It's a means of passing the time."

"Thanks for putting a name to my worst nightmare. I hate violence."

His mouth tweaked up at the corners. "Certain kinds of violence are recreational."

She narrowed her eyes at him. There was something about the way he'd said that, giving weight to the phrase, that made her nipples tighten and her stomach turn wobbly with sudden heat. Good Lord, that was such a bad idea, she didn't even know how to express it. She didn't need to be sexually attracted to a client. Especially since that client had already put a strange twist on their relationship by offering a fee that verged on bribery.

Business. Therapist and patient and nothing else. She pushed herself back into proper territory. "Get on with the story, please."

"You're a hard case, Doc." But he gave a little nod. "It sounds completely dorky, like a Gidget movie gone wild, but yeah, it practically was a surf off. They were talking smack, and I started talking smack back. I had a stack of borrowed boards anyway, since I'd left my favorites in Australia for the Margaret River Pro. The next thing I knew, we were all out in thirty-foot surf. It was just short of needing a tow-in."

"You were able to paddle out." She made a note on a small pad at the counter.

"I was even able to surf one wave. Then a second. But it was the third one. I dropped off the lip too hard and came down on the front. My knee twisted, and my board slipped. I free-fell into the front of the wave."

"I assume that wasn't enough on its own to cause the injury?"

He shook his head. "I had my arm out for balance. The wave pulled me one way while the ocean sucked me down."

"Were you concussed?"

"No. I didn't black out either. I remember every second of the pain."

"Did you receive treatment in Bali?" She scribbled more on the pad, but she wasn't really taking much in the way of notes. Every word of his story was scratched with more than just his pain—his determination and fire snapped through every word. She was doing her best to keep her head in the right frame of mind and not watch his eyes burn.

"Some first aid, but Coyote flew me back to the States as soon as possible."

"Good enough." She capped her pen. "Mr. Westin, I look forward to the next eight weeks."

He leaned forward, coming away from the desk. His shoulders were wide underneath his pale blue button-down shirt. The sling did nothing to dent his image. He hadn't taken even a nibble of her bait when she'd pushed him about the initial incident, but at this he suddenly seemed like a live wire. "Six weeks. I need time to get my game together."

"Eight," she replied calmly. "I won't promise you six. My program will be intensive, difficult, and, as it is, shorter than I'd like it to be."

He bit back a sigh. The lines of his neck were sharp as blades. "Then I suppose you should call me Sean. It seems like we're going to be spending a lot of time together."

Chapter 3

Sean knew he had issues. Plenty of them. Well, even that was hedging it a bit. More like he had a duffel's worth of issues wedged into an overnight bag. Things were busting out at the edges.

Like the fact that he didn't want Annie in his house. It wasn't anything personal against her. Actually, she seemed pretty cool so far. Less like a stuffy doctor and more like a . . . life coach, maybe. She was slightly snarky, and it almost seemed like her sarcasm oozed out around her words unintentionally. Sean liked that. His strange upbringing meant he sometimes missed that people put up false fronts. He took them at face value, accepting their word that they were exactly the person they presented themselves to be. If he believed the faces he was presented with, people would give him the same courtesy. And he'd had plenty of secrets to keep as a kid and into his teen years.

Which was still related to not wanting anyone in his place. He was sitting on the cement brick wall that lined his short driveway before it dipped into the underground garage. His legs bounced, heels lifting off the backs of his flip-flops. The fingers of his left hand sought purchase on the wall at his hips, but each digit only scraped over the concrete. He had a bad habit of biting his nails to the quick.

Telling himself to get a fucking grip didn't help much. The front of his house wasn't designed to be useful for pacing, but he pushed up from his seat anyway. He managed, going ten feet one way by picking around carefully balanced beach plants chosen to emphasize the local habitat. He'd paid a lot for the gardening. He'd paid a lot for the house, too, so it had seemed only fair.

He liked his place. It was custom built, and he'd picked everything from the land to the roof plus everything in between. The labor of love had been done long distance as he traveled to Bali and Teahupoo and Indo during construction. There had been walk-throughs when he was in town, and making decisions via Skype when he wasn't.

It was kind of ironic that he'd put so much effort into a home, considering what had once happened to the house he'd grown up in.

Annie's surprisingly beat-up Nissan Pathfinder pulled in alongside the curb. The SUV had once been dark red, but its fading topcoat made it look closer to gray, and the back right window had a two-foot-long crack running through it. When she hopped out, Annie craned her neck to take in the full view of the tall, narrow-fronted beach house.

"Nice ride, Doc," he drawled. It came out more sarcastic than he'd intended, but that was probably his nerves coming through. "At least I know my three million won't be wasted on fast cars and loose women."

She leveled a dark-eyed gaze at him. Her eyebrows lifted; then her lashes flicked back toward her SUV. "Maybe not fast cars. But I don't think we've ruled out loose women, have we?"

He choked down the laugh that sprang up from nowhere, but he wasn't sure why he bothered. She made him laugh. That ought to be a good thing. But there was something about her that left him slightly on guard and unable to drop his defenses. She was his therapist, and there would be forced proximity to navigate. She wasn't one of his usual, no-strings-attached sort of girls.

Why he was thinking even slightly in that direction he had no idea. She was about as far from those usual girls as possible. He liked them tall, so they looked appropriately dramatic when he walked the red carpet with one on his arm. Their blond hair helped balance his darkness when it came to the surfer image he carefully cultivated. He didn't *look* like a world championship surfer . . . and Annie didn't look like a world championship surfer's date.

In fact, she looked more like one of the street kids she sheltered at her center than anything else. Another pair of skinny jeans clung to her narrow hips. Her hoodie was still a dark color, but this time it had a silk screen that suggested a female comedy duo for presidential election. Sean would vote for them, considering the newest scandal pushing through Congress lately. They seemed more legit to him.

"You're too casual for loose women," he pointed out. "They wouldn't take a second look at you."

"Not you, though, right, Sean?" She meandered up the short walkway. "You're just right for that type."

"Maybe they're just right for me."

"Are you going to let me in?"

He kept his smile as casual as he could, but there was no denying his flinch. Christ, he needed to suck it up. He reached past her to push open the door. She was little, coming only to the top of his chest, but her spine never bent. She was steel and wire as they were knotted together in the small alcove. Her chin lifted up farther.

"I'm still not sure why this is necessary," he groused.

She sailed past him into the foyer. Her hair was caught up in another of those snubby ponytails, but the front was a dark fringe that hung into her eyes and covered her ears. She glanced back over her shoulder, but he barely got more than a flash of brown eyes completely ringed in black eyeliner and a smudge of black shadow. "If you're going to start arguing at this point, I might as well walk away."

"Three million."

She shook her head, shoving her hands in her back pockets. She stood in the middle of his living room, where slanted ceilings drew the eye to two-story windows. Though she wore shiny black boots, they had a little rim of pink between the top and the sole and pink laces up the front. "This isn't going to work like that, Sean. You're donating the cash to my center. Your choice. If it doesn't come from you, I'll go back to my five-year plan. No harm, no foul. I'm not going to become your lapdog because of the money."

"Seems a shame. You're about the size of a lapdog."

Her head tilted to the side, that dark brown hair shifting. "You're being childish. Is your injury causing you any problems? Does your shoulder hurt?"

His first impulse was to tell her to fuck off. He was being childish because she pushed him to extreme responses. She was *standing here*. In his *house*.

But since hitting adulthood, he'd made a conscious decision to not lie. He'd been so desperate throughout his childhood that he'd been forced to lie all the time. Constantly. Every breath in lunchrooms and at recess had been a lie while he pretended that everything was just fine, absolutely normal.

He didn't lie anymore. "Hurts like a son of a bitch. I tried to roll over when I woke up, before I remembered what an idiot I was."

"Not your best moment. Have you taken anything?"

He shook his head. "I don't like the pills. They're strong."

"They're strong for a reason. Because the pain is strong. Where do you keep them?"

"Kitchen."

That was enough for her. She spun on one booted heel and marched toward the back of the house, peeking in every room as she went. The kitchen was sleek and clean. The cabinets were glassed in, with an edge of chrome. He'd considered wood but wanted to avoid a cutesy feel. Even the fridge was glass-fronted, with stainless steel drawers beneath for the freezer.

Annie whistled. "Jesus. Between the size of this joint and this room, I don't even want to think about how much your maid service runs."

"I have a housekeeper."

Her mouth tucked into a smile on one side. "That doesn't really surprise me, somehow. Is she a little old lady with gray hair who leaves a cake out on your birthday?"

He snagged the bottle of pills from the cabinet next to the six-burner stove and leaned against the waist-high butcher-block-topped island. "Actually, she's a he. A twenty-seven-year-old guy named Keiji who usually leaves a bottle of Patrón out on my birthday. He's not one for cake, but he makes a really fucking killer chicken alfredo."

"Yeah. Okay, I suck for that one. Stereotypes for the win." She winced and sighed, rubbing her fingertips over her brow. "Ugh, I feel like shit now."

He touched his knuckles to her upper arm in the gentlest punch ever. "Nah, don't be so hard on yourself. I know Keiji is unusual. When I put out an ad for a housekeeper, I was expecting a little old lady too. Keiji was putting himself through his second year of college at UC Irvine and needed the money badly. Now he's worked for me for eight years."

"He stuck around after he was finished with school?"

"I pay really well." As well he should. Sean's standards were crazy high, and he liked his things in a particular order. Keiji had come with Sean from a rented apartment on Twelfth Street to this house once it had been built. Disruption was unnecessary.

Seemingly without thinking, she grabbed a glass from one of the open-view cabinets and filled it with cool tap water. She set it in front of him, took the pill bottle from his hands, and then consulted both the dosage instructions and her watch. "It's seven thirty. If one isn't enough, you can have one more at eight thirty, as needed. Otherwise about an hour after lunch."

"Yes, ma'am," he teased. But when she tipped one capsule into the lid and held it out to him, he took it obediently. "I just don't like how fuzzy they make me."

"If you don't take them, your body has to concentrate on mitigating pain rather than healing itself. You'll only delay the process. If you hurt, you take them. End of story."

"You're a bossy little thing."

She grinned. "You bought bossy with your three mil. Feel like a good bargain?"

His smile surged up in response to hers. "Depends. What are you doing here at half past seven?"

"We're going to have a purge." She opened the door next to the fridge, obviously banking on its being a pantry. "Normally I'm an advocate of balanced living, including balanced eating. But if you want immediate results, you're going to have to concentrate on a diet that operates at the highest possible nutrition level."

She was right, but his pantry was basically stripped bare compared to the average person's stores. Sean didn't cook much, preferring to dine out at expensive restaurants. When he was home, he asked Keiji to cook with locally sourced, fresh products. It kept things easier, with the added benefit of avoiding stockpiling too much of anything in his house. "You're not going to find a secret stash of Little Debbies, if that's what you're looking for."

She flashed a cheeky smile over her shoulder.

"Little Debbies are your weakness, huh? I'll have to remember that for an end-of-treatment celebration."

He could think of something else she could give him for an end-of-treatment prize. Maybe something involving the ass she was showing off by bending at the waist to look at the lower shelves of his pantry. It was a small ass but sweetly curved enough for his hand. He had the instant, absurd impulse to pat her.

Wouldn't that go over well? She'd probably punch him. Or maybe he'd get off lucky and she'd just walk out, probably with several snarky comments. He hid his involuntary chuckle against a loose fist.

She jerked upright. "What was that?"

"Nothing. What *are* you looking for?"

"No particular item. I'm trying to get an idea of your general taste and where we can proceed from here." She poked around in his fridge next, and that made his back teeth set on edge. He wasn't used to anyone touching his *stuff*. Which, Christ, sounded way too much like his mother talking inside his head. He took a slow, deep breath and pushed it out again. This was no big deal. Nothing to worry about.

Possessions were simply objects, nothing more. They weren't memories in solid form, and they had only the emotions people imbued them with. That was it.

Pity his mom had never been able to think of them like that.

Chapter 4

Annie had never been in a house quite like this one. It was . . . gorgeous. There were no two ways about it. Sleek and modern, every line was intentionally chosen for maximum impact. Glass glittered everywhere, but it didn't make the space feel cold. Touches like the butcher-block-topped island stretching seven feet through the center of the kitchen warmed the rooms. An abstract mosaic with Moroccan flavor topped the archway leading into the dining room.

The contents of the kitchen had been a different kind of surprise. She'd expected plenty of junk food, metabolized by his obviously devoted surfing career and crammed in among dinners out. Most of the pros she knew from her days before school had been like that. They'd justified eating crap and drinking their brains out by the fact that they surfed or swam or skateboarded five hours a day. They didn't take into account the long period spent chilling on their boards, floating on the water as they waited for the "perfect" set, or the long-term detriment to their cholesterol, kidneys, and liver. Especially their livers, considering the drinking.

She'd been there. She surfed with the best of them, for a while. The levels of indulgence were infuriating.

She should know. When she was fifteen, she'd been seduced by the bright lights of going pro. There was a well-trod path to the goal of sponsorship. She'd kept on that track for three years.

Getting screwed over in an epic way tended to clean the stars out of a girl's eyes.

It wasn't as if a gorgeous house like this would have come if she'd gone pro, anyway. The women's circuits had less than twenty percent of the prize money of the men's World Championship Tour. She'd have been fighting for accolades and attention, and that wasn't enough for her, considering the costs demanded in return. She needed more.

She needed to do more.

So she'd used surfing to nail a scholarship to UC San Diego. While she was there, she'd surfed her ass off in the National Scholastic Surfing Association for her team . . . but once she was done, she was done. She'd walked away from any hint of pro surfing and taken her shiny new degree off to med school. It had been the right thing.

Pro surfers had drive that took them to a higher level—and mowed over everyone around them on the way up.

But Jesus, if it got them houses like this, maybe she'd made the wrong choice. "Where do you keep the alcohol?"

He was so annoyingly smug sometimes. He slung a thumb in the pockets of his perfectly tailored slacks. "Why do you assume I have booze?"

She shot him a look that said she wasn't born yesterday. "Puh-leeze. You're Sean Westin. You're in the tabloids every other month, photographed at expensive clubs, with expensive women and expensive booze."

"Don't assume. Who's to say those glasses aren't filled with tea? Or tonic water with lime?"

Her stomach dropped. Had she misjudged him? She'd gotten enough of that shit herself, people who assumed her slightly tomboy look meant she was gay or butch or a shoplifter or antisocial. It sucked, but she'd learned the hard way that living for other people just wasn't worth it.

But then he broke into a laugh. Lines spilled out from the corners of his eyes. "No, I totally drink. No sainthood here. There are two bars in the place. A wet bar in the study and a less formal one on the lanai."

"Let's start at the lanai," she replied dryly. Keeping up with him had her on her toes, and that wasn't only referring to matching his long-legged stride.

At least following behind him meant that she could check out his ass. While she was fully aware that ass checking was the last thing in the world she should be doing as his physical therapist, it was a little difficult to strip her gaze away from that tight curve. His slacks were a fine material that pulled taut over his bum when he twisted open the sliding glass door. Damn, he dressed nicely.

If professional surfers usually dressed like he did, maybe she'd been hanging out with skaters too long. Her friends all wore board shorts and cargoes. Sometimes jeans appeared if the weather dipped below forty-five degrees. None of them had button-downs like the one stretched across Sean's shoulders. He was insanely fit, which went to show poor choices could make even the most fit susceptible to injury.

Man, she was going to have a hard time keeping herself together when he was undergoing physical therapy. At least she didn't have to be the one to administer it herself. She'd be a horrible therapist if this was how she looked at patients.

Not that any of them looked like Sean Westin.

Not that any of the men in the entire world looked like Sean Westin.

Annie's whole living space could fit into Sean's lanai. Considering that she lived on the upper floors of the same building that held her business, it wasn't saying *that* much, but she suddenly realized why this room was called a lanai instead of a patio. It had a roof, for one thing, and walls along two sides, though they were open-framed and lined with Japanese-style screens that would be enough to keep a neighbor from peeking at anything going on inside.

The furniture was low to the ground and upholstered in pale white cottons to match the screens. They'd be the perfect chairs for Sean to throw himself into after a hard surfing session. The bar wasn't hidden along a back wall, but instead installed as a central feature. It looked like something from a *Blade Runner* set, sleek black and knee-high with a recessed door in the center that was likely a fridge. The round arrangement would allow guests to grab what they wanted instead of having a designated bartender.

All of it paled compared to the space where the third wall would have been. Except anyone who'd put up a wall there would have to be smoking something made out of sinus medicines in the back bedroom of a trailer.

The only frame the room needed was the perfect, impeccable, gorgeous view. The water. The ocean. But more than that. It wasn't just *Oh, look at that blue strip* like so-called ocean-view houses in certain neighborhoods. Sean had a beach. He had white, pure sand that stretched for a mile north and two miles south.

Even the waves outside his lanai were perfect. He could grab a board, walk to the water, then paddle out into a right break that was currently six feet high on the front. "Jesus," she breathed.

"Makes you wanna hit the water, right?"

She might have expected him to be smug, but it wasn't there. His lips were slightly parted. His eyes were as wide as they went. Only in its absence did she realize the tension that had been held at his blade-high cheeks. He was softer here, looking at the ocean. Maybe he was one of those few people who actually seemed to understand the power the dark green water held. There was magic out there. Magic most people couldn't touch.

Magic she hadn't felt in a long time. "Wouldn't know. I haven't surfed in about five years."

He gaped at her. There were no other words for it. His carved jaw dropped and his whole body shifted toward her. "Are you serious?"

She shrugged, though there was so much tension across the back of her neck, it felt as if she were grinding glass together. "Haven't needed to since college."

He shook his head a little, then passed his free hand over the top of his skull. He scraped blunt nails through his short hair. She wondered what that hair would feel like under her palms. Probably scratchy. Maybe she'd get a little tickle. Definitely a lot of tingles. They'd probably work up her arms and into her chest.

Fuck, she was such an idiot.

"Surfing isn't about need," he said in a voice implying she might as well have spoken in Farsi. "Surfing is about a drive."

She pulled out the first three bottles lining the bar, and aimed her most beatific, bullshitting grin up at him. "Then I don't have the drive. Besides, I have my teens to think about. It's easier to keep an eye on five kids if they're all skating in my backyard. Our hiking trips are difficult enough in terms of logistics. Taking them to the beach would require different transportation, and I'd have to be stricter about maintaining control over them. Plus it's harder to store a surfboard than a skateboard."

Something dark flitted across his features. He hadn't shaved, so a shadowy growth covered his chin and jaw, but it did nothing to hide the twitching muscle. "I'll give you that one."

She sat back, spreading her elbows out on the armrests. It was probably the most comfortable patio furniture she'd ever planted her butt in and that was just not fair. She had kids who struggled to have enough to eat every day. Sometimes the snacks she provided would be the only calories they got. And

Sean Westin probably dropped ten grand on decorating a *lanai*.

"Really," she said, dragging out the word to an obnoxious level. But her speech sped up, faster and faster as she went along. "What exactly does a world championship surfer know about hiding boards so an obnoxiously drunk stepfather won't break it out of spite? That happened, you know. A boy named Mike stopped coming to my place after that, even though I got him a new board. He just gave up."

The crystal clear blue of his eyes muddied into something more like a dark river than the ocean at Cancun. She hadn't thought him capable of such changeable moods. The papers and talk about San Sebastian made him out to be way more of an affable, carefree playboy. He was the kind of guy who liked to have fun, and most everyone on the surf circuit loved him for it. "Maybe I didn't have a drunk stepdad, but my mom had her own problems. I kept surfboards at other people's houses most of the time. Usually they believed me when I said it was because they lived closer to the water."

"What was the real reason?"

As soon as the words were out of her mouth, he shut down. His eyes had been dark before, yeah, but that wasn't the same thing as blank. His mouth lifted in the *shape* of a smile, but it wasn't a real one. Even his posture changed as he rocked back on one heel. "Eh, there's no reason to get into that."

She didn't believe him for a second. There was a deep dark kind of thing behind those words and their studiously casual tone. But sometimes it was easier to get hints and work around to the truth later.

Her clients didn't always realize that they'd come to her for more than physical therapy. They needed whole-life overhauls.

She was just the woman to give him one. She smiled, pushing the bottles toward him. If he wanted to let it go, fine. For now. "There'll be no alcohol for the next eight weeks. How we go about it is your choice."

"What do you mean?" He almost seemed to hide a sigh of relief, but she had to be mistaken.

Sean might want to believe he was mystery and danger wrapped up together, but she was starting to think he was a whole lot easier to read than he wanted to be. "Either we pour the bottles out right now, together, or we load up my car and I store them for you."

She liked giving clients this choice. Their answer usually gave a deeper insight into their relationship with alcohol. Sometimes it was the easiest way to find out if they were closet alcoholics. Their *choice* didn't matter, but the way they delivered it absolutely did. Sean was frequently seen in clubs and had been in at least three bar fights that she'd heard of in the past two years alone. That wasn't even counting his current injury's being due to a bar incident that put his career in danger.

But he only gave a little shake of his head. "Really doesn't matter to me. It'd be some cash outlay to buy again once I'm better, but it's not like I have special scotch or fifty-year-old wine. I'm not really a wine type at all, for that matter."

"Wonderful. If it's all the same to you, then, I'd rather we pour them out. I could keep them safe at my house, but they would have to be locked up in my bedroom. I'd rather not bring that sort of temptation to my kids' doorstep."

He gave another of those soft, slightly wondering smiles. Her stomach flipped, and she told it to shut the hell up. He was absolutely not looking at her the same way he'd looked at the ocean. That was ridiculous.

"You call them your kids," he pointed out. "But they're not, right? None of them are yours biologically? They're teenagers who attend an afternoon drop-in center."

"That still makes them mine."

Chapter 5

Three days later, Sean had managed to drag Annie out to the beach. When she admitted that she hadn't surfed in five years, it had become his obsession to get her on the waves. He couldn't even fathom that. The idea was simply absurd. Who in the name of God would pass up on surfing when they were good enough to have been on a university team? He also knew players who'd come out of UCSD. They had high standards. Pros had been known to surf for them after their careers had ended, while they got degrees to carry them forward in life.

Annie had been that good and walked away. There had to be a story behind that.

Unfortunately, it wasn't his story to figure out.

She was his physical therapist. There was nothing in her job description that said anything about talking or having fun or dropping intimate secrets. It was better that way, since his secrets were of the incredibly distasteful variety.

The thing was, memories were crowding back. Partly because he knew she worked with underprivileged teenagers—and partly because he hadn't been able to surf for almost a week now. Surfing always rinsed out his brain and made him better able to deal with new shit that came his way. There was too much old bullshit that tried to hang on to him, and the water was the only way to push it away.

He had a beach house, for fuck's sake, and no one was out there in the ocean. He just sat on the back stairs with his toes digging into the warm, abrasive sand.

At least his big donation meant he got house calls from Annie rather than having to go into her office. Money did count for something.

Except the downside of training at his house meant they were training by the beach. It was bullshit. He was still looking at the one place he'd kill to be. Surfing cleared his head to make him feel like something more than a dirty little kid.

He'd lost that. He'd injured himself and lost that connection to the water.

He couldn't remember the last time he'd gone more than three days without hitting the waves. Even in January, he'd wear a full-body wet suit. Some of the best waves came when the weather was shitty and storms were rolling in offshore.

"When do I get to surf?" It was still difficult for him to breathe, which was hard to understand. All he'd done were some arm lifts and extensions. Under normal circumstances, he could run five miles against the extra resistance of soft sand, then do forty-five minutes of weightlifting. But sweat had sprung up across his forehead. He wiped it away with the back of his hand and slugged back some Powerade.

"When you can do five overhead lifts without breaking a sweat." She was folding up the table she'd brought along with her. He'd had to lie face-down on it and swing his arm up and down as if he were a kid playing come-get-me with the monster under the bed. He'd felt stupid. Worse than that.

His shoulder throbbed in a different way than it had over the past week. It was less sharp pain and more like a steady ache. "That's easy. I just won't drink any water the day before and there'll be no sweat."

"Oh yay," she said with a heavy dose of sarcasm. "Screw up your health in order to game the system. Good plan."

He capped his drink and put it down on the edge of the stairs. "I wasn't serious."

She sighed. "I know. Sorry. You didn't deserve that one. It's just been a long day."

"It's only eight. What could be wrong?"

Her hair was pulled back in her short ponytail, complete with a thick fringe of bangs. But she'd left off the eye makeup, and purple shadows clung underneath her lashes. She shook her head. "You don't really care."

He stood, his stomach giving a weird little flip. Was that what she thought of him? It didn't say much about him, did it? He gently stretched his arm, letting the pain burn through his muscles. It wasn't all bad pain. There was the sweet sting of muscles being able to do what they wanted for the first time in a couple weeks. The sun rose above the house behind them, streaking warmly through the air. The water called his name, but even he knew it would be foolish to grab a board and try anything stupid. "Maybe I won't care, but give me a shot. Maybe it'll be more like a distraction."

She sighed, but her hands stopped messing with the straps and struts of the table. She turned away from him. Her shoulders were narrow and her back even skinnier. She wore a T-shirt with shorts that showed off toned legs. Not surprising, considering how much she skateboarded. She had a skinned knee too, as if she were a kid. But the swell of her perky ass was all woman. "I've got this boy who comes by every now and then. Tim. He can grind for fucking miles. He's got shockingly red hair and pale skin. Turns out, skin that pale—it shows bruises really well."

"Shit," Sean muttered.

"Yeah." Her shoulders lifted and dropped as she sighed. "He came around at four this morning."

"His parents?"

"Dad." Her voice broke even on that tiny, simple word, but she stayed turned away from him. Her shoulders bowed in farther, almost as if she were trying to hide.

Sean turned toward the water. She obviously wanted a minute of privacy. A breeze on its way offshore tickled the back of his neck. At least his mom had never raised a hand to him. He'd been lucky in that respect. It had been part of why he'd never had a way out, which was the downside too. He'd always made the best of his circumstances, so the few times he'd been able to say something, no one had really believed him. He'd told a counselor in middle school. Mrs. Logan hadn't been dismissive, but she hadn't exactly moved heaven and earth to get anything changed. Sean had been put in foster care for a week while his mom had made the bare-minimum improvements. Then he'd been back again. He'd been hopeful for all of two days, until he'd come home from school to find out that his mom had been shopping at the Goodwill while he was in sixth period social studies. Bags of clothes they'd never wear covered the table where he was supposed to do homework.

He'd left that behind. Literally and figuratively. His house was clean. He had the life he'd dreamed of.

He stuck out a hand. "Come on."

She turned, but looked at his hand in the air between them as if he were offering her a handful of spaghetti. Not dangerous, but completely inexplicable. "But . . . where?"

"Down the beach."

She shook her head. "No swimming. You're not ready. You'll do damage."

"We're not going swimming." He flashed a shiny, cheeky grin. Distraction was a graceful weapon when wielded correctly. "You're not dressed for it."

"Like you've never talked a girl into skinny-dipping." She was wavering. A single step brought her close enough that she could put her hand in his if she wanted to.

He kept himself locked down. Fingers open. Stance easy. This was no big deal . . . but for some reason it felt like it was. He *liked* Annie. She was sharp and funny, and this morning she was hurting. He hadn't meant for them to have any sort of friendship, but he wasn't opposed to it either. "Sure I have.

But we've always done it after dark. It's morning. You're totally safe."

She laughed. "No woman is safe around you."

He didn't mean to, but he took a step closer to her. They were shrinking the distance between them. He felt his spine tilt, his chin come down just a fraction. "Why, Baxter, does that mean you like me some?"

"A woman would have to be *dead* not to think you're hot." Except she said it with more of that disdain of hers. Like his attractiveness was a fact, but not one that mattered. "You know that. Of course you do, or you wouldn't have been in ads for those expensive watches. There's surfing sponsorship, and then there's wider appeal. You've got it in spades."

"I like money." He'd never considered that a bad thing. He did what he needed to do in order to build his portfolio. The sport of surfing and his own corporate image could become something bigger. Better. Surfing was fucking awesome. If he could make money and help other people realize that, no one lost. There was the chance that his split focus was the thing holding him back from the top ten, but he'd calculated that as an acceptable risk. He still had to stay in the game, however. "I also like the water. Come on. Come sit with me."

He could practically see the internal battle she waged. Her eyes were the same chocolate brown as the stripe down the surfboard he'd had his senior year of high school. That had been a good year, when he'd first entered Prime events.

"Fine," she said with a decisive nod, almost as if giving herself permission. She tucked her hand in his.

He closed his fingers around hers immediately. Her hand was smaller than the hands he was used to. Smaller than he liked, honestly. It took some thought to realize that all the vibrant personality he dug was packed into a tiny capsule. If she were as big as she lived, she'd have been six foot five.

They walked to the edge of the water in silence and sat below the tide line. The damp sand immediately soaked through Sean's workout sweats. He stripped off his shoes, tossing them behind him to the white dry sand. She followed suit, ditching her tennis shoes. Her toes were elegant, with navy-painted nails.

He didn't say anything. He knew from experience there was no point in pushing if someone didn't want to tell a story. He hadn't known Annie long, but she seemed like the ultimate in determination and control. The cold white froth of the very edge of the waves tickled their toes. When a particularly large surge swept beneath them to lick at the sand they sat on, Annie squealed. Sean laughed at her, but only a little bit. He had a feeling she didn't mind.

There weren't many surfers out, mostly because conditions were predicted to go off later in the day. They'd double the surf in the afternoon, so most people were probably getting other shit done so they could have free time when the surf was banging. Not Sean. He had all the free time in the world. Lately that had chafed him, but at this moment, it was something of a relief.

"He's not a perfect kid, of course. It all started because he'd been drunk and out until two on a school night. Plus I bet he mouthed off when his dad tried to get onto him." She spoke without looking at Sean, but that was fine. At least she was speaking.

Sean knew what it was like to hold on to something important and have nowhere to vent. "Still, that doesn't make it okay."

"God, no." She sighed. "His father hauled off full force, and he's got at least fifty pounds on Tim. He's lucky he doesn't have a fracture in his orbital socket. It was a really hard blow."

"Plus he's lucky he had you to come to."

She shook her head. Her hands dangled between her upraised knees. "Sometimes I don't know about that."

"I'm sure of it." Sean would have killed for someone who gave even half as much a shit about him. But there was no point in heading down that road again. It only caused pain.

"I should get going. I have an appointment in less than an hour, and I still have to get all the way across town."

He liked the way sand felt under his feet. Comforting, even when it was cold and damp. Sand was home. Sand shifted; it could always be swept away by the ocean and cleaned before it was dumped back on the beach. "Go ahead." He winked. "It's not my fault you feel the need to check up on my clean living."

"Clean living." She gave a derisive snort. "Sure."

"I swear it. Like a Boy Scout or something." He crossed two fingers over his heart.

Suddenly, an idea hit him that was brand-new and ridiculous, but he'd never had a better one. "You know what? You should go with me to an event I have Friday. Just so I can prove how good I'm being."

"I'm not going anywhere with you," she replied immediately. She shoved up from her seat and brushed off the clumps of damp sand from her ass and the backs of her legs. "Don't be silly. It wouldn't be professional."

"I disagree. In fact . . . I think it would be entirely professional. These are the types of movers and shakers who are always looking for new charity projects to support. It's a red-carpet event for the opening of a new magazine. It'll probably shutter in less than a year, because who the hell buys magazines anymore, but that's not your worry."

Her eyebrows lifted. "What *is* my worry, then?"

"What to wear."

Chapter 6

A nnie didn't do parties. Not the way Sean did parties, at least. He had his fancy on, that was for sure. His suit was an indefinable gray, and he'd paired it with a pale pink shirt with the faintest plaid pattern. His brighter pink tie should have looked awful. The combination should have made him look slightly effeminate or unmanly.

It didn't. God, it didn't.

Annie wanted to wrap his pink-dotted tie around her fist and haul him six inches down so she could kiss him.

The colors made his tan stand out, the darkness of his hair even stronger. All of it was contrasted by his bright, neon, unfairly blue eyes. That wasn't even counting the blade-sharp cheekbones and jawline. He had lines around his mouth that only men could pull off and behind them, his cheeks were barely hollowed.

It was unfair. He was too beautiful.

At the moment, he was talking with a perfect blonde who had the whole package down pat as well. Sean had introduced the woman as Gloria, Nate

Coker's girlfriend. They obviously knew each other quite well and Sean kept things to a perfectly honed level of pleasant conversation. He never dipped into flirtation territory with his teammate's girlfriend.

And yet . . . Annie could tell something was off between Sean and the other woman. She kept touching him, for one thing, despite the way that Sean was practically waving a no-swim flag above his head.

Gloria swatted Sean's shoulder. "We're going to miss you in France. What was the name of that bar you took everyone to last time?"

"Chanteclair." He gave it the perfect French pronunciation. "But I'll be competing by the time the circuit gets to France."

He was so coolly collected that Annie felt like digging her toes into the dirt and ducking her head whenever she was around him. Standing at his side while he charmed the event's coordinators made her feel about as gauche as a terrier at the opera. She was so out of her depth.

Her dress had seemed like a good idea when she was in Nordstrom. The handkerchief hem flirted around her thighs, and she'd loved the fabric's gold shimmer. But now that she was the three-foot-tall munchkin surrounded by seven-foot beauties in sleek black dresses, she regretted her pick.

"Well, if you don't make it, we'll have a round in your name," Gloria promised, ignoring Sean's potent determination to be surfing in time for that competition. Then she flicked the shortest glance possible at Annie. "Nice to meet you."

Sean waved as the other woman slipped away between the closely packed bodies dressed in tiny scraps of silk and cotton. Oddly, more than one person was wearing a scarf wrapped around and around the neck, as if the sixty-five-degree spring weather in Southern California actually necessitated extra warmth.

"You look like you could use a drink." Sean leaned toward her, ducking his head to create a private space between them.

"Make it three drinks and you've got a deal."

Sean threw his head back to laugh, and she was mesmerized by the strong line of his throat. He was all strength and sinew. Leanly attractive. When he hooked an arm around her shoulders, his thumb came to rest at the cap of her shoulder. "You're in luck. It's an open bar."

"In that case, I want six."

They worked their way through the crowd toward the equally packed bar. People were . . . people. Everywhere. Laughing and chattering and talking with flying hands. They were all the fancy people too. Annie had barely made it through med school with all these Type As and the *big* way they lived.

"You like keeping a low profile," Sean said once they'd squeezed in at the bar. It was made of opaque white Plexiglas lit from behind to make clouds of color that gradually shifted through the spectrum.

Annie faced the bar, tucking her elbows in close to herself. The guy to her right was a dapper man wearing a tailored three-piece suit, but he kept rocking back on his heels as he told a story about a gardener, a pool boy, and his ex-boyfriend's coke habit. His suit jacket brushed Annie. She scooted closer to Sean. "What gave me away?" she asked dryly.

He braced his left hand on the counter, carving out breathing room for her. He sheltered her, and though she'd buck up against that sort of male-female protection most of the time, for the moment, she needed it. Her chest was closing in, and she had those awful tingles down the back of her thighs—the ones that said she was getting way too wound up way too fast.

"I dunno," Sean said. His cheeks hollowed as he tucked away a smile. "Maybe the fact that you're a millimeter from plastering yourself to me."

She waved for the bartender. "I'm not that close."

Half a step between them. Not even that. A shift. He took one deep breath and was touching her, his chest against her shoulder and his hip against hers. Her lips parted. She sucked in a breath. Then another.

No. This wasn't going to work. She couldn't do this. Couldn't be that kind of therapist. He was her patient. She'd worked him through a round of mobility exercises that very morning, having him hold one end of an elastic band to work on resistance.

The tingles down the backs of her thighs turned into full-blown shivers. Her chest was tight. "Who's Gloria?"

"I thought I said during introductions?" Sean replied blandly. "Nate's girlfriend?"

Annie shook her head. Tendrils of hair skimmed her temples. "No, who is she really?"

Sean's mouth tweaked into a subtle smile. "My ex-girlfriend as well, Ms. Observant. Points to you."

If Annie had thought her chest was tight a moment ago, it was nothing compared to the wrenching pressure on her lungs. Gloria looked right for Sean. Tall and beautiful and polished, they'd be like the surfing world's Barbie and Ken equivalent.

"What can I get you?" the fresh-faced bartender said, popping up in front of her. She smiled blankly back at him, glad for the sudden distraction.

"Two vodka gimlets." She might have been teasing about needing three or six, but this was definitely a multiple-drink moment. She really wished she'd renewed her Ativan prescription. But years of therapy after Terry and that disastrous night had finally helped her work through the need for antianxiety meds. Or so she'd thought.

"And a Corona with lime for me," Sean added.

"No, he'll have a cranberry and soda."

The bartender pursed his lips. His gaze flicked from Annie's, up over her shoulder, to Sean. He had both hands spread, wiry shoulders leaning into the bar. When he tilted his head, his short Mohawk didn't move. "Sir . . . ?"

"Cranberry and soda," Sean echoed. But as soon as the bartender was gone again, he leaned down close enough that Annie could feel his breath on the skin below her ear. "You're gonna owe me for this one."

That was certainly one way to beat away the threat of an anxiety attack, wasn't it? Distraction worked, but it wasn't something she could provide on her own. Sean, though. The way he touched her was like ice water to her system. Her breathing still felt tight, but God, in a different way. An exhilarating way.

She twisted, turning to face him. The periphery of her vision swam with darkness, but in the center there was Sean. His eyes. The way he looked at her, with that graceful mouth holding still. Concern narrowed his brows and traced lines across his forehead. "Are you all right?"

She ignored the question. "I warned you there'd be no alcohol under my watch."

"You were having two. I figured it was worth a shot."

"Here you are, ma'am," the bartender said, pushing two slender-stemmed glasses across the bar. He set a squat tumbler of cranberry and soda next to it. He'd stuck a jaunty paper umbrella through a cherry.

"Thanks," Sean said dryly, before removing the umbrella and cherry without comment. He dropped it on the paper napkin.

"Thank you." The drink was cool against her sticky palms. Medicating herself with alcohol was a piss-poor idea. She knew that, but she sucked it down anyway. The vodka sizzled against the back of her throat, balanced by the lime juice and sugar. "Come on, Sean. Let's make this trauma fest worth it."

She tried to push past him, but apparently, even with one injured arm, there was no making Sean shift if he didn't want to. He was a wall. A handsome, gorgeous wall. She stretched up to her full height, but that left her still craning her neck as she attempted to look him right in the eyes.

"Only if you tell me what's going on."

She was using her best poker face, but her cheeks felt heavy and her skin clammy. At least the fire of the drink had curled through her body, warming her from the inside out. "No."

"Annie . . ." He drew her name into something she

shouldn't want to hear again . . . but she did. She'd think of his deep, determined voice at three in the morning; she knew it. Her brain would replay that sound, only add in a different context and different hopes.

And she was an idiot. "I'm your physical therapist, Sean."

"You're obviously upset."

"Then why don't you tell me what you think is wrong." It wouldn't count as inappropriate if he was just guessing, right?

Fuck, she deserved to have her license taken away.

"I think you're on the verge of a panic attack." He braced himself against the bar, blocking her in. Between the suit and the tie, he looked like something out of a fashion magazine instead of a surfer. But she still wanted to let her head rest against his deep chest.

"Not anymore." She held up the drink. "I've successfully self-medicated."

"You're not supposed to do that."

"I'm also not supposed to be having this conversation with a client." The washes of sensation down the back of her thighs were gone, at least. That was a bonus. Except she wasn't sure if they were gone due to the vodka, or due to Sean's obvious worry. "Let's make tonight worth it, okay? Can we do that?"

She wasn't sure how he would answer. Sean had a reputation for being a flashy playboy, and the way he navigated the night's crush hinted at why. But most people hadn't seen him sweating through a physical therapy session. Apparently they hadn't seen the dark, determined look in his eyes. Otherwise they'd have entirely different ideas about him.

The moment he decided to let the charade go was so obvious. His smile built slowly, pulling up on one side farther than the other. His eyes sparked with blue.

"What would make tonight worth it for you, Annie? I have a few ideas. But I doubt you'd agree much with my choices."

"You're not supposed to flirt with me," she replied automatically. Really, she wanted to clasp his face between her hands, feel his scruffy stubble across her palms, and plant a smacking, relieved kiss on his mouth. Just as a giant thank-you for letting her change the subject.

"I do lots of things I'm not supposed to."

She scoffed, the noise slipping right out of her mouth without thought. Challenging a wild animal wasn't a good idea. "You're practically a pussycat."

"Are you gonna make me prove it?"

"Only after you get me that introduction you promised. Mover or shaker, either would do."

He smelled good. It was expensive cologne, sharp musk that wove beneath the press of bodies all around them. But under that was the tangy scent of salt water. He lived and breathed the ocean. "Maybe I've changed my mind," he said. "If I introduce you to this life-changing person, you won't need my money anymore. You'll discharge me as a client."

Maybe she should do that anyway. She was an idiot for even letting this continue. Therapist-patient restrictions existed for a reason. She sipped her drink to hide the flush of guilt making the back of her neck prickle. "Does he have another three million I can have?"

"He might." Sean had lost that cheeky tone, the one that said he'd hauled them into flirty, fun territory. He had dark holes in him, Sean Westin did.

She lifted her gaze to his. "I'm not greedy. Six mil would probably be too much for a fledgling foundation to manage."

"Ever dream of quitting your day job?" he asked solemnly.

She snorted. "No. With as hard as I worked for my degrees, you've got to be shitting me. I'm never walking away. I'll be practicing physiotherapy when I'm ninety-three. That much funding probably *would* allow me to hire a full-time center director, though."

He washed her over with a sudden, blinding grin. "Leaving you more time to skateboard with the kids?"

"Totally. That's the fun part."

"You're a good person, Baxter."

She'd disagree with that. She tried to be good, but she was pretty messed up all the way through. Apparently she could add having no idea of therapist-patient propriety to her list of sins. "You're stalling, Westin."

"What if I am? What if I wanna keep you all to myself?"

She shook her head, because that was the last thing she wanted to happen. She was happy where she was, leaning against the bar in the shelter of Sean's body. Which meant she had to get away. "You're out of luck, then."

"But you're in luck. Because our quarry is coming to us."

Her spine jolted, nerves slamming into the base of

her back in one abrupt punch. Her neck snapped tight. "What? Who?"

"Frank Wakowski, the owner of WavePro."

Bewilderment made her gaze dart around the room. It was a packed wall of women's bare backs and deep cleavage and men's suits. "But you don't surf for them."

"Nope. I know Frank, though. He's a good guy, and he's looking for a new pet project."

She scrambled through her knowledge of Wave-Pro. From what she could remember, they put most of their donation money into exclusively surf-oriented causes, such as beach cleanup or runoff prevention. "I run a skateboard clinic."

"You run a safe house for teenagers." Sean caught her hand and her gaze at the same time. "That's important, Annie. I wish I'd had someone like you around when I was young. It might have saved me."

Chapter 7

Sean apparently had a loose-to-negligent setting on his mouth. Because, Jesus, where in holy hell had that little saccharine drip come from? He hadn't said anything like that in . . . ever. No one on the 'CT knew where he came from. They didn't need to. No one needed to, except his personal physician and his manager, who knew to watch for signs of mental imbalance. There'd been none. Sean was about as well-rounded as anyone. Some worries crept in when he hadn't managed to go surfing for days, but that was about it. He'd made the mistake of telling Gloria a hint of his past when they were dating, and she had very quickly moved on to Nate, deeming him a much less shaky bet. Sean had sworn to not even think about telling anyone else.

Annie had been in a bad place in her head. He'd always been a sucker for women in need, so he'd done what he needed to in order to make her feel better. That was it.

He tugged the bottom hem of his suit coat. An uncomfortable feeling slithered up his spine. Annie was . . . different.

Annie was better than he was. That was the truth. He'd have liked nothing more than to cup her face in his hands and kiss her better, but that wasn't his right. She'd have freaked out for sure. She was his physical therapist, and she seemed to take that responsibility seriously. But what they had between them was more than that.

He'd let himself slip around her. Said things he shouldn't have. Since she was so clever, she probably already had started putting pieces together. Things in his past were better left there, and he couldn't afford the trouble that came with a serious relationship. Girlfriends tended to need honesty, and he'd had problems with that. Sure, he always stayed on the up-and-up with where he went and the kind of man he was. He didn't *lie*. But he also didn't give away all his truths.

He'd never been able to tell a soul about his mother. Not even Gloria. Those days were long ago.

Sean ruthlessly stomped down buried memories that wanted to explode. He needed the water, and soon. It was the only thing that could clear his head. That his shoulder wasn't aching at that very second made the desire worse. Unfortunately, it would only take one wrong move to hurt it again.

He smiled at the owner of WavePro and shifted so that he was shoulder to shoulder with Annie. "Frank. It's good to see you."

The older man verged on skinny from a life spent surfing. He held out a hand. "Sean. I was sorry to hear about your injury."

Sean nodded, but his back teeth ground together. "I'm sure you'll understand if I don't shake hands."

"Of course, of course," Frank agreed, waving it off. "Sorry. Wasn't thinking."

Frank was a nice guy, and as easygoing as the head of any multimillion-dollar company could be. He likely hadn't meant anything by offering to shake hands when Sean was nursing his injury, but the reminder still grated. For now, it would have to be enough that Sean felt better day by day. Annie's treatment had plenty to do with that, he was sure. But it made his bones scrape with discomfort that he wasn't at a hundred percent.

"No worries. But Frank, let me introduce you to Annie Baxter."

Her mouth curved into a slight smile. "That's *Dr.* Baxter."

Shock left Frank's mouth hanging open. "You barely look old enough to be a coed. I can't imagine where you managed to squeeze in all your schooling."

"I've had people ask me that before." There was nothing wrong with the way Annie replied, and her expression never wavered. But Sean could see her pulse flicker into triple speed behind her ear.

How often must she hear that? Too often for it to be even remotely amusing anymore. He wanted to put a hand at the base of her spine, but he resisted the impulse. Putting women at risk of gossip had never been his favorite hobby. "Annie runs a teen drop-in center focused on peer outreach support systems. She teaches skateboarding as a medium for contact," Sean said smoothly.

If he hadn't been quite as focused on Annie, he'd have missed her rapid blink and the way her lips parted. Just as quickly, she recomposed her expression into a serene smile. She looked gorgeous enough to eat. The gold dress skimmed over her with a modest bodice, but it put a killer expanse of back on display. She was sleek and lean, the body that had looked boyish in jeans and a T-shirt suddenly wholly feminine. It seemed that she hadn't expected him to so easily reel off her foundation's principles.

"Is it in San Sebastian?" Frank asked. He had salt-and-pepper hair, and he'd recently cultivated a short beard and mustache. He rubbed the beard. "I'm always looking for projects in town. Keeping development local shores up our roots in the community."

Sean knew that already. He couldn't have leveraged his surfing into the healthy investment portfolio he'd managed without keeping his ear to the ground. Sean surfed for Coyote, but that didn't mean he was unaware of WavePro's growing status in the surf community. They wanted good press, and they wanted it in Southern California. Charity donations created a healthy tax write-off for them as well.

"My ad hoc location is in San Sebastian," Annie agreed. "We're hoping to be able to open the permanent center off Seventeenth Street, since there's a former bowling alley that could be easily converted. But it would depend on meeting our funding goals."

"What are your goals?"

"High-end figures are two point seven million. We can do it for less, but we'd rather not."

Sean smothered a grin behind his cranberry and soda. He didn't miss how she avoided mentioning that Sean had already pledged enough to cover all those so-called funding goals. She was ruthless. He pretty much dug that about her.

"Skateboarding, huh? No chance there's any interest in surfing?" Frank winked.

Annie's narrow shoulders lifted in a shrug. "We've had interest, naturally. It's hard to run a teen center in San Sebastian without having kids who want to surf. After all, you sponsor Tanner Wright, who's also a local. The fervor for the World Championship Tour is at an all-time high."

She didn't seem to have any personal interest in surfing, though. Sean didn't understand that. How could she have left it so cleanly in her past? Unless she'd had a shitty wipeout or some other sort of trauma. He knew plenty about leaving unpleasant stuff behind, but to him, surfing was life. Surfing was what cleaned away all the nasty.

He watched her profile as she continued chatting with Frank. It was hard to believe the pixie who'd almost had a panic attack in the middle of a party twenty minutes ago was holding her own with the owner of a multinational company. She was badass like that. Her nose and chin were rounded from the side, her cheeks soft. Her lashes were dark and lush, casting shadows across her upper cheeks under the party's dramatically colorful lighting.

"Well, naturally I can't promise anything," Frank eventually said, "but if you contact Adin Lund, our new director of operations, I'll take a look at your prospectus."

"I'd be happy to, Mr. Wakowski," Annie said, every inch the graceful professional.

Sean thought there would probably be a much more significant reaction from her as soon as Wakowski walked away, though. She was vibrating, but quietly. Her muscles popped into tight alignment along her spine. The hint of ribs at her midback suddenly became more visible, three definite swoops revealed by her electric tension.

"Sean, it's been wonderful to see you," Frank said, clapping Sean on the back. "I must say you're dealing with those strange rumors fairly well."

The world tilted. Sean's fist curled. Some part of him had been subtly terrified this moment would eventually come. There was nothing in Frank's words that guaranteed he was about to say something horrible about Sean's past. Not at all.

But Sean knew. He knew with a perfectly incontrovertible irrationality that was all sorts of convincing. There was only one thing in his past. One allegation that had haunted him for life. His mother's ruin. Everything else was practically sunshine and roses when held in perspective. "What rumors?"

Frank flushed red. His jowls pushed up as he shook his head and held out a hand. "No, that is . . . if you haven't heard . . . You haven't heard?"

Sean shook his head. "I've been keeping my head down the last two weeks. Well, collarbone, anyway."

But he should have been dialed in. His smartphone had all the addresses and phone numbers of every person on the 'CT, as well as their Instagram accounts and sponsor-mandated Twitter. If no one had told him what was going on, this was bad. He'd been here before, the one on the outside when the slightest hints about his mother leached into his high school's rumor mill. His stomach coiled into a chilled knot.

Annie set a hand on his forearm. The suit and his long-sleeved shirt meant that he couldn't feel the softness of her skin, only the weight of her touch. "Sean," she said softly.

"What's going on, Frank?"

"Son, maybe we should sit down."

"Maybe you should just spit it out." He was losing his grip on the spike of anger that had his fists clenching, both of them. There was no pain from his shoulder, because the rest of him didn't even exist.

"There's talk that a documentary maker has found something interesting about you. They aren't saying great things. Rumors are saying the topic might be doping." Frank held up both hands. "But they're mostly just rumors so far. No one's even attached a director's name to the picture. I wouldn't put any stock in the idea."

Sean gave a bitter huff. His stomach twisted. No one had come to him with a request for a documentary lately, which could only mean that they'd intended from the beginning for it to be unauthorized. "People are putting plenty of stock in whatever the hell they feel like. Otherwise someone would have told me what was going on."

He'd been left in the dark. Fuck, he hated that. He'd felt helpless and ignorant when his mother's illness pushed him around. Not her, not the *stuff* that she accumulated, but the mental illness that pushed and pulled her around. He'd never been able to help her conquer it, not even at the dark end.

That was why he'd avoided being helpless once he'd had his own life. He conquered the damn ocean, and he'd been so close to a world championship so many times, he could have kissed the damn silver trophy. Yet he'd missed it.

He was close again this year, but between injury and these new rumors, he could feel things slipping out of his grasp. All his plans, all his work. Fucked again.

He ground his teeth together, and his spine felt like it was made of metal. "Frank, there's nothing in my past worth making a documentary about." That was a lie, but he wasn't going to tell that to the head of a rival company.

"I know, Sean," Frank agreed, giving a conciliatory nod. "But . . . well, things have gotten tough lately. Everyone's scrutinizing athletes for doping history. Hell, look how long Lance Armstrong got away with it until they really started clamping down. . . . If there are any sorts of drugs in your past, things might get a little tough."

Sean muttered curses under his breath. This was not good. "Why me? Why are the rumors centering on me? I'm a midranker at best."

"I think it has to do with this recent injury, and particularly the circumstances of it. It's drawing you extra attention. Combined with how closemouthed you've always been about your past . . ."

"Man, this is bullshit. These are just rumors." And they were way off the mark. So far.

Frank's expression turned mournful. His mouth turned down at the corners, and his eyes deepened with sadness. "Sean . . . I know they're rumors, but you really should cover yourself. Maybe you should talk to your attorney."

Chapter 8

Annie had never played with fireworks before, but sitting next to Sean in his car felt like being strapped in next to a rocket launcher. He was dangerous and explosive. Part of her was tempted to reach out and touch him. His grip on the stick shift left his knuckles white with strain. The tendons along his neck stood in stark relief.

Sean Westin didn't take things as lightly as she'd thought. Even his vehicle was something of a surprise. She'd have guessed Porsche or Lexus, but instead he drove a late-1970s Bronco. True, it had been fully restored and improved so there were butter-soft leather seats and a dashboard that rivaled any new car. The in-dash GPS was so fancy, she was surprised it didn't do the actual steering. But the body was all business, and Sean even had two boards in the back, both of them midsized shortboards good for a wide range of surf conditions.

"Should I ask where we're going?"

Sean had insisted on driving to the event tonight. It had seemed the most sensible option at the time, but now she regretted that she'd be an extra problem when Sean didn't need any more shit. She couldn't even imagine what he'd be worrying about. The calls he'd likely have to make.

"No. Yes. Fuck. Sorry, Annie." He smacked the steering wheel. "I should take you home, but I just hit autopilot to my place."

"It's all right." She twisted the hem of her dress around her pinkie. Hopefully he wouldn't notice the shot of nervousness overtaking her. "Head home. I can always call a cab."

"No, you don't have to do that." He sighed. "I'll take you home after I make one phone call, yeah? That work?"

She nodded, leaning into the corner between the seat and the door, watching him. Part of her knew if she said a single word in protest, he'd change course and take her to her place. But he'd just been given a hell of a wallop, so she was sure he needed to bring in his cavalry. As quickly as possible.

He drove with one hand atop the steering wheel and the other on the gearshift. His motions were small and efficient. On the way to the party, he'd been a good driver, but the way he kept his calm now, when he was this upset, was appealing. She wanted to watch him drive in more extreme circumstances. Off-roading in Baja, maybe. Or driving one of the fast cars she'd pictured him in.

"I'm so surprised you don't have a sports car."

"I do." He cracked out a smile, almost unwillingly it seemed, because he quickly doused it. He flashed a quick glance at her. They were rolling down wide, smooth highway, and the streetlights surged and waned between, but it never was completely black. Such were the benefits of California toll roads. "I have an Audi R8."

"Then why aren't we driving that?"

"You didn't seem like the sports car type."

For some reason, she went stiff, wedging herself out of her comfortable corner. The back of her neck tightened. "I'm not cool enough for the fancy car with the non-name?"

"You sure do get sullen fast." He reached into the space between them, covering her hand where it rested on her knee. "I thought you'd like my Bronco better. That's all."

She stared at his hand. The bones were long, and he was full of grace. He was so tanned that she looked even paler than her normal shade of porcelain by comparison. Her heart took a sickly lurch. He was dealing with so much. His injury was bad enough, and she'd put him through a wicked workout this morning, culminating in side arm lifts that had stretched his shoulder to its full capacity. As reward for her physical punishment, he'd brought her to a glamorous sports-world event, thinking they'd have a great time, but then he'd been delivered awful news. With all that on his plate, here he was, comforting her because she'd been unreasonable about which overly expensive car they were driving.

"How much did the Audi cost?"

He chuckled. "Has anyone told you it's rude to ask stuff like that?"

She rolled her eyes. "You're paying me a three-million-dollar bribe for physical therapy. I think we've moved beyond rude."

"You don't even know rude, sweetheart," he

drawled, completely taking the piss out of the words. There was nothing serious behind his intent. Just more and more teasing until Annie thought she might strip out of her skin.

"You'd be surprised what I know," she retorted. Except she didn't know shit, not really. She wasn't the flirty type. There had been that long period after she'd been on the competition circuit, through college, when the thought of sex and flirting had been more terrifying than intriguing. Therapy had worked her through lots of those issues, but it had left her with a different problem. Guys either thought of her as their little sister or they were hot-shit players who didn't glance at her even for a second.

It was completely obvious which category Sean fell into. He was too gorgeous for words, much less for Annie.

Yet his hand still rested on hers. The cuff of his shirt hinted at dark, crisp hair. His wrists were thick. Man wrists. The kind of hands she'd been scared of a long time ago. But Sean's were different.

Or at least they felt different to her.

She swallowed the tight knot in her throat. "The car," she prompted again, because that was so much safer than where this conversation could end up if they didn't have nearly as many barriers between them. "How much was the car?"

"Close to a quarter mil. After taxes, at least."

She nodded as if that made perfect sense in her everyday world. She struggled to pay her bills in addition to the center's bills. The groceries alone were enough to make finances downright painful. Part of the goal of turning her ad hoc backyard setup into an official center on Seventeenth was splitting her life more definitively. Her days were absorbed by either work or the kids. The plans included a salary for a director, and though Annie intended to keep direct control, she couldn't wait for a little more time off.

She wasn't asking for much. Maybe one Saturday a month, to start with. She'd had to jump through hoops to get things covered so she could come out tonight. After all, she'd have to slowly relearn how to actually occupy herself when she wasn't surrounded by a half dozen teenagers. Maybe she'd have time for lunch with Tabitha and Rebecca, her best friends since their third year of college, when they'd randomly ended up as roommates based on a message posted on a coffee shop bulletin board. She *missed* Tabs and Becky. They were funny, and she could do with some funny in her life.

She could also do with some sex. It had been entirely too long since she'd had a man. The last time she'd been out on a date had been with Brad a year and a half ago. Brad, a music producer, had ridden a crotch rocket motorcycle and knew how to pick a delicious bottle of wine. Annie had been pretty impressed with him . . . but not impressed enough to return his calls.

Sean would have eaten a guy like Brad for breakfast. On toast. With marmalade.

There were no lights on in Sean's house, but when they pulled in, the garage door opened to reveal bright white. Even Sean's garage gleamed. The few yard tools he had, like a rake for the pebbled postage-stamp front yard, were perfectly aligned and hanging from Peg-Board like soldiers at attention. There was a red highboy Craftsman toolbox, with a work-bench next to it. Overhead, there was an organization shelf from which glass jars hung, arranged by size. Annie squinted. Were they filed by color and type too? Because everything on the left shone silver under the fluorescent lights, and things on the right were darker in hue.

Parked at the front of the garage was the sports car she'd quizzed Sean about, but they didn't linger long enough for Annie to admire it. Sean bolted upstairs to the kitchen, giving her a fast brush-off before heading up another level to the second floor.

Annie shouldn't have followed him. Casting aside her better impulses, she stepped through an open door upstairs to find his office. She ignored the trembling knot of nerves in her stomach, but she was very aware of a damp prickle taking up the center of her palms.

She knew better than this. She thought about him too much. She liked him too much.

She had to regain some distance.

Somehow.

The money he was offering was a lot, but losing it wouldn't be the worst thing in the world. She could return to her original five-year plan. It was doable; that was why she *had* the plan.

She needed a way to understand this man.

Crossing her arms low over her stomach didn't hold in the quibbly feeling that made her warm and oddly fuzzy. Though Sean established himself at a desk on the west side of the room, she stood in the middle and turned in a slow circle.

This room was . . . a war room. There was no other word for it. Battles could be mounted from the place. Sean's U-shaped desk was covered with three PC monitors across the left and a Mac on the right. The space between had a couple hard drives, and two small televisions were mounted on the wall to the right. As he sat, Sean flicked them on with a sweeping gesture on a smart remote. They came on muted, one tuned to the weather channel and the other to a financial network.

The entire stretch of the left wall was covered with maps. Her arms still laced over her stomach, Annie stepped closer. There were squiggles and data points all over them that she hadn't the slightest clue how to read. Nautical charts. Her nose was six inches away from a map of the Azores, a little chain of islands in the Atlantic that were west of Portugal.

Annie had wanted to surf the Azores, but she never got there. Terry had promised there'd be a chance, if she kept up her end of the deal and did everything she could to retain her surfing sponsorship with Leslie Sunglasses, but it had never happened. Of course. Nothing Terry claimed had happened. She hadn't been destroyed by him either, but she'd been the one to see to that.

Even though she'd been exactly the good little girl she'd been expected to be.

She spun on the balls of her feet, which were aching. She couldn't remember the last time she'd been in heels this long. Sudden awareness of the way her feet throbbed also set her up to notice everything else that was wrong with her. The backs of her knees ached, and so did her lower back. She was hungry. Something like pissiness settled in the knot between her shoulder blades.

Sean wasn't even looking at her. He had pulled up two computer screens, plus he had just put his phone to his ear. If she left, he wouldn't notice.

Except for some reason, she couldn't do it. This was the last place she should be . . . but she couldn't think of anywhere to go.

She slipped off her heels instead.

"Hey, bro," Sean said into the phone. "Crisis mode over here. And no, I'm not overreacting."

She didn't intentionally listen in while he gave the person on the other end of the line a fast but efficient rundown of what had happened with the owner of WavePro. The guy had been doing his best, but he'd had shit information to pass.

She turned her attention to a different set of charts, these ones color coded and covered in names she'd heard. Slater. Wright. Crews. These were all the members of the 'CT. Westin had all their stats posted, from all their points down to their height and approximate weight. He had listed the types of boards they rode and where they got them from. He charted sponsorships, team divisions, and coaches.

It was all there. Charts and spreadsheets. Covered in ink from handwritten annotations.

"Didn't I ask you to stay in the kitchen?" said Sean's curling, stroking voice over her shoulder.

She spun. Her skirt whirled out. She kept her arms locked over her stomach by pure force of will. "Sean . . . you're a fucking fraud, aren't you?"

Chapter 9

"I don't know what the fuck you're talking about, but you're not supposed to be in here."

"Why? Is it your private space?" She made her eyes wide and, leaning forward, dropped her voice as if she were telling a secret. "Have I stumbled into the bat cave? You're not hiding a cape and a utility belt, are you?"

He lifted a single eyebrow. "You've got a fetish for superheroes, don't you? Tell me, Annie. Does Superman get your panties wet?"

She made a dismissive noise, wrinkling her nose. "God, no. That guy wouldn't know his way around Lois Lane's panties if she tied them to a stick and waved them like a flag."

Rather than laugh at her, he buried it. "If I'm remembering correctly, I left you in the kitchen."

"All you said was 'Feel free to get a drink.'"

He crossed his arms over his chest, only to realize that meant he was mimicking her posture. He didn't shift, though. There was no sense in giving her more power than she already had. "I did. When I left you in the kitchen."

"I didn't realize it was a prison." Apparently she could give her mouth a stubborn cast when she wanted. The babydoll bow disappeared, leaving behind a sultry, displeased woman. "You're going to have to work on your skills if that's how you mean to keep women confined."

"I don't generally intend to go into kidnapping as a hobby," he said, rubbing the back of his head. "It didn't seem like that much for you to stay where you were while I made a call."

Her mouth opened, then closed again. She pinned him with a look from under her straight-line brows, but dashed it away.

"Spit it out." He wanted to touch her. But she had all the signs that said *Hands off*, and for all his shortcomings, he'd never once touched a woman who didn't want it. There was enough nasty shit in his history, things he'd done that made him an awful human, without adding taking advantage of women on top of it.

She shook her head.

"Spit it out," he repeated.

She dropped her hands to her hips with a heaving sigh. "You didn't leave me when I needed you."

"You were nearly having a panic attack. I wasn't about to leave you alone." He sputtered as the rest of the implication caught up. "And I most certainly do not *need* you."

Dark hurt flashed in her eyes, but she quickly buried it. Here and gone in a second. She was a woman who knew about hiding behind a mask. "You got shit news tonight, Sean."

"Thanks for the reminder, Baxter." He had done what he could for the night. His call to Max Sherwood, his manager, would start the ball rolling in a hundred directions. The rest he'd have to deal with in the morning. Including a visit to Tanner Wright. When Tanner's half brother kicked up a giant storm of scandal, Tanner had managed to coast through and ride it out. He might have advice for Sean. That Tanner had left the circuit made Sean slightly uncomfortable, but at least he'd be a trustworthy, unbiased source.

If Sean had anything to say about it, heads would roll. He'd shut down this documentary and do it instantly. There was too much in his past that needed hiding. He'd had a major fuckup, and he'd gotten lucky when it was time to tidy it up. More than lucky. But there was one thing he could say with one hundred percent assurance. "I'm clean."

"I know," she responded instantly.

His chest blew wide on a deep breath. Fucking hell, that had felt good. A weight stripped from him that he hadn't even known he'd been carrying. Max had been on his side, but that felt like a given. Max was paid to be on his side. He was paid a hell of a lot of money, as a matter of fact, a percentage of Sean's greater earnings. So it was in Max's best interest to ensure that Sean's career progressed in a positive manner.

Annie had no reason to believe him. No invested motive. But she looked up at him with wide, sincere eyes. Her lips were slightly parted in a serene smile.

"How do you know?" He couldn't help but ask.

Faith was something he'd never managed, not easily. Definitely not blindly. But she seemed like she had it for him, and they'd known each other—what? A week? That was kind of hard to believe in itself. He'd have thought he'd known her longer.

"This room."

"You said this room made me a fraud." His office was probably the most cluttered room in his house, but that wasn't saying much. He had two shelves of reference manuals, most of them pertaining to climate and weather patterns. The multiple computers were an indulgence. Technically he could do what he needed on a single screen. But the setup made it easier to monitor conditions in three different areas at once. He not only needed to know about where he'd surf the next week; he liked to keep an eye on the next two 'CT destinations as well.

She spun away, leaving him with a view of her shoulders. She had dressed relatively conservatively, showing little skin until tonight. He wondered if she realized what a temptation even her shoulders were. She was made of muscle and elegance, and when she lifted a hand to touch the list of his competitors, she created a divot at the cap of her shoulder. "How much work do you put into these rankings?"

He shrugged, then reminded himself that she couldn't see that. "Some. Most of the process is automated. Downloading information from the Internet."

"You're a competitor, Sean Westin. Not a playboy." Her head tilted, and dark hair shifted across the tops of her bare shoulders. She was cream and chocolate, blending her personality's sharp edges.

Her hair was thin, but it looked butter soft. Touching it would be like touching spider's silk.

"Can't I be both?"

For some reason, that made her turn around. The gentle oval of her face was tempered with that silken hair. Her eyes were widely spaced, her cheeks soft. "Don't you eventually have to decide what you are? Isn't that part of growing up?"

He knew better, but he put a hand on the wall by her head, right between his analysis of Rowdy Mc-Millan's second heat at the Hurley Pro and the overall standings of the last Billabong event. Leaning in was so damn stupid that he tried to stop himself, but he couldn't. She didn't move. Didn't flinch. Kept staring at him with those eyes that he wanted to drown in and that mouth that he wanted to taste.

He tested the tight limitations of his right arm to let the ends of her hair skim like feathers over his fingertips. She was worth the pinch of pain. "Growing up is bullshit. That's why everyone wants to be done with it as soon as possible."

Her head tilted. "I don't think that's true. There are lots of people who hold on to their high school years with an iron grip."

"The star football players. The homecoming queens. The ones for whom everything worked." The words spilled out with a hefty dose of bitter ashes.

"You weren't one of those, were you, Sean?"

When his shoulder pulled with fatigue, he put his hand on her waist, framing her in. She shied away from his touch as if she wasn't the one in charge. He'd seen that when he tried to take her hand at the party. Even in the middle of a crisis, she'd held safe within herself. But crowding her meant that maybe she'd stop asking stupid questions about his background. He wasn't ready to answer, because the answers blew. There was nothing lovely about being trapped in a house with a crazy woman. "No. I wasn't."

"You're certainly making up for lost time lately then, aren't you?" She lifted her face toward him, defiantly raising her chin. She wasn't completely unaffected, though. Her hands flattened against the wall at her hips. The pulse at the side of her throat fluttered like a butterfly's wings. "Putting on the playboy act. I don't think that's real. I don't think that's who you really are. Maybe a hard-drinking, bar-fighting surfer would take drugs to try to catch up. But you're this Sean Westin, the one who devotes hours to research. Who knows your competitors inside and out. Who's made himself an industry. You wouldn't risk any of it by doping. Steroids would defeat the purpose."

"You don't know anything about me," he growled. Fuck, he needed to shut his own mouth up, because what was he arguing for? She was saying good things about him. But at the same time, it felt like she was going too far beneath his surface. Crawling under his skin. He didn't know what to do with that. How to respond. She assumed his biggest concern was doping rumors. How cute.

She smiled serenely. "Sure I don't, Sean," she agreed, except she laced her words with doubt, teasing him. "But I also know you're about two seconds away from kissing me."

The hand he had braced against the wall clenched into a fist. He dropped to his elbow, crowding her even more. He had to pull back his bad arm, which made the nerves across the back of his skull crawl with frustration. She smelled like pure skin and soap and the faintest hint of flowers. No perfume for her. She didn't put that type of work into herself. "Shouldn't you run, then?"

Her head fell back against the wall. Her breasts pushed out with the move, her hips bending away. "Do I seem like the running type?"

He hated when other people were right about him. He'd made it his mission to defy expectations in so many ways. Otherwise he'd have a house piled to the rafters with trash, if he'd even had a house at all. He might have been homeless. It came close to being a viable option more than once when he was young. He broke stereotypes about surfers being laid back and lazy. He was neither of those.

But Annie was right about him. He was transparent as glass, because he couldn't think about anything but kissing her, not anymore. Part of him wanted to blame it on her because she'd planted the idea in his head, but he knew it wasn't true.

He'd been fixated on her mouth for hours, ever since she'd shown up at his front door in her demure dress with the gold straps. She was a demon meant to torture him.

So he kissed her.

If he'd thought she'd melt, he had another thing coming. She made a welcoming sound, a gasping moan in the back of her mouth, and rose on her toes so that she pushed up against his mouth. Her breasts brushed his chest, but he didn't touch. He didn't move his hands from their fisted position at the wall.

Kissing her was like kissing a whirling dervish cloud. She was energy and fire, but if he tried to grab on, he thought she might flit away. Disappear like so much mist. She trembled under him. Her bones were made of wire and held together with lace. But the lace was made of steel as well.

He tasted vodka on her and regretted it. He wanted only her pure taste. She was wet velvet against his tongue. Every move of his lips across hers was temptation. Keeping his hands still became harder and harder with the pounding echo of his blood in his ears.

The roar was almost enough to drown common sense. He wanted to tell himself to move on, to take more, to cup her breast in one hand. Or at the very fucking least, her tight, slim waist.

But he didn't move. Only poured his every thought into their mouths, into their kiss. They were something incendiary.

And she was someone who'd been bruised at the edges. He'd suspected it before, but the way she moved and sighed at his kiss confirmed it. Her hands fluttered at her waist, as if she wanted more but didn't know how to take it. That didn't sound like Annie in usual circumstances. The way she stood boldly and challenged the world to come at her was one of the things he dug about her.

Sean was used to women touching him, used to them immediately twining their arms around his neck and pressing lithe bodies against him. Hell, sometimes they wrapped their leg around his hip before he'd even gotten to the point of opening his lips.

Not Annie. She was waiting. She was hesitant.

And he was the worst shithead in the world for liking that.

Chapter 10

Annie didn't flee. She wasn't the fleeing type. Instead, she made a strategic exit as quickly as she could. It might be a matter of semantics, but they were words that mattered to her. Fleeing sounded weak, and she didn't want to ever feel weak again. She'd left that feeling long behind. Considering how delicious Sean's mouth was . . . maybe that exit wasn't done as quickly as it ought to have been.

She insisted on a cab, despite Sean's protests. There was no way she was getting back in a car with that man when her whole body wanted nothing more than to climb him like a spider monkey. And how strange was that? She couldn't remember the last time she was more than vaguely turned on, and that had been intentionally created as part of therapy, by trolling Tumblr for the very best in smutty-men pictures.

But there weren't pictures of Sean Westin on Tumblr. Or rather, there probably were, under the #surfing hashtag, and in every one he'd be wearing board shorts at the least or a wet suit at the most. On a board. On top of the world.

Not obviously worrying over the vagaries of his career. Except even that was an understatement. This was a crisis that could destroy his entire career and with it his name. He didn't need her experimenting all over him.

But God, she could use an orgasm that wasn't self-directed.

Except not from him. Not from him. Maybe if she repeated it to herself a hundred times more, she'd believe it.

The man could kiss like a god. Not rape-minded marauding Zeus, but one of the gods invested in making their human targets seduce themselves. He'd teased responses from her, his lips on hers promising all sorts of things.

Hence, cab.

She was a professional. She wasn't supposed to be messing with him.

But when she stood at the start of the walkway to her back door, all she wanted was Sean. She didn't want to walk into her house. There was no quiet there. No privacy. She looked longingly at her ramp and pool.

Skateboarding could fix her. Could get her out of her head and into her body. She bit the edge of her thumb where the cuticle met her nail.

"If you want to skate, you'll at least have to come inside and change your clothes," said a voice from behind her. "If you wreck that dress, I'll be so annoyed. Do you know how hard it was to find an actual *dress* that you were willing to wear?"

Annie's shoulders released from their anxious climb up toward her ears. "I know, Mom."

"Twelve. Twelve dresses. That's how many I had to take back to the store. Because it's not like you could be bothered to go shopping, even when you're the one with the fancy schmancy event."

"I know, Mom." Her tension was slipping away. This was a conversation they'd had a hundred times. A million. "What are you doing here, anyway? Your town house is two miles away."

"Two point six. You might as well call it three miles."

"You say three miles like it's some giant hardship." Annie finally turned around. Her mom was leaning a shoulder against the open doorway. She had on skinny jeans, awesome boots with buckles that went up to the knees, and a cowl-necked sweater. Annie's mom had style, which was why it was kind of pointless for Annie to go shopping. Denise had it covered.

"You know there are people who live *thousands* of miles away from their families," Annie continued. "They leave for college and never come back."

Denise waved a hand, her nose curling. "Those parents obviously did something wrong, to make their kids run away."

Annie rolled her eyes. "You don't believe that."

"I don't." Denise flashed a grin. "But I like having you living nearby."

"Easier to spy on me?"

"You know it." She stepped back in the doorway, letting Annie move past her to the stairs, and they both climbed.

Annie loved her bedroom. It was on the east side of the house, which meant it got gorgeous sunlight in the mornings. The bed was huge for her. There was no reason why someone who was only five foot one needed a king-sized bed with a half-canopy headboard. She'd piled it with all sorts of blankets, from a fuzzy fleece to a black-and-gold afghan that her grandmother had made. The pillows teetered haphazardly.

She was at least a little bit self-aware. She'd made her bed into a nest, a safe place where she could hide from the world. Nothing was wrong with that as long as she didn't hide forever.

Ducking into her closet, she pulled the stupid dress in question off over her head. "What are you doing here, anyway?"

"I can't hear you, darling. Stop talking with your mouth full."

Annie stuck her head out the door and shot her mother a look. "We're not at the dinner table."

"Fine, don't talk with a face full of fabric."

"Does Dad know you're here?"

Denise wasn't easily shaken. She was an inch shorter than Annie, but she'd always been able to wrap Annie's dad around her little finger. Andy adored Denise, and he had since they'd met in college. She rolled her eyes and said with droll emphasis, "No, he thinks I'm working the corner."

"Come on, Mom." Annie shuddered as she pulled on a pair of cotton pajama bottoms and a camisole. "Don't be icky."

"Don't ask stupid questions," Denise said with a laugh.

"Did you just call your only daughter stupid?"

Denise sat on the love seat that Annie had strategically placed in front of the fireplace. She only managed to use the fireplace about twice a year, since temperatures in Southern California seldom dipped low enough. But it sure looked pretty in the meantime. Annie dropped onto the love seat next to her and leaned her head on her mother's shoulder.

She was tired. But more than that, she was a twisting mass of contradictions and nerves. Her fingertips tingled with anxiety, but her lips were tingling as well—for an entirely different reason. "Why *are* you here?"

Denise passed a hand over Annie's hair. It had been a long time since her mom had petted her head, and it said a lot about the place each was in. "The last time you went to a surfing industry party, you came home pretty upset," Denise said quietly.

Annie chuffed a laugh at the understatement, but it wasn't actually a funny subject. That night had left Annie a mess, and it was the reason she'd had to work through so much. Her entire life shifted that night. "I proved I could protect myself, at least." It was the one bright side to what had happened—the bright side she'd sometimes clung to desperately.

"You did." Her mom squeezed her shoulders. "My brave and amazing baby."

"I was eighteen."

"Exactly."

Despite her age, she'd thought she could conquer the world. She'd been on the Prime circuit for women's surfing for two years already, and a sponsor had come calling. Terry had been the rep for Leslie Sunglasses, and he'd told Annie how much they liked her look and her skills. Then he'd told Annie how much he'd liked *her*. On a personal level.

"Sean isn't Terry. He was a perfect gentleman." Even when he'd kissed the hell out of her. That had been all about being devoured by his mouth. Nothing else. He hadn't touched her. Even though he'd sheltered her against the wall, she could have ducked away anytime. It was nothing like what Terry had done.

Denise's fingers dug into Annie's shoulder with remembered upset. Annie patted her hand. "I still say I shoulda killed that man. Your daddy has a very big hammer. If I'd come up on him from behind . . ."

"Murderous doesn't look good on you. And that was a long time in the past."

"Is it?" Denise's eyes were lighter brown than Annie's, since Annie took after her dad in that regard. But when they filled with concern, they darkened and turned luminous. Annie knew love from the way it was filtered through those eyes. Pure and undiluted. "I still worry about the effects. You've never had a long-term boyfriend since that dick."

"He and I dated for three months. I'm not sure it counted as long-term."

Denise pulled a frown. "It was the summer after you graduated high school. Anything more than three days is long-term when you're that young. But he was a smarmy, too-old-for-you, good-for-nothing."

"He was twenty-three." Just out of college, he barely knew what he was doing himself. But he'd known enough to trade in expectations and disgusting favors. Annie had thought he made her feel special. Instead, he'd been trying to artificially build her up, the better for tearing her down when the time came.

"I know exactly how old he was. I still regret letting you even *talk* to him." Denise squeezed Annie. "I'm sorry for that, Annie. I should have kept you safer."

Annie jerked back far enough that she could look her mother in the eyes again. Her jaw dropped open. "You are an amazing mother. You have nothing to apologize for."

"I thank God that ass didn't win at turning your head toward a pro career. You didn't give up your slot at San Diego."

Annie was thankful for the same thing. She'd had to surf long enough to keep her scholarship, but after that she'd been able to walk away from the entire riddled, corrupted system.

She bit her lip hard enough that a wash of pain ran through her. "Sean's in trouble. He found out some bad news tonight."

Denise's eyebrows flew up. "Something happened while you were with him?"

Annie found herself recounting the entire story, including the way that she'd almost lost her shit to a panic attack, since her mother knew every bit of her history and treatment. But when she moved on to the part where her positive conversation with Frank Wakowski had turned sour for Sean, Denise sat up straight.

"Annie . . ." Her voice was laden with warning as she shook her head. "This isn't something you need to get involved with."

She sighed, dropping back against the arm of the love seat. "I know, Mom. And really, there's nothing I *can* do. But Sean's in a world of hurt."

She knew she'd be in the same world if she didn't back away. Kissing him had been foolish. So ridiculous that it felt like a farce. If she had even a modicum of sense, she'd walk away from him immediately. But how would that look? She didn't want to be the kind of person who left when the shit hit the fan.

He seemed to have so few people on his side. His first call in times of trouble had been to his manager, and he had definitely not followed it up with any sort of family call. Maybe he'd saved that for after she left, but she doubted it. There'd been nothing in magazines or articles over the years about his family. He didn't talk about them. It was as if he'd sprung fully formed into the surfing world at eighteen, kicking ass through the Prime.

If she abandoned him, he'd be alone. Part of her warred with that idea, arguing that it wasn't as if they were *real* friends anyhow. She was hired. Practically an employee.

An employee to whom he was offering three million dollars. She hated that it was even a concern. It made her feel dirty and sticky, as if she were one of those people with screwed-up priorities. But the money wasn't even *for* her, not directly. It was for the center. That was different.

Keeping her mouth to herself wasn't asking too much.

"You can't take Sean on as a project," Denise insisted.

"I'm not intending to." Annie drew her feet up on

the couch, knees in front of her chest. She wrapped her arms around them. "I'm going to do my job and get out."

Her mom didn't believe her. Annie knew that look from the few times she'd tried to slide by on schoolwork in order to go surfing or skateboarding. She drew a cross over her chest with two fingers. "No project. Nothing more than work. I swear it."

Chapter 11

Sean didn't get many visitors at his house. He certainly didn't get unannounced visitors. But when he pulled open the front door, he felt a small smile curve his mouth. "Annie. What are you doing here?"

"Way to sound inviting," she said with a cheeky little smile. Dark lashes ringed her eyes, and her mouth looked like it had been colored pink with some gloss. She ducked past him, under the arm holding open the door.

"But we don't have an appointment." It had been two days since the Saturday night party. The night Sean had kissed Annie like the idiot he was.

The thing was, he couldn't get that kiss out of his mind. He kept running it over and over in his head, as if he could re-create it if he thought about it enough times. Like he could actually taste the sweetness of her mouth, rather than just remember it. That wasn't going to happen again.

"I know. I wanted to come by and make sure you were okay precisely because we *don't* have an appointment." She shot him a severe look. "Calling my office voice mail in the middle of the night? Seriously, dude. That's a douche bag move."

"Something came up."

"Yeah, I figured that much, considering the weight you put on your recovery." She perched on the edge of a cherry-stained coffee table and picked up its only decoration, a crystal paperweight. She held it up to a ray of sunshine, and the embedded gold flecks rained sparkling light on her features. "You think I don't understand that you've got things you need to deal with?"

He ran his palm over the top of his head. He'd cut his hair bristly short about a year ago, on a trip to Bondi Beach, Australia. The feeling of sand encrustation had finally gotten to him, so he'd had a go with a pair of clippers. Coyote had spit nails over changing his "image" without consultation, but the new look had nailed him pages in a national non-surfing mag. Good enough for him, and good enough for Coyote too.

But this whole situation was a lot more dire than shaving his hair off. He could get booted from the Coyote lineup. He could get dropped by any or all of his sponsors, even before the rumors were verified. Image was half the gig. Ranking in competition was the other half, and fuck, he still hadn't won anything. For that matter, he was having a hell of a time hanging on. If the distasteful aspects of his childhood came out, he'd have an unsavory taint. And that wasn't even counting his brush with the law.

There might be less pressure on him if he'd won a title. Unfortunately, he was a long way from that.

As if on cue, his shoulder throbbed. "I can't do this now."

"Which this?" she asked calmly. She set the globe down slowly, then crossed her legs. "Physical therapy or kissing? Because only one's up for offer."

"You didn't come in with your usual bag of tricks, so maybe you mean kissing." He shouldn't be snarly, shouldn't be an awful ass. But he both dreaded and anticipated her tote bag full of equipment. At least it would be the devil he knew, rather than the meeting he was headed for with Tanner Wright.

"That won't happen again," she said with a voice so even, he almost thought she believed it. He *wanted* her to believe it, because maybe she could convince them both.

She stood, and he moved closer. All he wanted was to frame her face in his hands and kiss the everloving hell out of her. He wanted the freedom to touch her this time, to twine his fingers through her hair and see if it was as silken as it looked. As he'd dreamed about last night.

She was wearing another T-shirt, this one with the four horses of the Apocalypse. Pony style. Little-girl toys with snarling, vicious muzzles, ranging in color from bloodred to pale green.

Annie was a work of art.

The growing heat meant she'd left her usual jeans at home and wore dark khaki shorts. He wished they were a little shorter, because her legs were pale but lean with muscle and subtle strength.

He had to be losing his mind. This was just a way to distract himself from the holy-fuckin-hell levels of trouble coming down on his head. Annie was sweet and levelheaded, but he shouldn't be thinking of her quite so much.

His crazy had hit new levels. Any woman who got involved with him at this point would either be doing so because she was the same sort of crazy, or because she felt oozing pity toward him. His stomach turned at that second option. He wanted to impress Annie, wanted her to think of him as a guy with his shit together.

There was no way he was letting her in. Not that way. Fuck it, not for any reason.

Letting people in only led him to trouble. Led him to arson, if he was going to be fucking honest with himself. "I have to go, Annie."

"Do you mean figuratively? As in, trying to run from this discussion we're having? Or literally?"

"I have to meet someone." His throat was tight with something thick. He forced a cough, then another. "I just . . . I have to go."

But he didn't move. And neither did she. Her mouth parted, and he was so shit at resisting temptation. Because he kissed her. His hands slipped around the back of her neck. She came closer, then closer still. His body brushed hers. She was lithe and hot under the sun's warmth.

He wanted to absorb her.

She grabbed his shoulders, fingers digging in tight. They breathed together. Fast and then faster still. That easily, they were part of something new, something they could build together.

Something he wanted to believe in.

But then, she yanked her mouth away from his

and pushed back. She lifted the back of her hand to her mouth. Her fingers were trembling. "I quit. I can't take care of you anymore."

He wasn't surprised. When things went to shit, they tended to go off the pier all together. "Yeah. Fine."

"Doesn't mean I'm done with you."

He looked closely at her, but he'd never been a mind reader. He didn't know what to make of the expression in her dark eyes or the way her tongue slicked across her bottom lip. He touched her only because he couldn't resist. "Don't make decisions you'll regret, Annie. I'm going out now. If you're here when I get home . . ." He took her mouth fast and hard. His tongue plunged between her teeth and she welcomed him. "There won't be any going back. Not for either of us."

She'd fired him as a patient. The mixed relief and annoyance he had at that made his head swim. He wanted the best for his rehab, sure. Whatever it took. But that wasn't the only way out. He'd gotten where he was through his own sweat and determination. He might not have been scoring the way he liked last year, but as soon as he got over this injury, he'd fix that. The rewards that might come with the risks, though. Jesus, they'd be worth it.

Sean started walking toward the beach. Considering that his house was only steps from the pier, it didn't take him long to get to Wright School so long as he ignored the pure need rushing through his body. Tanner had left the circuit in December, and since then everyone knew he'd poured every bit of his energy into the school he was opening.

The place had once been a surf shop run by Tanner's mom and stocked with the usual run of things. Sean abided by the principle that you didn't need much to surf. A decent board, a pair of shorts, and go. Wet suit only when necessary. It was what he'd survived on, after all. By the time he was fifteen, board wax felt like a luxury.

Wright Break had been one of the better stores, at least. They sold good stuff, even when it came to the California-emblazoned T-shirts for tourists. Theirs didn't fall apart after five washings.

The store was empty. Brown butcher paper covered the inside of the big plate glass windows. Not abandoned, however. A two-by-four propped open the front door and music poured through the crack.

No one was expecting him, and he'd taken a risk by showing up unannounced. But there was no telling whether Tanner would have answered a call from him. The best thing they could be called at one point was rivals. The worst was acquaintances. Sean didn't have much call for friendship with Tanner. He knocked briskly on the door anyway. He'd never exactly been put off by expectations.

Tanner answered the door. He was a big guy, with really wide shoulders for a surfer and incredibly thick thighs. Sean had researched his competition, so he knew where Tanner's epic air came from. The man had been known for power moves, and his hefty body had been the force behind them.

He also had a bright smile. "Hey, mate. It's good to see you."

Sean gently tongued the inside of his bottom lip.

Did Tanner mean that? His expression was open enough. With paint splattered up his arms, and a roller still in his hand, he'd obviously been in the middle of a project. His expression seemed happy enough, but that could just as easily be attributable to his most excellent girlfriend, Avalon Knox.

Sean didn't like the part of him that doubted everyone, but he'd been proven right more times than not. "Wish I could say the same, bro." It made life easier if he tried to suss out motives ahead of time.

"Ah." Tanner nodded. "You've finally heard."

"Then you did know."

Tanner's wide shoulders lifted and fell in a surprisingly helpless shrug. "Come on in, dude. I've got a few beers in a cooler."

"Can't. Training regimen," Sean said, and fuck, did he feel like an idiot of the first magnitude. He ought to be fucking grateful that Tanner was stepping to the side to let him in. Turning down a drink from the man was hard to do.

"Got some fruit juice too. Sage shoved them in there."

"That'll do." A flicker of relief licked at Sean like a tiny wave.

The interior of the building had been fully gutted since the last time Sean had been inside it. Where there had once been a counter and two registers was now bare floor. The clothing racks were all gone. With all the empty space, the place seemed bigger and brighter. The front third had three rows of cafeteria-style tables, and full-color photographs of famous surfers on giant waves had been laminated directly to the wall.

"That's the study area," Tanner said, pointing to the front. "I'm painting the gear storage right now."

"Study?"

"Yeah. We're going to work on the fundamentals of tides and oceanography, but they're also going to have time to work on school studies. Get help if they need to trade it around. Weather ain't always the way you'd hope. They need to learn their limits."

Sean felt his mouth twist. "You can say that again." He'd busted his shoulder by ignoring his limits. He subtly stretched, drawing his shoulder blades together in the way Annie had taught him.

Tanner put the paint roller down in a bucket and traded out for their drinks. "Rumors are just rumors. You don't have to let them get to you."

"I got a call from a media company this morning. They were asking to do an interview. Didn't say specifically what they wanted to talk about."

But he had his guesses. He took a swig of the cold juice. The mango chilled his throat . . . but not the little kernel of fury burning away inside him. He'd worked so fucking hard to get where he was. Now someone was trying to take it away from him. "Tanner, you're the expert. So many years on the 'CT and fuck, now we all know what you were hiding for so long."

Tanner shook his head. He pointed at Sean with the neck of his bottle. "You trying to tell me you've got something as heavy as I was carrying around?"

Sean swallowed. He was proving crap at not giving hints lately. "No."

Tanner's gaze turned solemn. His blue eyes dropped to consider his feet in their worn sandals.

He had specks of paint down his legs too, a decorative addition to his cargo shorts. "Then you don't have to worry about it. You need to learn to let it go. Secrets carried only get heavier as you go along."

Sean's eyebrows felt like they were doing their damnedest to fly off his face. "Come on, dude. A few months ago, you were so pissed at your dad, you'd have believed it if someone told you that he'd shot Gandhi."

"That was then," Tanner said simply. "I've let a lot of stuff go. And don't get me wrong, I know my dad was a shithead. But I did the wrong thing, keeping it all under wraps. I called my mom this morning— well, it was morning for me. Evening for her."

"She's still in China?" Sean sat in a camp chair next to the cooler. He stretched his legs out and kept his head down. It was easy for Tanner to be so damn Zen. His mom, Eileen, was a gracious, graceful woman who was finally doing exactly what she wanted to in life.

"Nah, she's in Cambodia now."

"Jesus, aren't you worried about her?"

Tanner pushed the front door open wider, letting out some of the paint fumes. "She's in Angkor Wat. Me worrying about her doesn't matter. She's seeing the things she's dreamed of. She's better off now."

A part of Sean was tempted to ask if maybe he should call Mako. As Hank Wright's illegitimate, half-Tahitian son, Mako understood being punished by the past. But he was still a sore spot for Tanner, and Sean didn't much feel like alienating the man who might currently be his only friend.

Sean shook his head. "I don't understand what's

going on. A documentary on me? I'm practically a no one as far as the 'CT goes. There're two dozen guys who're ranked better and have done bigger things."

"I don't know." Tanner leveled a direct stare at Sean. "But if I were you, I'd start with anyone who's got it out for you."

Chapter 12

Annie walked away. The second Sean strode off down the street and left her behind, she piled into her car and fucking *bounced*. She wasn't a doormat. Had never, ever been something even remotely close to a doormat. She took an hour-long drive down the coast, to a little hole-in-the-wall that served the best chili cheese fries she'd ever put in her mouth. It was the avocado ranch sauce that made them special. They were worth the drive, but she only made it when she had major decisions to work through. Carbs and cheese always seemed to make thinking go easier.

They didn't fail her this time either.

Then she went back. She sat on his front step. Exactly where a doormat went.

Except this was different. All the decisions she'd made last night had flown right out the window. After she'd talked things through with her mom, it had all seemed set in stone. By the time she woke up alone in her bed, dreams of Sean barely fading into the background, she'd thought she was happy with her choice. When he'd bailed on their physical therapy appoint-

ment, she'd only gone to his house in order to hold him
to the schedule, like she'd threatened him when they'd
started this journey. Just because he was progressing
rapidly and healing at a remarkable pace was no reason to slack off.

But he'd been a mess. A complete, under-the-
surface head case. He'd been . . . accessible. Vulnerable, though, good God, she'd never say that word to
his face. He'd probably snap. But he needed someone
right now, and that made her . . . need him in return.

He was a dick. But she wanted to play with his
cock.

Normally, she'd think poorly of a woman who
made a sweeping decision based on gonads. There
were plenty of penises in the sea, and they all worked
more or less the same, with varying levels of attractiveness. Or so she'd figured.

With Sean . . . everything was new. She was
tempted in a way she hadn't felt in years. Since Terry,
if she was really, really honest with herself.

At least the way he was healing meant she
wouldn't feel guilty about turning him over to a different physical therapist.

She'd thought she didn't get those butterflies in
the chest, stomach-swooping tingles anymore, because they were a teenager sort of thing. Maybe
other women kept getting them, because God knew
she'd heard plenty from her friends. And she wasn't
completely immune to attraction and sexuality,
which was why she'd thought she was okay. She'd
thought she was healed.

Maybe she hadn't been.

The way she felt when Sean kissed her gave her

stronger feelings than she could remember . . . ever. She was someone new with his mouth on her. Someone who wanted everything.

She was someone who thought she deserved everything.

Starting with Sean.

The sun had dipped behind the house at her back by the time Sean trudged up his front walkway. He looked exhausted. His shoulders drooped, and he walked with his head down, which was not at all like him. His hands were shoved in his pockets. He was ruining the line of his handsome trousers.

That he didn't care said something terrible about his mood.

"Didn't get the answers you wanted?" She was sitting with her back against the door and her knees up. Her hands fidgeted, nail digging into cuticle. She put a hand flat on the wood. Only when she felt how the sun had baked the pale gray paint did she also realize how fucking sweaty her hands were. Her stomach had taken up residence somewhere around her clavicle. The blood roared in her ears in a swoosh-swoosh that said her pulse was high. Stupidly high.

"Why are you still here?"

When she couldn't make herself answer his question, he gave a laugh that wasn't anything close to actual laughter before unlocking the door. "Pretty sure that when someone dismisses another person, they don't see each other again. I've been here before, after all."

"Who's ever dismissed Sean Westin?" Incredulousness felt like weightlessness. She darted around him, stopping in the foyer to rise up on her toes. Or maybe she felt weightless because she was breathing too fast. She was going to make herself pass out if she kept it up.

His mouth twisted in a bitter smile. "Plenty. But they've got another thing coming if anyone expects to do it again. I'm not putting up with that shit anymore."

He was in a bad place. That much was crystal clear. She couldn't help herself; she looped her fingers around his wrist. Well, not that she could wrap her grip completely around him. He had a man's wrists, the bones solid and sturdy, perfectly contrasted with the smooth cuff of his expensive dress shirt.

What if her traitorous girly bits had aimed too high? What if last night's kiss had been an anomaly, born of his shitty night and her invasiveness in trespassing in his office, and this morning's had only been about that vulnerability she'd seen? Maybe he didn't actually want her. He'd been off his guard. Rattled.

She'd just have to rattle him again. "Come on," she said, tugging him toward the stairs.

Even in something so simple as stairs, the existence of Sean's money all but glared at her. They looked like glass, supported with only the tiniest slivers of metal that did absolutely zero to hide the view of the floor dropping away beneath them.

"I almost wish I were wearing a skirt." She darted her best cheeky grin over her shoulder.

Sean's confusion had disappeared, giving way to something thunderous. His eyebrows lowered, and those bladelike cheekbones were even sharper as the skin drew taut. Bright slashes of color across the tops made him look like a savage prince. But then, he always looked like a prince.

"No, you don't," he said in a low voice. "You're not the type. In fact, I bet if *I* had been the one to suggest that, you'd have given me the finger."

"You're probably right." Her throat felt so tight, she was going to choke on something as simple as words. There was a difference between wanting something and being bold enough to take it.

It had been so long, and to be truthful, it had never been like this. Her fingers were still looped around his wrist, but she wasn't sure if that was her pulse or his she felt rushing at her fingertips.

When they came to the open door of his bedroom, she almost chickened out. She froze for a half step but then just as quickly stumbled over her own feet to keep going. His bedroom was sparse to the point of being a little frightening. Only one picture on the wall, of a wave that Annie couldn't identify off the top of her head. No surprise, since she'd never really gotten to the traveling phase of competition. She'd been only a young local when she'd been all but broken by the pro industry.

His bed was huge, but it hit the very opposite end of the spectrum from hers. His was stripped down with only a couple extra-long pillows and two carefully layered blankets in shades of blue.

"What are we doing, Annie?" His voice was a growl that stroked down her back and made her skin tingle. But he wasn't pulling away. There was no real way she could drag him along if he didn't want to go.

She stopped with Sean still behind her. Still attached by her hand and his wrist. Blindly, without looking, she twisted her palm around and laced their fingers together. Pulled him closer behind her. He stepped near enough that she could feel his presence with every one of her cells straining toward him.

Her breath, which had been so frantic moments ago, stuttered to a stop.

"I won't touch you, Annie," he said. No, that wasn't mere words. That was a growl. A low-down dirty promise made with innocent words, even when he was saying the very opposite of what she wanted.

A little smile pulled at the corners of her mouth. She bit it back, but it was a good thing Sean was behind her. He'd have seen it in her eyes, and he was treating this moment as if it were dire. Like they were about to jump off the edge of the building. Even though it was soft beach sand beyond the edge of the deck, the three-story drop would still hurt.

She'd never been suicidal. Not even when she'd thought everything was lost. She sure as fuck wasn't about to start when she had a man like Sean Westin so close to her grasp.

"I'm serious," he continued. "I'm the last person in the world you want to get involved with right now. I have no idea what kind of shit is coming down on my head."

"None of that says you don't want to be with me."

His harsh intake of breath was enough for her. She knew what that meant. He wanted her as badly as she wanted him. "I don't take things lightly, Sean. People will wonder why I've stepped away from you as a client, and it won't be a reflection on you. They'll say I couldn't hack your situation."

"Then why?" He rasped the words. His hand clenched on hers. A flutter of sensation over her right hip was his other hand seeking her out.

"Because I can't stay away from you." That was half the truth, at least. She turned so she could face him. His eyes were bright and blue, and she wanted to drown in them. "Because I think you're just as damaged as I am."

He shook his head once, then again. "Fuck, Annie, you're not—"

She lifted her hand and put her fingertips across his mouth. His lips were soft, but she pressed hard enough that she could feel the resistance of his teeth behind them. She wanted to test his limits. She wanted her own boundaries blown away.

Stepping back a foot, she slipped free of him. She hooked her thumbs in the hem of her T-shirt. "You're not my client anymore."

"You've made that more than clear." A muscle twitched at the side of his jaw. His gaze was locked on her hands like a missile on its target. His fists opened and clenched at his sides.

"Then I can do this now." She pulled her shirt off in one quick move, but she didn't let go of it. She held it in front of her hips, and her arms framed her breasts. "I'd have worn a prettier bra if I'd known what I was gonna do today."

He had a cheeky, smart-ass smile. When he took a step toward her, the intent behind his eyes made her heart take a fluttery tumble and do its best to escape her chest.

His fingertips grazed the outside curve of her breast through the plain white fabric. Then he followed the arch of her flesh up and over, stopping at the tiny white rose in the depth of her cleavage. "I don't know. I can't picture you in black lace."

"I'm not the type, am I?"

"You're not." He lowered his head slowly, as if giving her the chance to pull away. Which was completely ridiculous, since she'd been the one to start this.

He was practically a gentleman. A lamb in rogue's clothing, maybe. Except the way he kissed her collarbone said he still had plenty of expertise to go around.

She dropped her shirt, and it fluttered around her shins before catching on the edge of the bed. Maybe her last connection to sanity, floating away. The sun was setting at her back, the last rays kissing her skin with their warmth. She was floating too. When he finally kissed her, his mouth gliding over hers, she knew she was lost.

In the best kind of way.

Chapter 13

Sean had made some foolish choices before, and part of him kept insisting this was one. The rational part of his brain, or what was left of it, kept saying that Annie didn't know what she was doing. There was no way she could give up the three million he'd offered for her teen center.

Flat out, he wasn't worth it.

But he couldn't pull away the way he should. He couldn't stop touching her. He couldn't, couldn't. Couldn't. He was strung tight as wire trying to hold himself back.

And then fuck it, he *wouldn't*.

He snapped, wrapping one arm around her lower back.

She was made of flesh and skin and bone. He kissed the upper swells of her breasts. Yeah, her bra was plain, but it framed the most perfect set of breasts he'd ever seen. She was pale and soft. When he opened his mouth at the top edge of that bra, she gasped. Her hands landed across the backs of his shoulders, but lightly. So lightly he could almost ignore their touch.

Yet he couldn't ignore the way she trembled. The shaking worked all the way through her, a fine vibration that had her operating on some higher frequency.

"Are you all right?" He kept his head down as he asked, his mouth on her flesh. If she said no, he'd stop. But he wouldn't want her to see his face. He'd probably give away how hard it would be to stop. He'd heard about his self-indulgence too many times to count.

"I'm good," she whispered. "I'm good. I'm fine." She sound determined more than anything else. Her voice shook to go along with her body, and he darted a glance up to see her dark eyes.

She was a creature torn in two. Her mouth opened on a silent gasp when he cupped the fullness of her breast, but her gaze was troubled. The flush across her cheeks spread to her throat. Her porcelain paleness turned pink.

He could see it in her eyes. She was using him to explore something that had once hurt her. He was free game to so many women, the kind of guy they took for a spin or two before tucking him away and moving on to a real relationship guy. He could do that. He could give her the freedom she needed to try to move on. He *wanted* to do that.

He twisted the two of them so that Annie's back faced the bed. The sun streaking in through the westward window painted her with an impressionist's brush. Delicate art blended with the strength in her wiry muscles. Her stomach was taut and drawn hard with her mixed tension. He wanted to see her softened. Relaxed.

Dropping to kneel before her was easy. Surprisingly so. He'd always thought of himself as a balanced lover. Not selfish, but not in the least subservient.

Except now. The carpet beneath his knees, he framed her narrow hips between his hands. The pose earned an openmouthed smile from her. The tip of her tongue dipped into the corner of her mouth. The reverence in her hovering hands made him want to give her everything. Anything he was capable of.

"What are you doing?" Her voice had dropped to a whisper, and in the empty room she sounded a little lost.

He took her hand and placed a kiss in the center of her palm. Her skin was soft, with texture from the lines of her life. She closed her fingers around the edge of his jaw. "I'm taking what I want."

"What's that?"

"Don't you know?" He flashed a good smile up at her, one that had creamed the panties of plenty of models and wanna-be actresses. He had game. Time to use it. "I want you to come so hard you see stars."

That smile of hers turned incredibly cheeky, making her jawline softer. He cupped her rounded chin in one hand, turning her mouth down for a kiss that snatched away her gasp. But then she pulled her mouth away. "Seeing stars is usually just a sign of oxygen deprivation. If you concentrate on increasing oxygenation and breathing evenly, an orgasm can be enhanced or even increased."

"Damn you're cute when you talk smart."

She stuck her tongue out at him. "And you're a smart-ass when you talk all dumb."

He wrapped both hands around her rib cage but kept his grip loose. She was as skittish as a wild animal, and though her mouth could keep going all cheekylike, he couldn't escape the fear that she'd bolt if given half the chance. He stretched up toward her mouth and she bent down. Their kisses were soft. Gentle. But her mouth tasted like spice and sugar, and he wanted more. Holding himself back was a bitch.

His muscles locked tight, and something like anticipation made him about as rational as a shark. He'd intended to taste her from there, pulling her shorts down and nudging her legs apart. But when he opened his mouth on the curve of her waist, she jumped. She needed more control than that, even.

He dropped to his heels, pulling her forward. She squeaked. "What are you doing?"

"Come here."

He pulled and tugged and stripped her shorts. She hopped from one foot to the other, letting him, but giggling with a slightly nervous tone. Then he took her mouth again. It seemed so simple. Kiss, kiss . . . explosion. They burned. Her mouth clung to his when he tried to move away, so he kissed her more. Again. Until his brain swam. He cupped the softest part of her ass through her panties, which were plain white to match her bra.

Leaning again, enough so he sat back on his heels, he nuzzled the tiny white bow at the top of her panties. She smelled like a woman, and though he kept his hands away from her pussy to intentionally give her time to warm up, he could tell she was wet. He buried his face against her stomach, then licked a trail across her skin and left goose bumps in his wake.

Hands on her hips tugged her down, over him. "You're unbelievably hot."

She was. The tight tendons between her thighs and the seam of her body twitched with his words. She was *strong*. Her stomach wasn't just flat; she had a faint line of muscle down the center. He spanned the side of her rib cage with a single hand, and beneath his palm were sinew and bone. She needed pampering, and she needed to be taken care of. He knew the pressure she put herself under—the need to keep going without being able to rest because rest was closer to failure than she could afford.

"You don't have to say that."

"I do. Because it's true."

Her gaze troubled, she rubbed her hands over his jaw.

He hadn't shaved that morning. He hadn't shaved yesterday either, but that had been calculated. He'd wanted to be artfully stubbly for a photo shoot for a line of board shorts—a stylistic choice that felt faintly self-centered and foolish now. What were a well-chosen suit and *GQ*-level stubble when the entire industry had turned on him?

But now his beard was softer. She left tingles in her wake. She was her own sort of magician. Someone he'd have never known if not for the strange twist his career had taken. For a moment, he was actually grateful for that argument he'd gotten into at the bar in Bali. The guys had been loudmouths and not worth it . . . but the fight had brought him to Annie.

He pulled her down until she straddled his waist, and then he lay on his back. She had a wiry strength, but she looked half-stunned as she stared down at him. "What do you want, sugar? Anything I've got, it's yours."

Her hands spread wide over his chest, and the position pushed her breasts together. Her knees barely grazed him. She was all strength and completely dynamic. He framed her hips, stroked down the length of her thighs. She dropped her chin to her chest, then looked up at him from under her lashes. "I want . . . I want to lick you."

He froze. His thumbs dug into the soft flesh at the inside of her thighs, below those tendons that stood out in stark relief. "Well. That's not exactly what I expected."

"Is that a no?"

"Fucking hell, it's not a no."

She laughed, though she still seemed strung so tight, she could explode. But she jerked him straight up to her same level of twisted up when she spread her knees and dropped to balance on him. Her pert little ass pressed against his cock, which was hard enough that he throbbed. He groaned.

"Bad?" Fuckin' A, she was teasing him. She lifted herself high enough so that she wasn't making contact anymore. "Should I stop?"

"You should do absolutely whatever the fuck makes you happy." He managed to keep his hands loose on her hips and didn't haul her ass down to grind on him, but fuck he was close to doing just that. He settled for letting his spine curve up so he could brush over her delicate flesh.

Those panties were soaked, the white fabric turning almost translucent. He could see the seam of her lips, a hint of trimmed hair. He nudged both thumbs under her hem. Taunting could go both ways. Her flesh was damp with her need for him. His stomach clenched on want. He pushed his hips up, and fortunately she came down at the same time. Then bent all the way down, until her breasts rubbed against his chest.

The way she kissed him could almost make him think this was something special. But she was distracting herself, trying him out. This didn't count. Not in the scheme of things. Not as something big.

Her mouth traced fire over his shoulder, over the tops of his pecs. Her fingers dug into the sides of his chest. Holding still enough for her to explore was going to make him snap. He could roll her over and shove her down into the floor so he could fuck her fierce and hard and *more*.

But this was Annie. She was still strung so tight, he could snap her with one thump. Her hips were making little thrusting motions under his grip. Most women would be writhing, pressing into him in pure demonstration of their willingness. But she was constrained. Tiny movements. Tiny grasping.

Tiny but steady. She traced her tongue over the top of his abs, and he clenched so hard, he could have been getting ready for a magazine photo spread. This was . . . Fuck, this was temptation.

"Annie, I'm not sure . . ."

"You said anything." She wrapped her fingers around his hands and pulled them away from her hips. He tried to lace their fingers together, but she spread their arms and pinned his hands to the floor. Even with her full weight behind it, the pin was a joke. It would take barely a jolt to shake her. But her breath rushed in a hot wash over his chest. A matching pounding pulse fluttered at the base of her throat.

The red across her cheeks hadn't faded in the least. He concentrated on that. She was pushing herself hard for some reason. Her lips parted, lush and wet. Her eyes were so dark that sometimes he couldn't read them. But the skin between her brows was tight, and she bit her lip. He was laid out on his fucking back in the middle of his floor. This was for her. Asking him for some restraint wasn't unreasonable.

"I *meant* anything." He swallowed hard, pushing his own turn-on away. He'd get plenty, especially if what she wanted so badly was her mouth on him. Still, his voice came out hoarse. He was rewarded with a brilliant smile.

Her touch trailed up his arms, tickling the inside of his elbows and then digging into his biceps. She stopped at his shoulders. Kissing her smile was heady. A deadly kind of delicious.

"Besides," she said against the underside of his jaw as she trailed her open lips over his skin, "I'm begging to go down on you. I can't imagine a single guy in the world who'd complain about that."

He chuckled even though his chest felt like he was burning his way through the last of his oxygen. "Yeah, no. Not protesting. Not at all."

"Good boy."

Chapter 14

God, Annie felt high. She'd smoked pot exactly
once, when she'd visited friends at UC Santa
Cruz. It had been her freshman year, when she was
still dealing with the fallout of walking away from a
pro surfing career. And yeah, *dealing with it* had
mostly meant reordering her own oddly broken
brain and trying to make sense of what had happened.

She hadn't liked being high. She'd felt out of control, and fuzzy at the edges, as if she'd been erased
just a tiny bit. It had been her control issues at work,
probably. But she'd never forgotten how particular
and individual that feeling was. Nothing had come
close to it.

Until now.

The second she called Sean a good boy, he laughed
and jackknifed up. All that power, all that strength
and the muscle under her thighs, bent up at once. She
was lifted off her knees, but he had her safe when he
wrapped an arm low around her ass. He was laughing, but she knew calling him a *good boy* was pushing
him too far. She was laughing too, because when

amusement was a man's response to something so ridiculous, she felt . . . safe.

She wrapped her arms around his head and shoulders. "No." She giggled. "You promised."

"Oh, you can blow me, sugar." He buried chuckles against the top of her sternum, his mouth leaving traces of sensation in its wake. "But not with names like that. I draw the line."

"You're putting your foot down?" she teased. "Blow jobs on your terms only?"

"Hey, you're the one who wants it. I was offering my own oral sex."

"Were you? I missed that?" Except she hadn't. When he'd been on his knees in front of her, she'd known exactly where things were headed. This wasn't her first rodeo.

But it was the first time she'd felt so blurry. So out of control.

She wedged her hands against his shoulders, and took a moment to appreciate how damn hard he was. Her fingertips were hooked behind the caps of his shoulders. Pure muscle. She held back against the hot surge that went through her.

He was so damn gorgeous, it was unfair. He twisted the two of them around so that his shoulders were resting against the end of the bed. He was a swoop of muscle, a comma made of temptation.

That he was still wearing pants was unfair. She fumbled with his belt, and the smooth leather slipped free eventually. The button went next, and she could barely hear the teeth of the zipper beyond her own raspy breathing. When she wrapped her grip around the waistband of his pants and pulled, he helped by lifting his hips, which made the muscles of his chest and arms and shoulders bulk out even more.

He was built. She sometimes forgot that for brief seconds because he was also lean and graceful, but his muscles stood out in stark relief. Holding his body weight up on one hand next to his hip in order to let her pull his clothes off—that did it. His shoulder had to be tender still, but he wasn't letting that affect him.

He could probably hurt her. Physically. He could hold her down and take what he wanted. He might not even break a sweat while he did it either, despite his limited range of movement on his bad shoulder. She could fight back and probably could make a little dent in him. She wasn't completely helpless. But he had ten inches and sixty pounds on her, and if he used them in any negative way, she'd be screwed.

Yet she wasn't frightened of him at all. He was just this side of harmless, only dangerous enough to make a woman know it would be a hell of a ride. He wouldn't dream of hurting her; she knew that from the way he studied her, the careful way his gaze had tracked her every movement at first. The fact that he'd tried to resist her.

His briefs were shorter than boxer briefs, but longer than tighty-whities. The dark gray material clung to his narrow hips. She traced her blunt fingernails across the top band. "What are these?"

His brows lifted in the center when he chuckled. "Underwear. You're wearing some too."

"No, I'm wearing panties." She lifted on her knees enough that his mouth was almost level with said panties. She cupped her hand over her body, pressing against the tingling ache. The last time she'd been *this* damn turned on had been . . . never. "You're wearing something else."

The thin material stretched so tightly over his cock that she could see the outline of his head, the fullness of his shaft. She squeezed him, gently at first. Then a little harder when he sucked in a harsh gasp. She liked that. Holding him, holding herself, listening to the little noises they passed back and forth.

"You can call them whatever you want. Just keep doing that."

"Don't wanna."

He groaned. His hand lifted to the edge of the bed, beside his head. In that position, his arm looked even bigger. Crisp, dark hair dusted his armpit. He was a man. No boy. All big and bold, just like the cock in her hand. But even though his hand fisted in the blanket, he didn't say a word of protest. He nodded. Sure, it looked like he'd had to force his neck to bend, but he still got out a nod.

"I wanna lick you. I wanna feel you in my mouth and taste you."

"Fuck," he breathed. Then again, and again.

She pulled his briefs free, and he was so gorgeous. His shaft overspilled her hands. The flush, red head had a gleaming drop of precome at the very end.

Ducking her head, she created a private world for herself. Her hair slipped down to shield her from his gaze, and so her eyes could drift shut when she licked him clean. Bright and salty moisture. She liked the taste of him as she pushed farther, licking around that ridge between head and shaft.

Licking the webbing there made his hips twitch.

Just as quickly, he yanked himself down again. He was so tense, the arrows of muscle going from his waist to his groin popped. She traced him with her nails, then the tips of her fingers. He had rougher skin than she did, a little hair too. She liked it that way. She liked knowing he was a man who held himself contained for her.

A thick ridge ran up the underside of his cock. She rubbed it with the flat of her tongue in long strokes, then longer. Up his whole length. He tasted like a hint of salt, like the ocean infused him. He lived for it, lived for the water and surfing. She wanted to see him there. If he could really make magic, maybe he could carry her away.

She filled herself with him. Both hands wrapped around his length, she opened her mouth over his tip and took him in. But when she looked up, she couldn't see him past the curtain of her hair. Suddenly she didn't want to be safe. Didn't want to hide.

What she needed was to see his face when he gave a low, tortured groan.

She released him from her lips with a sucking pop. After one quick lave of her tongue across the thin slit decorated with wetness, she flicked her hair back over her shoulder. His fingers were gentle when he tucked a slick sheaf of hair behind her ear.

"You're really good at that," he said with a low voice. His eyes were burning hot. She felt more solid, connected to her body in a way she hadn't had in a long time. He had done that. He had done that *for* her. With the astonished, enticed way he stared at her.

"I bet you say that to all the girls."

Women she didn't want to think about. Tall, gorgeous things who had probably rolled and posed all around the bed behind him. Hell, they'd probably strutted naked all through his house. The women he'd been photographed with were always the tall, leggy type. Blondes with more hair than Annie would know what to do with.

She refocused on him, wrapping her hand around his thickness, stroking up through the wetness left by her mouth and his eagerness. Each stroke made muscles in his stomach shift and tighten. Each individual section of abs stood out.

"You're better than any of the other girls." Sean stroked her hair, then turned his hand over and traced her jaw with a soft, gentle touch. She couldn't help the quiet noise she gave, the way she leaned into his hand.

"At least you're not a liar," she said. But then she dipped her head again, took him into her mouth. Distracting them both. She was about as transparent as a pane of glass.

Hell if she didn't love the way she held him. Touched him. She'd needed this. There was power in it, in the way he was leashed and tied and holding himself down.

She sucked him deep, then deeper. He was skin and flesh. Swollen with interest. Quiet moans filled her ears, delving down into her body. Her chest clenched first, then her stomach, and finally the wet and aching flesh between her own thighs.

Her fingers crept into her panties. She didn't want him to notice, because this was all so new and strange and she'd never been this turned on from giving head.

But when her gaze flicked up, she knew he'd seen. His blue went hazy. His eyes first locked on her shoulder, then traveled down to the line of her hand behind her thin panties.

She touched three fingers to her clit, pressing against the throb that was tied to her rushing heartbeat. He was firm between her lips. There was so much wetness, it slicked her fingers and made the way she touched herself send shivers under her skin.

Annie barely felt attached to her own body. Her eyes drifted shut. Sean throbbed in her mouth. She throbbed under her own fingers. The rhythm she found was fast and unrelenting. Her free hand followed her mouth, adding an extra layer of sensation into each stroke over him.

At first, she thought the roar in her ears was only the pulsing, pounding force of her blood. She had nothing left in her brain but him, nothing left to think of but the way he tasted and the way her finger circled her clit to wind her tighter. She went up and up, and his gentle touch on her shoulders only pushed her up higher.

Even the way he cupped her shoulder was reverent. His fingers stroked across the back of her neck, and her spine curled with tingles and shivers. She was on her knees, curled over his torso, her fingers hidden between her thighs.

So much of this was new to her. Not the particular actions, but in the way he made her dizzy. She was high on endorphins, probably, but that was fine. Better than fine. She needed this. Needed a chance like this, to feel as stupid and giddy and ridiculous as any other woman her age.

He cupped her jaw. Not restricting, just feeling her. His thumb rubbed over and over her cheek where it hollowed from holding him and sucking him. "Right there," he breathed. "Like that. Harder. Can you go deeper?"

She wouldn't have thought she could have, but she tried for him. His head stroked over the top of her mouth. She breathed through her nose, let her eyes close. His expression was enough to send her over, but she actually didn't *want* to come. Not yet.

She took him deeper. Enough that he brushed the back of her throat. Her eyes burned, and God, that was all it took. She couldn't hold off her own pleasure any longer. It broke like shards, each burst of her heartbeat slamming more sensation through her. Her pussy clenched, even as her toes curled. Her hand tightened on the base of his shaft and his hair was crisp against her palm. This was more than sex; she was free.

They were free. Together.

Tomorrow there might be hell to pay, but for now . . . oh, for now there was his exploding flavor across her tongue. The way his cock got a fraction bigger in her mouth and her hand and the way she swallowed him down. His hips thrust up for the first time, and he pushed deeper in her mouth and she didn't care. She loved it. There was no boundary too far at the moment, no place she couldn't follow him.

Nothing she wouldn't give him.

Chapter 15

Sean's spine had been ripped out and seared to ash. He was breathing as hard as if he'd been deep in the tube of a perfect curl, all hard work and balanced timing. One hand still framed the back of Annie's head. Her fine silk hair tangled in his fingers. His other hand was locked tight in the woven blanket hanging off the end of the bed. Sweat prickled at the base of his spine.

That had been one of the best orgasms of his life. Maybe the best.

The physics were the usual. He couldn't even say what it was that had made her so damn good. The way she seemed so tentative at first, as if she were practically new at it. Her later enthusiasm, maybe. "That wasn't the first time you'd given head, was it?"

She slumped to her stomach, her cheek pillowed on his thigh. He traced the bones between her shoulder blades. "If it was, would you have done anything differently?"

A breeze worked over his skin. He rubbed his knuckles down the center of his chest and cracked a yawn. "Nope. Not a damn thing."

Laughing, she buried her face against his thigh. "Good to know, Westin."

"What can I say?" He liked the feel of her. Maybe she was small, but there was a lot of her packed into such a little bit of a human. Even her back was firm and smooth under his fingertips as he kept petting her. "I'm a gentleman."

"You should feed me, then. Offering a guest a meal and all."

It was the middle of the afternoon. Sean hadn't eaten lunch either. Maybe not even breakfast, since things had been a little hazy. He'd been hip deep in phone calls, attempting to figure out who was heading the mythic documentary. Talking to his business manager and coach. It had only been after they'd washed out that he'd come up with the idea of going to Tanner. Thank Christ for that, since he'd been the one to point out that Sean might want to look for the source of the stories, instead of just trying to find the person doing the research.

Result was, Sean was starving. "I know exactly where we should go."

She twisted onto her back, stretching. She'd never even taken off her bra and panties, though the front of the latter was dampened through. Her rib cage lifted toward the ceiling and her stomach dipped. "I think you should bring me food. Considering what I just did for you and all. We could call it tribute."

He pushed to his feet and held his hands out. "Nope. Come on, Baxter. What we're after doesn't travel well."

She rolled her eyes, but she put her hands in his instantly. After he hauled her to her feet, he locked one arm around her shoulders and dropped a kiss on her temple. "That was . . . Thanks, Annie. Thank you."

She swatted his shoulder and twisted away, grabbing her khakis. "You're not getting soft on me, are you?" She flashed a smile over her shoulder, but he didn't think it matched her eyes. "That's not what we're after here."

He watched her while she pulled the shorts up over her hips. Even though her ass bounced with particularly pert enticement, he wasn't buying the extra swish. She was fronting, and hard. Maybe she didn't want insta-serious, but this had to have some kind of weight behind it for her to risk her business. Her reputation pivoted on her professionalism and the results her clients could rely on. Throwing it away for a quick bang that wasn't even an actual bang didn't seem likely. Didn't seem logical, for that matter. Why risk everything?

But if she wanted to play like that, he'd let her. He knew about keeping things close to the vest. "We're after lunch."

"Is it still lunchtime? I'm pretty sure this is a dinner date by now." She shrugged into her T-shirt, and he scooped up a pair of jeans from the bottom drawer of his dresser.

Impulsively, as soon as he had them on and zipped, though not buttoned, he grabbed her by the hand and pulled her close enough to wrap a hold across the back of her neck. He kissed her deeply. Because he wanted to. Because she was Annie and they'd done something mind-blowingly intimate minutes ago, but she was still so damn laid back about whether they were even going on a date. "Yeah. Dinner date for sure."

She looped her forearm across his back and leaned up toward him. She nuzzled the underside of his jaw, her lips soft. "You're paying for mine, then."

"Of course I am. You fired me as a client. Saved me a boatload of money."

He took her to Manny's, a bar and grill a couple blocks north on the beach. This early in the spring, not as many tourists filled the outdoor patio as they would in July. Instead, the balance went the other way, with locals sitting at butcher-block tables inside. Still, Annie and Sean were able to find an empty booth near an open window.

When Annie slid in first, he promptly dropped in beside her. He pressed close so their shoulders brushed, their knees touching.

"You have personal-space issues." Annie leaned against the back of the booth. Her head tipped so far that her face pointed up toward the ceiling. She looked dead relaxed. Probably the orgasm. Shame Sean hadn't been the one to give it to her.

That'd have to change next time. "Considering where our body parts were thirty minutes ago, I think maybe it's you with the personal-space issues."

She laughed and ran both hands through her hair. She'd put her T-shirt back on, but he knew what was underneath there now. Modest underwear and a body made for sinning. "You have no idea, actually. I have so many issues, I need a monthly subscription."

"Tell me one." He hooked an elbow on the table.

The breeze wafting through the windows was crisp with salt. The fact that it was coming into shore from the ocean meant that there was awful white-water froth on the waves. Hence, so many locals in the restaurant. They were all waiting for an offshore. This was San Sebastian, after all. Only had to wait a little bit and the surfing conditions would turn from good to awesome.

She shook her head, her smile going wider. "No way."

"Why not?" He grinned at her, then slipped his hand onto her thigh beneath the line of the table. His fingers flirted with the hem of her shorts. The skin of her inner thighs was thin and delicate. "I've trusted you with my most favorite body part. You've put me through two-hour workouts to strengthen my shoulder. You can trust me too."

"You have a point." She didn't pull away from his touch, but she didn't exactly purr under his attention either. Her smile was more dark and mysterious than coquettish. She wasn't exactly the flirting type.

Which was exactly why he'd been so damn shocked when she'd tossed it all over in order to play with his cock. He had a decent ego, but that was simply ridiculous. "We'll play tit for tat."

"I think that's what we just did."

He mimed a drum rim shot, but that only made her stick her tongue out at him. He liked her. The snarky, subtle flavor of her personality was one he hadn't tasted in a long time. Before he had a chance to push further, the waitress stood at the end of the table. She had a little pad of paper, a pen, and a smile that was about as fake as the racks on Sean's usual girls.

"What can I get you?"

Annie leaned around Sean. "A menu might be nice."

"You mean a drink menu?" The waitress tossed a thick sheaf of hair back over her shoulder. The tangled, tousled look and damp roots said she was probably a surfer when she wasn't waiting tables.

"I was promised food," Annie said to Sean. "Your batting average is dropping."

"There's no menu here." He hooked his arms across the back of the booth. "It's either wings, and then there's only hot or hotter, or fish tacos done Manny's way."

He was kind of curious how well Annie would deal with this. She didn't always seem to be the loose and roll-with-it kind of girl. She liked things the way she liked them. There wasn't always much middle ground.

Lots of women wouldn't like Manny's. In fact, Sean had only ever brought a woman here once and that had been a complete accident. He'd picked up a chick at a martini bar, only to realize she lived two houses down from Manny's and had never been. Sean had been so astonished that he'd insisted on going—only to spend the next hour swamped by subtle whining and mock surprise that a San Sebastian bar would be so down-market.

Annie speared him with a single, searing look. "Do you swear I won't get food poisoning?"

He traced two fingers over his chest, then held them up. "I swear it on my history as a Boy Scout."

"I'll take the fish tacos, then." He liked the way her mouth tweaked up into one of her little smiles as she leaned her elbows on the table. She was a go-to sort of girl after all.

"Good choice. I'll have them too."

It didn't take long before the waitress was back again, this time carrying two plates that looked more like trenchers than china. They were dark wood, lined with time-tempered metal and each piled with half a dozen tiny tacos. She set them down, along with the sodas they'd also ordered and a stack of napkins two inches thick. "Enjoy."

"Dude, I plan to." Annie's eyes were wide. "These look great."

Each taco was only the size of Sean's palm. The fish was seared and grilled, with cabbage and Manny's secret dressing—which Sean was pretty sure had something to do with yogurt and coriander and a half dozen other herbs and spices. "Manny grows the tomatoes in a rooftop garden."

Annie glanced up toward the ceiling, her expression doubtful. "Here? On a commercial property?"

"Yeah, his apartment is upstairs. The garden's on the roof. He throws wicked parties up there sometimes." Sean took a sip of his soda, leaning back in the booth. "Try it."

Annie wasted no time in obeying. The tacos were a little gooey, causing white sauce to dribble out the back. But the first bite made her eyes drift shut and her cheeks soften in bliss. "Oh. Oh, that's really good."

"Good. Now I can tell you that I was never a Boy Scout."

"I know." She licked a bit of sauce off her pinkie.

"You did not." He scooped up his own taco, inhaling half in one bite. Spice exploded across his tongue, clearing out his sinuses.

Her smile was supremely confident. "Did too."

"I could have been an Eagle Scout and you'd have no idea."

"You weren't." She kept tucking into her food as they teased. He liked a girl who could eat, and in Annie's case, that was especially respectable, considering her size. She couldn't afford to lose any calories. "In fact," she continued, "I'd bet you were the type of kid who avoided any organized sports or groups."

"You're right." He wiped his hands with a napkin, slowly getting each of his palms. "I grew up rough, actually. Mom discouraged joining . . . eh, she discouraged joining anything, pretty much."

"How about your dad?"

"Gone." He gave his best rakish grin, the one that had dropped panties worldwide. He knew he was good-looking. Hard to be in magazines and ads without recognizing that on some level. Sean's mom had always said his looks came from his dad, though. "You're looking at the bona fide product of a one-night stand. Old-school bar-style pickup, to boot. Mom never knew his last name."

"Ouch." Annie put her hand on his knee, and the simple gesture oddly eased the sting. "Did you have a good mom, at least?"

"Nope," he said with an artificial injection of cheeriness. "She was batshit crazy. I loved her lots, but she was completely around the bend."

Annie's eyes went wide. She breathed his name and her fingers tightened on his leg. Fuck, he hadn't meant to say that much. There was something about simply *being* with Annie that made everything easier. And made keeping secrets harder.

But he couldn't stand the pain on her face. It was totally time for distraction mode. "Whatever, though. How did you know I wasn't a Boy Scout? Don't I have an honest face?"

She studied him for another long, quiet moment, but apparently decided to give him a minute and let the subject drop. "The Boy Scout salute is done with three fingers raised." She demonstrated, holding up her three middle fingers and folding down her thumb and pinkie in the direct opposite of a surfer's *hang loose* gesture. "Not two."

"Damn. Guess that Eagle Scout dream is shot."

Just like his chance of holding his past private would be shot if he didn't get something done about those rumors.

Chapter 16

The problem with firing Sean as a client was that it left Annie with no ready excuses for seeing or talking to him. She had to admit to herself that she simply *wanted* to see him. To hear his voice. They spent hours on the phone—until late—simply because they had been goofing around. The phone pressed to her cheek had become warm at the edges. "The Beatles or the Stones. It's not like choosing a thesis statement."

"I didn't go to college. Don't you use them fancy thesis thingies on me."

She was lying in her bed, her head piled on three pillows and her feet propped up on two more. Twirling the fringe on a pale blue afghan, she stared up at the ceiling and pictured Sean's face. So handsome. He verged on beautiful, but it was the sharpness to his features that drew her. When they'd said good-bye three days ago, he'd kissed her on both cheeks with the aplomb of a world traveler. She'd rolled her eyes at his put-on sophistication, especially since minutes earlier he'd been licking taco drippings from the side of his hand.

He was . . . complicated.

"Yeah right." She made a scoff noise in the back of her throat. "You're not dumb."

There was a moment that drew out like taffy, and all of a sudden she regretted that she couldn't see his face. There were a lot of hints she read in those sharp blue eyes and in the hold of his mouth. The scruffy beard didn't hide the way the muscle in front of his ear jumped when he was displeased. "No, really, Annie. I didn't go to college at all."

"Oh." On one level, she had to have realized that. The trajectory of his career meant that he wouldn't have had time to go in the traditional way. But he'd been surfing on the circuit for around eight years. "You didn't go online or anything?"

"Didn't need to. I've got an excellent manager, and I've built what I need to."

She scrunched her eyes shut. He'd certainly made plenty of money, hadn't he? And she wouldn't have gone to college either if Terry had organized her career the way he'd wanted. "I didn't mean to sound like I was judging or something. It's just how smart you are. I assumed."

"I figure I'll go when I have more time. After I've won a championship and I've retired from the circuit." His chuckle came through as clearly as if he'd been sitting right next to her. Her breasts tightened and tingles lanced her nipples at the sound of it. "It's a little hard to manage a pro career and an academic career at the same time."

"I bet." She sat up and pulled her knees to her chest. "But still, I think your inability to decide between the Stones and the Beatles speaks to a significant drawback in your personality."

"Is that right?" He paused for a beat, and then she heard his voice drop into a purr that did wicked, melty things to her insides. "What are you wearing?" He'd said he was sitting on his back patio while they talked, watching the dark waves roll in.

"A tank top and panties." Heat flashed across her cheeks. Thank God she was alone in her room, because her blush was incendiary.

"What's on the tank top?"

"On?" She shook her head, suddenly confused. "There's nothing on it. It's just white."

"Damn," he muttered with another little laugh. "I had a bet with myself whether it'd be a comic book reference or a television show."

She jumped, clapping her hand over the front of her panties, as if he could see through her cell phone. But she must have made an involuntary squeak, because he pounced. "What? What is it? Is the tank top modeled on a show or something?"

Well technically, she did have tanks that were designed in the layered look of *Battlestar Galactica*, but she actually wasn't wearing those. "No. It's nothing. There's nothing on my shirt." She was talking too fast, the words coming out in a clatter.

"Nothing on your shirt," Sean repeated. She could practically see his eyes narrowing, see him edging forward. He'd put his elbows on his knees and lean into her. "That leaves your panties. What's on your panties, Annie?"

She shook her head frantically, only to realize he couldn't actually see her. She clapped her arm over her eyes. Hidden in the dark, she was tempted to tell him. "Nothing."

"Annie. Please."

She squeezed her arm tighter over her eyes, but then she was laughing. "I can't fucking believe I'm going to tell you this."

He laughed too, almost in solidarity. "Come on. Tell me. You know you want to."

"I'm the biggest sucker in the world."

"You should tell me, and you should come to the beach tomorrow with me. The new therapist said I was cleared. Gotta keep to relatively small waves, but I can give the shoulder a try."

She stopped laughing as suddenly as if the air had been sucked out of the room and out of her lungs with it. She sat upright. "Define what you'll expect from me at the beach."

"You'll come to my house, and then we'll go all the way into the water." There was a pause, and then something that sounded like Sean clearing his throat, except that would mean he was sort of nervous. "And I'll have a board waiting for you."

"Sean . . ." She drew his name into something more than only a name. Asking him not to do this to her, maybe. Except that wasn't all of it. She was tempted; she had to admit it. It had been almost six years since she'd been surfing.

She'd always thought she was happy with skateboarding. It gave her the rush, and it involved her whole body. The tricks she'd learned were epic, considering that she'd taken up skateboarding only after she'd given up surfing.

Seeing the ocean every time she went to Sean's

house was wearing on her, though. To be so close without actually being in it . . . She was starting to crave the salt water.

"Okay, let's start small." Sean's voice slayed her. He was so intense. "Tell me about the panties."

"They're thin white boy-cut, with a little Xbox 360 emblem, and they say 'achievement locked.'" Telling him about the panties did really seem minor compared to the taunting, tempting idea of surfing again. "Gaming reference, not comics or TV. So both sides of you lose."

"Fuck no. I get to picture you in your panties. Neither side of me loses."

"Are you going to think about me later? With your hand on yourself?" She was desperate to think of anything but the idea of going back to the ocean. Once it got ahold of her, she probably wouldn't be able to walk away again. Maybe that wouldn't be a bad thing. She didn't have to be involved in the pro world just to be able to go surfing again. There were tens of thousands of people all over the world who surfed regularly and didn't even read surfing magazines.

He saw right through her. "Come to the beach. I'm not going to pick you up and put you on a board or anything. Just waves and water. It's supposed to be above eighty. Pretty warm."

The first really warm day of spring, heralding the coming summer. Spending it at the beach would be just the thing. Not an expectation in and of itself. And he was right. It wasn't like anyone could actually *force* her to surf. "Yeah. I'll go."

"Wonderful," he purred. "It's a date."

*   *   *

So he'd talked her into another date. She suddenly didn't like calling them that. Why did they have to put names on what was going on? They were grown adults, almost thirty. It wasn't like their dates were to the school dance or anywhere dumb.

Instead, she was waiting for him at the edge of the beach, where the scrub plants gave way to sand, and she was wearing a swimsuit.

She put her hands flat over her bare stomach. The bikini had come from the back of her drawer, and she couldn't remember the last time she'd put it on. Maybe two years ago for a picnic with her drop-in kids? She had managed to avoid going in the water that day. It hadn't been that hard, since she'd volunteered for the volleyball tournament. No mess, no fuss, and she got to keep the ocean in her peripheral vision.

She was an idiot. A full-blown idiot. She was throwing so much of herself up in the air for this man, and it was only going to be a temporary thing. There would be no happily ever after for them. It was one thing to agree to a single afternoon at the beach, but she'd stayed away from the ocean for reasons—important reasons.

Drawing a deep, burning breath into her lungs, she intentionally turned to look at the water. In Southern California, the water always kept a green tint. That was due to the depth and the temperature of the water, and the accumulated masses of beings that lived and existed in the ocean. Being out there in the water was like touching an alien world. Surfing was like conquering that world.

Which, in the end, was why she was here after all. Sean might have issued the invitation, but he hadn't thrown her over his shoulder. He hadn't forced her into anything, because she was a grown woman in complete control of her mouth. She had to admit she wanted that rush back. She wanted to know if she could have it pure and free of all the rest of the bull-shit of the pro world.

"If you wanted to body surf, I'd really, really try not to think too badly of you."

Annie jumped, her hand flying to the base of her throat as she spun. "Jesus, Sean. I didn't hear you come up."

He shrugged, but the gesture was contained by the two boards he had hooked under one arm. With careful movements he stretched out his bad arm, then moved it farther as no pain registered on his face. "It's the sand. Hid my steps."

"Duh." She winced. She hadn't meant for that to come out so harshly. "I mean, yeah. I'm sure that's right."

"Come on, sugar," he said, striding out past her onto the white expanse of sand and toward the water. "Let's stake out some land before it gets too crowded."

"It's a Thursday afternoon. Shouldn't be too bad."

"Perks of being self-employed." He had a gorgeous grin usually, but now it was ridiculous. He was so energized, in a way she hadn't seen in him before.

The board he presented was perfect for her. Plain white with the classic ". . . lost" logo in the center, it was under six feet and had the usual deep V-tail of a fish. Her hand lifted on its own. The bottom was slick and glassy, in perfect shape. The top had been waxed to perfection. Its bumpy pattern was familiar under her fingertips. Sean stood there patiently, not saying anything while she petted a surfboard.

Something stung the back of her eyes. "I used to have one just like this."

"I'm not surprised," he said. His words were businesslike, but his eyes were shining with compassion. "The RNF 5 is a really traditional model. It's been around more than twenty years."

"Is that new wax?" She traced the pattern.

"Did it last night. Didn't want you to have any excuse to pass. Warmed up my shoulder for the evening too."

"Diagonal crosshatch—isn't that fancy." Her smile felt wistful. "I used to do straight ups and downs."

"Everyone's got their own style."

She bit her bottom lip, looking up at him. He wasn't pushing. He wasn't insisting she should do it. He'd only presented her with the perfect board. Years ago, she'd slowly sold her boards one by one, as she left her past behind her. For a little while, she'd thought maybe she'd surf again, so she'd kept her RNF 5. Then it gathered dust in her garage and made her sad every time she'd seen it, and she'd assumed she was done with that part of her life. So she'd sold it on eBay.

She took the board from him and stood it on its pins. Looked past it to the water. This was . . . her. Part of her. If she could use Sean to reclaim the sexual part of herself she'd thought long dead, then she could do this too.

More than just do it. She could kick ass at this. The surf was small, only a few feet, but she'd once been damn good. She might be out of practice, but she sure as heck wasn't out of shape.

She gave a little nod. Her cheeks tightened against the grin that wanted to come out. And then, fuck it, why shouldn't she smile? This was going to be awesome.

Tucking the board under one arm, she walked out into the cold, crisp water.

The welcoming ocean took her back with arms wide.

Chapter 17

Sean had put a worrisome amount of time into wondering if Annie would still be a decent surfer. He hadn't wanted to embarrass her if she wasn't. He'd wanted to be able to give her back the thing for which she'd been longing. He didn't think it was too egotistical of him to think he knew what she wanted. It wasn't as if she'd been particularly surreptitious about it, nor had he been spookily observant.

She'd stared at the water from his back deck with longing apparent in her eyes. You could even call it desire. She had that look a woman got where her mouth went slack and her eyes went needy.

There was no reason to look like that when it had something to do with the water. Not in California, when the ocean was what made the state bright and great, and people came from all over the world to be in it.

Sean had surfed the world. Washed out more sand from his shorts than he'd ever had bits of sense. When it came to getting back in the water after his injury, there was nowhere he'd rather be than San Sebastian. It was home. It was the place that had washed all his problems away the first time around. The movement of the ocean was subtle this afternoon, but that was half of San Sebastian's appeal—its wide range of conditions.

Today was perfect for testing out his recovery.

She waded out into the water, diving in when it got deeper than her hips.

Sean followed closely behind. She'd worn only a bikini top and board shorts, so he got to watch the pale expanse of her back shift with every swim stroke. "Did you put on sunscreen?"

She paused long enough to shoot him a completely perplexed look over her shoulder. Her hair was already soaked and plastered to her forehead. She'd worn most of it in a ponytail that had turned small and scraggly in the water. "Wasn't born yesterday, Westin. Why?"

"Because I like your skin." He let every bit of his intent and desire for her shine through his eyes. "I'd like to lick every inch of you, and I can't do that if you're sunburned."

Her breasts lifted on a fast inhale. Bright red slashed over her cheeks to her ears. "Yeah. Okay. I can work with that."

She dove headfirst into the water, disappearing under a wave break, only to pop up again on the other side. Sean followed close behind.

The water was cold, the way it usually was this early in the season. Most of the surfers in the lineups had skipped wet suits, though one or two had on shorty versions.

"Hey, mate," said Nate Coker, sitting on a board

and floating with the bob of the ocean. "Good to see you out."

"Just got cleared," Sean answered with a wave of his good arm. "You remember Annie, right?"

"Sure." Nate nodded toward her. "Gloria was talking about you after we met the other night."

"Was she really?" Sean lifted his eyebrows. He knew Gloria and knew the tendency she had to tear other women down. It was her default mode.

Nate had the good grace to look chagrined. "She goes on a bit. Said she had no idea how Sean managed to hire you for his therapy."

Annie had easily mounted her board. She was sitting spread-legged on it, hands planted between her knees. The black bikini had metallic squares at the top hem, giving it an almost punk-rock look. But her board shorts were dark red, and all Sean wanted to do was pull them down her legs. From there, things could go whichever direction they liked. He just appreciated Annie naked.

She cast an easy smile toward Nate. "Technically, I've released Sean from my care anyway, but I don't usually work with surfers."

"That's what Gloria said. She's done reams of research the last few days on you. Says you're the best, and Sean must have worked some kind of black magic voodoo to get you to work with him." Nate's eyes crinkled at the corners. "When I tell her you were actually surfing, she's gonna have a coronary. Says you ain't done it in years."

"She'd be right."

"Dude, your girlfriend sounds like she's becoming a private eye." Sean shifted back on his ass, but not too far, so that the board didn't go flying out from under him. He usually didn't even have to think about balance in that way, but it had been four whole weeks since he'd been in the water, and his shoulder was still sending up occasional twinges to remind him that movement on the ocean wasn't like movement anywhere else in the world. He didn't want to make an ass of himself in front of anyone, but not in front of Annie most particularly. "She needs a chill pill."

Nate shrugged. "She's intense sometimes, but she means well."

Sean had his own opinions about that, but the chick wasn't his girlfriend anymore. There was a hell of a reason for that. He much preferred Annie's laid-back style, the way she was subtly full of nudging. Gloria supervised Nate's manager to the point of micromanaging. Annie would never even dream of doing that; Sean was sure of it. "How much does she expect out of you this year? She realizes the championship isn't magically up for grabs just because Tanner retired, right? You're in tenth, and once I'm back on the circuit, I'll be launching right past you."

"You sure about that one?" Nate arrowed a deliberate look at Sean's shoulder. "You clear enough to surf competition? The heats are harder than fucking about on a Thursday afternoon. I leave for Fiji tomorrow. Last I heard, you were sitting that one out."

Sean bared his teeth. "I'll be there, Coker. Don't worry about me. But here's the thing—even if I wasn't going to be there, I'd still eat you up in the points once I did show up. That's what matters."

"If you say so." Nate seemed pretty relaxed a lot of the time, but half of it was an act. He was a hard driver. Someone who meant to make it to the top, and he'd only been on the 'CT for two years.

"Gentlemen, stand down," Annie said. "One more exchange and I'm going to have to insist you guys meet for pistols at dawn. I'm here to catch my first wave in years, and I don't want to be distracted."

"You win," Sean agreed. Even the ocean was behaving. He could feel the water drawing back, preparing for a new set of waves to pour in. The surge and give was subtly heart-stopping. He loved it, every time. "The next set's coming too."

"I know," she said dryly. "It's been a while, but that doesn't mean I've forgotten every scrap I knew."

He flicked water at her, just to watch her dark lashes flutter. She wasn't normally the fluttering type. "Excuse me for trying to help out."

"You can help out by watching my spot in the lineup."

"You're good if you wanna go next," Nate provided.

A few words down the lineup cleared the way through those waiting. They'd stretched out the length of the right-breaking wave, but since they liked seeing women surf, they let Annie go. For some of them, it came from a sexist, watch-the-ass kind of place, but for Sean and plenty of others, they moved back for women because there ought to be more of them in the surfing world.

He'd always figured surfing was an equal-opportunity sport. If he'd been able to rely on it as a scrawny, desperate teenager who was underfed half the time, then anyone could do it. While women surfers had a little less power, they usually made up for it in artistry. Sean didn't know why the women's section of the World Championship Tour wasn't better funded. They made less than twenty percent the prize money Sean and his buddies did on the regular 'CT.

Because as soon as she paddled out with the wave, Sean knew this was going to be a treat. Something gorgeous to watch. Her strokes were perfectly smooth despite it having been years since she'd employed them, reaching for the shore as if she were slicing into first in a swim competition.

"Right on!" Sean yelled.

Nate cheered too, as did a spatter of other surfers.

The wave was going to be a good one. He could tell by the way the water pulled and rushed, the way Annie and her board were snatched up by the force. She was there at the crest of the wave and popped up first to her knees. She balanced, shaky for a second—and Sean wondered if she'd stop there. Or even fall, maybe.

Sean almost cursed himself in that second. It was asking a fucking lot of her to expect her to be awesome on her first go. She hadn't even warmed up, not really.

But somehow, he had known what was coming. He had known she'd be amazing.

She hopped to her feet a half second later. Her hands balanced at her hips for a heartbeat, but then she lowered into it. Her knees bent. Her ass tipped back as she offset her weight.

But he hadn't expected Annie to be a goddess in the water.

Diana, probably. The one who held a bow and went for blood, because damn did Annie look determined.

Sean smacked the surface of the water with an open palm, sending up a celebratory splash. "Fuck yeah!"

She didn't try for anything too fancy. Her board slipped across the front of the wave in a dropping arc, her waist and shoulders dropping out of view as Sean remained behind the wave, while she owned it.

Sean paddled after her during the very next wave, not wanting to miss the aftermath. He wanted to ride it as a matter of course, since surfing had always been as easy as breathing and because he could already see her onshore. She'd dropped her board to the sand and was standing facing the ocean. Her hands were stacked behind her head, her elbows pointed up toward the sky, and he couldn't quite tell what her expression was. His stomach clenched. Had he fucked up, bringing her here?

Maybe he'd let himself get carried away on a hard shot of ego. Rising to his feet on the board was harder than he expected. As he balanced himself and hopped up, his shoulder twinged at holding half his body weight. He barely had control of his own life, considering the rumors and accusations he was facing. It was asking entirely too much to think that he could show Annie what she'd been missing out on in a single afternoon.

As soon as he balanced on his flat feet, riding the wave like he'd been made for it, he breathed easier.

A knot released from the base of his neck. His shoulders were tight, held firmly, but it wasn't more than he could deal with. The pain itself was a subtle warmth that edged him toward a wince. Nothing compared to where he had been.

When he got there, she was laughing. Her face pointed toward the bright sun, her ribs in stark relief. Laughter fell from her like a strand of pearls. Her joy lit her expression, opening her eyes. "Holy shit, that was awesome."

"Yeah? It was good?" He dropped his own board to the sand without even looking to make sure he'd aimed the wax up. Because fuck, he couldn't resist touching her.

Her skin was hot beneath the sheen of chilled ocean water that still clung to her. She was trembling under the surface. Holding his hands at either side of her waist was like containing fire within his palms. She was light. She was *lightning*.

"In my head, I know I've had better rides. Better waves." She shook her head, flicking away water from her ponytail. Her lashes looked even darker than normal. "But right now, from right here . . . God, I'm not sure any of them matter."

He spread his fingers across her bare waist. The sun shone on them, quickly warming her skin. Or maybe that was her from the inside out.

He kissed her. There was no way he could look at that beaming smile and not know what it tasted like.

The answer was salt and sugar. She pushed up into his kiss, rising on her toes. Her breasts brushed his chest, wet on wet, and her arms locked around the back of his neck. She didn't weigh much, but even that slight weight drew her close. He could feel each tender ridge of her spine under his fingertips.

She broke away, then traced openmouthed attention down his throat. He managed to hold back his pleasure-spawned shiver, but goddamn, it was a close call. Her fingers dug into the tops of his shoulders, and she made a little noise in the back of her throat. "You're going to take me inside later, Sean. And we're going to make each other feel really damn good."

"But not yet?"

She shook her head without moving her face from his skin. "Nope. Not yet." She drew back far enough that he could see her liquid-fire smile. "I need something else first."

"You need to surf."

"You got it." Her smile faltered for half a second. "Do you mind?"

"Why the hell would I?"

Her gaze darted back out to the water, past his shoulder. Something knotted between her brows, two little lines that he smoothed away with his thumb. "Gee, *I wanna bang you, but I wanna go surf first*. Some guys would be pissed at hearing that."

He laughed, because he couldn't help it, then locked his arm low around her back and lifted. "Those guys would be idiots if they didn't recognize what I just saw."

"What's that?"

"You're gorgeous out there, Annie. You're beautiful everywhere, but this time I'm going to sit onshore for a few minutes and watch your next couple waves, because on the water . . ." He paused for a moment, nuzzling aside damp hair from her cheek while he thought. "On the water, you're more than beautiful. You light up from the inside out. You're . . . incandescent."

Chapter 18

Even on her borrowed board, feeling the ocean snatch away her control and give her back the gift of riding a wave, Annie couldn't get Sean's words out of her head. She didn't want to. Incandescent. *Incandescent*.

When had a man ever called her anything remotely as amazing as that?

Terry had tried. He'd been full of sweet words and promises. He'd talked about how she'd be the next big thing on the pro circuit because she had the moves and she had the looks. He'd praised her little frame, saying that she'd be inspirational for some of the younger grom girls who wanted to see surfers who looked like they did and weren't blond bombshells. Even when he was talking her up, she felt like she was hot in an also-ran sort of way. Second-best, even to a guy who was supposedly breaking rules to date her.

Annie bobbed on her board, beyond the break. Her arms burned from swimming out past the lineup and then from paddling to catch waves. She'd already done it more times than she could count this afternoon. This was what surfing had once been like. Consuming. Obsessive.

But before, she hadn't had Sean at her side. He cheered her on like *whoa* and *damn*. He was . . . amazing also.

True to his word, he'd watched her surf for a good half hour. Every time she'd come close enough to see him, he'd had a slight smile and a stunned look in his eyes that made her feel as dazzling as a superstar.

Taking slow, deliberate breaths, she turned her face up to the sun. Even that yellow glow felt different on her shoulders when she was in the water. She hadn't been an indoor person in the intervening years. She'd skateboarded plenty, plus done occasional hiking. But this was . . . different.

This was what she'd needed.

Sean had given it to her.

Maybe she was foolish for having thrown away the cash Sean had offered. Firing him would set her teen center back five years. To make matters worse, there was no chance of this thing they had actually going forward in any way. As if she weren't screwy enough, Sean was exactly the opposite of the sort of guy she wanted to settle down with. He had more secrets and issues than she did, and that was fucking saying something.

She needed someone who could balance her. Someone who could calm her down at the end of the day and make her feel safe.

Not someone who made her tingle as she came back into shore at his side. She was practically high, her endorphins rushing and turning the tips of her fingers numb.

Throwing herself to the sand was safe. The way Sean flung himself down beside her was hot. Every inch of her knew where his inches were—and where they would line up.

The sand had started to absorb the heat of the day's sun, but an inch below the surface it was cool with the remembered chill of the water. She dug her fingers in. The stickier, damp sand beneath provided her with more resistance, but it wasn't as if she could get a full grip anyhow. Grain by grain, sand didn't provide resistance. You could poke and dig and scrape right through it. It was only when you smacked the shore bluntly that you were stopped by it.

Maybe Annie didn't want to be stopped. She pushed up to her elbows, looking down at Sean. "Thanks."

He had his eyes shut, but his mouth curved in a faintly smug smile. Golden sun kissed his forehead and his nose, but his hollow cheeks were shadowed, and not just because he hadn't shaved. "I did good?"

"Yeah. You did."

"Good. You're welcome." And with a deep breath, he let it go. That easily. He had his own shit to deal with, but at least he never put it on her. It was his own tangled mess.

She rested one hand in the center of his bare chest. He was thick with muscle, strong enough to withstand her whole weight, if she wanted to throw it at him. The water had beaded up on his skin, outlining the arc of his pecs and the sweep of his lats. A droplet broke free, sliding down the center of his chest to his abs. She wanted to follow it with her tongue. He'd taste like ocean salt. How long before she could make him taste different? Like fresh skin, licked clean, like something more?

She swallowed against the sudden clenching deep in her body. Her eyes felt too heavy to keep open, and her fingertips wanted to dig into him.

"You shouldn't be looking at me like that. Not here."

He was watching her. Except his gaze wasn't trained on hers. It was somewhere around her throat, or her collarbone. When his gaze dipped, she could feel it like a caress over the swell of her breasts.

"Not here means I *should* do it somewhere else."

He pushed so that he was sitting fully upright, leaning on his good arm. Even though he'd gone pretty easy, he had to be nursing some pain. She withheld myriad questions about his regimen, exercises, and range of motion. He wasn't her patient anymore. He *couldn't* be.

Her grip dropped from his chest to his upper thigh. Even his legs were strong and well muscled. Through the rapidly drying material of his board shorts, she couldn't feel the texture of his skin, which meant her entire brain stop-stuttered on the fact that he had like zero body fat. Not even there. He was so damn fit. All of him.

She squeezed her knees together against her ache.

"I want to fuck you, Annie," Sean said in a voice that was *almost* businesslike. Almost. It was certainly miles away from that rough purr he could give at times, but the words were weighted with enough promise that she still shivered. "I want to walk you into my house and into the shower. We'll wash off, and if we don't make it to the bed, I won't mind."

She swallowed against a sudden knot in her throat. He was looking at her with the sort of intention that made her insides liquid. She wound a finger through the bottom hem of his shorts, and his skin was just as hot as hers. "You sound like you're trying to warn me."

"I am." His hand rose to the side of her face, tucking a lock of hair behind her ear. He cupped her cheek, and his hands were so big, they swamped her. She shivered, in direct contrast to his cheeky grin. He was such a changeling. Sometimes she wasn't sure what was the real Sean Westin and what was games. "I wasn't sure if you wanted to get another set in."

"When you're looking at me like that?" She rose to her knees and balanced her hands on his shoulders. They were close enough to do dirty, naughty things, even though they were surrounded by rapidly growing crowds of tourists. Despite the temptation, she only brushed a soft kiss across his mouth. His short bristly beard sent a tremble through her. "Then I'll ask if we really, really need the shower."

Three nights ago, she hadn't been quite ready. She'd needed to know more about fooling around with Sean, if it would be everything she hoped for, or if it would be something to scorch her through. Now . . . Now all she could think about was having him inside her.

"Yes. Shower is mandatory."

"Persnickety."

He laughed against her neck, which, holy shit, did things for her. If she'd thought she was ready before, all of a sudden her body was demanding him. Craving. Her nails dug into his shoulders as she gave a little whimper. He didn't pull away. Instead, his chuckle turned into a growl as he drew patterns on her skin with the tip of his tongue. "With the way I'm going to fuck you, Annie . . . sand in crevices is a bad idea."

She groaned. "Oh, ouch. Crevices? That's about as unsexy a word as possible."

"You'll take that back when you see my shower."

"Promises, promises," she said, but Sean was already getting up and putting out a hand. She let him grab both her hands and haul her up.

She also let him pick up both the boards, because why not, when a man was offering to be chivalrous. It wasn't something that came from Sean all the time, but he tucked both boards under one of his arms and waved ahead of himself with the other. She hooked her flip-flops and . . . strutted. The sand made it hard, but she let the sex she was thinking about drop into every swing of her hips.

She did a good job, if the soft grunt Sean gave from behind her was any indication.

He made her feel good. He made her feel like she could do anything, anytime. Since she was facing the house and not him, she let her grin shine through. Maybe it wasn't mature to grin on the way to mind-melting sex. But her chin was as high as it had ever been, and she felt every movement of her body like it was something she held in the palm of her hand.

Like she won the damn world.

Sean tucked the boards into a rack at the back of his garage, but then he led the way upstairs three flights, and through his bedroom. He stopped at the archway to the bathroom, then leaned against the pale gray wall. Right in front of them were two free-standing wall panels covered with corrugated metal, each holding a square sink. Behind them was an open area divided roughly into two sections. On the left, multiple showerheads mounted in the ceiling would create a rain-shower effect. On the right was a tub that matched the gray wall tile. The room encompassed the entire narrow end of the building, and the windows ran the full extent, wrapping around three walls. But they were so high that all they showed was pure blue sky, none of the buildings across the street or next door.

She sauntered past the sinks to the shower. She could feel his gaze pinned to her ass and the dip of her spine, so she made him work for it. Twisting her ponytail free, she wound her fingers through her hair and gave it a shake. It fell to skim the base of her neck. "Okay," she agreed. "You do have a really nice bathroom."

"I know," he agreed.

"Though I deny the assertion that it balances the use of the word *crevice*."

"No, but I think your use of the word should balance out mine." He shrugged. The way he had his arms folded across his chest emphasized his strength. Even the thickness of his throat drove her crazy and made her want to sink her teeth into him. But she didn't really need that. She needed to be chased. She needed to be needed and wanted for herself, not for what image she could project.

The top of her bikini, tied at the neck, came free with a couple negligible tugs. His sharp intake of breath as her breasts came into view was payment enough. She released the band around her ribs. The scrap of material fell to the tile floor, but neither of them watched it go.

Sean pushed away from the wall, but only a step. "The shorts."

She swallowed her smile. "What about them?"

"Take them off." He dropped the order as easily as he surfed—with command and intention. He didn't come any closer either, only waited for her to do as he said.

Which she did. The shoestring-style ties first, and then the Velcro. The shorts pushed off her hips, caught on her ass. She wiggled, which made her tits bounce. His gaze shifted from them to her mouth to her hands on her ass, and she was winning at life, dammit.

He was so gorgeous, it hurt. She looked at his bright eyes and her nipples went tight. When she focused on his mouth, her body readied itself for him.

"The panties next."

"Technically these aren't panties."

"I don't care. I want them off."

She wasn't sure what impish impulse took hold of her. Spreading her feet slightly, she put her hands on her hips. Not grinning was so damn hard. She bit her bottom lip. "Why don't you make me?"

Chapter 19

Sean found his feet moving completely of their own accord. A part of him thought that maybe he should give her more time. He'd wanted to keep this slow and enjoy every moment. It wasn't as if he'd get a lot of chances with a girl like Annie. He didn't want to speed past the good stuff.

But her tightly budded nipples lifted toward the sky when she put her hands on her hips and gave her hair a toss. The pure pride in her movements was enough to make him want to grab and snatch and hold her. Because she was more than beautiful, she was aware of herself on a level that she hadn't been close to a month ago.

He wrapped an arm around her waist, yanking her close. They pressed together from shoulders to knees, her rack soft against his chest and the welcoming curve of her hips cushioning him. He groaned against her neck. She tasted like the ocean, salt and spice. She felt the way a woman should.

Reaching past her, he tapped the buttons for the shower control. She had her hands laced across the back of his neck, scraping her nails over his closely shorn hair, so he was glad the controls were autoset to his preferred temperature.

Water poured from three spigots lined up across the ceiling. He walked Annie backward, until they were drenched. It only made her taste better as the ocean's salt washed away to leave the purity of Annie's skin. She was the embodiment of calm and rest, but he wanted to drive her crazy.

When he kissed the end of her collarbone, she gave a little gasp and a wriggle. She came up on her toes, pushing closer. "There. God, there."

His hands clenched on her hips. Water added another layer of warmth, rolling over his shoulders. Drops pattered against the tile, filling his ears with the white noise and leaving room for obsession. He could hear every tiny breath she took, the way her teeth clicked together when he cupped her bare breast.

Her nipple was tight against his fingertips. He circled it once, twice, enjoying the contrast of her pointed flesh to the resilient undercurve of her breast. She wasn't the fullest handful he'd ever had, but she was the most enticing.

He'd always liked the things he'd had to work hardest for. Working made it easier to believe in the results. Surfing hadn't been half as easy as staying home would have been, and he'd given that his all. Annie would get nothing less from him.

He took her mouth in a kiss that made all sorts of promises. Delving past her teeth allowed him access to the soft rasps of her tongue. Then he pulled back, taking her bottom lip between his. Over and over again. They were explosions in tiny inches of skin and bodies. The repercussions threatened to spin his mind upside down. Where would he be when she moved on? With someone different. He wasn't sure if he wanted that.

Through the years, he'd been a survivor. So he'd be able to survive once again. He'd become a shell, in the best, most protective kind of way. There was nothing wrong with a person taking care of himself.

He wanted to be *better* when she was around.

He tucked his fingertips under the thick band of her bikini bottom. The material across her ass was skinnier than he'd have expected, considering Annie's reluctance to bare skin except as necessary, but then she'd had shorts on the whole time they surfed anyway. He wasn't sure why. She was perfectly formed, with no reason to hide any part of herself.

He'd hold her up to the world, if she'd give him half a chance.

When Sean pushed down her swimsuit bottom, the tiny squeak she gave wasn't supposed to be funny. He stifled the laugh that wanted to rise against her mouth and their kiss. It wasn't hard, considering the way her body cradled his and the way he throbbed with need for her.

He liked her modesty. He appreciated that she didn't throw everything she had out there for the world and that, instead, her body was only theirs to share.

It made him appreciate the way she allowed him to cup her behind in both hands. He felt like the king of the world, for a moment.

"You have to get clean," he managed to rasp. He

only managed to bring his head up to her temple, trailing his mouth across the shallow dip.

"Just so you can get me dirty."

"Exactly so."

They were twined together and slip-sliding. His every move wrenched a breathy moan or soft sigh from her body. She liked it when he cupped her breast and pinched her nipple between his thumb and forefinger. That move made her fingers dig into the back of his neck. She was holding on by a thread.

He scooped one hand over the globe of her ass, fingertips slipping low and lower, until he found the crease where her thigh met her ass. The heat there was enough to sear him. To lay him flat as if a huge wave had pounded him during a set. He was on his own with Annie to please. And fucking hell, did he like it that way.

He teased the seam of her body. She was shaved close, smooth and slick lips underneath a trimmed portion. Her pussy creamed to ease his way into her. His fingers danced over her plump and swollen lips. She was everything alluring.

He kissed her again, because her mouth was something he could dream about. Perfectly responsive. He wanted more of her. More and more, in any way he could get her. This was a fun distraction from the rumors swirling around him, and that was it. He had been fucked over too many times growing up, and the permanent scars had left him useless for anything but this. But damn, he meant to do his duty up, down, and sideways.

He rinsed her. Shower water sluiced down on both of them as he ran his hands over and over her, swiping the sand away from her skin. It pooled at the tile around their feet. Her hands tangled with his under his suit, and he sucked in a harsh, deep breath. He had wanted to make her as needy for him as he was for her, and this sort of active proof of her desire was exactly what he'd been looking for. Their fingers twisted as he yanked his ties free; then her hands were all over his ass, his thighs. Everywhere but where he wanted them most—his cock.

But that was probably best. If she touched him too soon, he'd explode. He knew backup methods to make her feel good, but there was no way he'd lose that kind of face. Not with Annie.

He ran his hands down her slender arms, stopping at her hands to lace their fingers together. When he lifted her arms, she went with it, letting him do exactly as he pleased. Her gaze burned from under her lowered lashes, and she slicked her tongue across the plump inside of her bottom lip. Her teeth were dead straight and perfectly white.

He was a little self-conscious about his bottom teeth, the way they slightly crowded in on one another. It wasn't the imperfection, so much as what they said about his childhood, and the fact that no one had taken care of him.

Not Annie. She'd been well taken care of, but he could tell that something dark and off and noxious had happened to her. She'd reclaimed herself, but only parts. And parts of her, like the core that loved to surf, had been hidden so long that she'd seemed to have almost forgotten about them entirely.

He couldn't believe how fucking lucky he was that she'd decided to give him this piece of her. It wouldn't be forever, that much he knew. But there was something to be said for being half-naked in the shower with a fully naked woman plastered to his front.

She pulled his mouth from hers, letting her head drop back far enough that the ends of her hair brushed the arm he had locked around her back. The damp tendrils made him shudder and hold her closer. Hold her tighter, even as she shifted away.

"It's been a long time," she breathed. Her eyes were closed. She swallowed hard enough that he could see her throat clench.

"I know," he said against the arch of her sternum. He moved his mouth to her breasts.

He used one hand to plump her small mound to his lips, then pulled her nipple into his mouth. She gasped, nails digging into his shoulders hard enough to bite. He liked it. He'd finally gotten through to her.

His cock brushed her soft hip. She widened her legs enough to cradle him between her slick thighs. He pushed, holding his head against her swollen flesh.

She made another little noise, this one slightly louder. More of that. He wanted to hunt those sounds, find out what new ones she could make. Last time she'd come, it had been due to her own fingers, as her mouth had been wrapped around his cock. Not that he was complaining, but it hadn't afforded him much of a chance to be the one to please her. To find out what she sounded like in the throes of an orgasm.

He meant to fix that.

He kissed her and at the same time he dipped his fingers into her pussy. She was soaking wet. For him. He liked that, naturally. He wanted more.

He controlled their every movement. When he felt like it, he wrapped her wrists between one of his hands, at the small of her back. Her body arched, breasts pointed toward the ceiling. But even sucking and kissing her nipples from that position got barely a response from her. She was an impenetrable fortress. There, but practically absent.

He wrapped his hands in her hair and held her tight, turned her face up toward his. "Tell me what you want."

She almost looked drugged. Her lashes were heavy, and not only with the droplets of water that glimmered on the tips. But her mouth curved in a mysterious smile. "Aren't you supposed to be the expert?" Annie didn't struggle against his grip on her wrists; she only let her neck bend back as well. He had her contained, but he didn't have her at all. "How many women have you slept with, Sean?"

He shook his head. He didn't want to answer that. Hard numbers felt sordid in their contained rainstorm. They were something beyond that, weren't they? Except maybe not. Maybe she was all body and that was it. He kind of liked her mind as well, but maybe he hadn't been granted full access to that part of her.

Yet.

He wasn't exactly the sort of man who took no for an answer either.

He wrapped his entire hand over her pussy, cupping her tightly. Tucked two fingers between her lips and found her opening. She was hot and wet and clasped his fingers tight. He groaned in response to his wickedly fast mind, which was busy imagining what it would be like to be inside her.

But then he let go of her. That gave him a whimper. Her hands rose as if to hold him close, but he grabbed them and placed a kiss in the middle of one palm. "Patience."

"I don't like being patient." Her mouth twisted on a sardonic expression. "I tossed away a whole career based on one night. Patience isn't exactly my strong suit."

"This'll be worth it."

"Promise?"

"Absolutely."

Chapter 20

Sean Westin making promises to Annie Baxter.

This was a moment that ought to be written down in the record books. Maybe she'd go home and inscribe the date on a calendar . . . except she didn't keep a paper calendar anymore. Damn it. Besides, sometime a few weeks from now, Sean would be done with her. By then they'd have burned out this strange combination of magnetism and chemical attraction, and she'd only be able to look at the annotation she had once made. Better to take the memory out and turn it over and over in her mind. This wasn't going to last into the future; no part of this would keep going.

But this was now.

And she sure as fuck liked now.

"Don't leave me hanging long, Sean," she said, and even to her own ears her voice sounded sultry. Sultry! She didn't do sexy, not anymore. Not since she'd been too young to know what to do with it.

"I'm not going far."

He matched actions to words, heading for the seemingly blank wall panels in the middle of the room. The sinks hung on the other side, and she was surprised when he pressed a spot on the left side and a cabinet swung open.

"So damn slick," she couldn't help but say. "That was totally hidden!"

He flashed a grin over his shoulder. "And here I was hoping you'd be staring at my ass."

It definitely was an ass worth staring at. Heat attacked her cheeks. She blushed so often around him, it was as if he had some personal button of hers. He was so lean that his cheeks had twin dimples. The backs of his thighs were hard with muscle. He'd developed his quads to the point they could take a woman's bite without notice.

Or maybe he'd notice but like it.

Inside the cabinet were all the usual supplies found in a bathroom. Bottles of over-the-counter medicine and Band-Aids and rubbing alcohol. The curious part was how precisely ordered everything was. "Does your housekeeper tidy your cabinets too? I can't imagine living like that."

"No," Sean said. "Well, he does, but it's according to my orders."

"You've got a thing, don't you?"

He lifted a single eyebrow, his cheeks tucking so tight against his grin that something nearing dimples popped up. "We're grown-ups. I'm pretty sure you don't have to call my dick a thing."

She stuck her tongue out at him, even while she practically withered up and died of scorching embarrassment. "You're a dork."

"I know." He wrapped his hand around his cock. His flesh overflowed even his big, broad hand. The head was bright red, probably about the same color as her cheeks. "But I'm a dork who's going to make you feel so good, you won't know what hit you."

"Seeing-stars kind of orgasm?" Hope bubbled in her chest. She knew how to make herself feel good, but she didn't know how to make herself feel . . . transported. In her few relationships as an adult, she'd never really hit that spot where she could give up control.

She had a feeling Sean was going to completely wrest control from her. Her heartbeat throbbed in her ears and took up a resounding thump in her chest. She didn't know if she could handle this, so she struck out, though gently. "I meant the cabinets. Everything in your house. It's so tidy. Sparse. If I didn't know better, I'd say Spartan."

He cocked his head, approaching her with more swagger in his step than any man ought to have. It helped that he had a body to die for. If the strong chest wasn't enough, there were always his flawlessly carved abs. Or the thighs that had more power than she probably had in her entire body. His cock rose from a tight nest of pubic hair and stretched nearly to his navel, without any support. Just his . . . enthusiasm.

She swallowed down her own excitement. Otherwise she might start drooling, and that wasn't the least bit appealing in a booty call partner. Or it shouldn't be, at least.

"I like my place tidy. Isn't that better than bachelor-style trashed?" He stepped back under the heat of the shower. He came close enough to touch her, and he trailed the backs of his fingers over her jaw. Down her neck. All the way across her chest to the tips of her breasts. Her hands curled into fists against the urge to simply jump on him. "Would you prefer if I had to shove pizza boxes under my bed before you arrived? What if I had to sniff the sheets to see if they're clean?"

She giggled. "Ew, no."

"Then I'm not sure what you're complaining about."

Her hand looped around his neck, but she quickly pulled it away again. "It wasn't a complaint. More like . . . I was pointing out that I noticed."

"You notice lots of things, don't you, sugar?" He stroked his cock with one big hand, starting at the base and squeezing the swollen head. His grunt made parts of her perk up in answer.

"Is that bad?"

"Fuck, no." He kissed her, this time a soft nibble of mouth to mouth. Their lips clung and slipped away again and again. His fingers traced over her, again and again.

She tried to take the condom from him, but he noticed and pulled it from her reach. "Nuh-uh," he said, a teasing note to his voice. "I want you to watch me."

Her chest thumped with need. She backed up enough steps that the tile wall cooled her shoulders. She stacked her hands behind her ass, one on top of the other, and leaned back, thrusting her chest upward a little. Her breasts were small enough that they could use any help they could get. She swallowed down her pure nerves and concentrated on the show he was putting on for her.

He stroked his shaft again, this time staying away

from the head for a few movements. Then he ran his thumb over the ridge that defined him. "See the way I want you, Annie?"

She tried to answer, but her voice cracked. She wet her lips. "Yes. I do."

"I'm going to make you feel good." He opened the condom, leaning out of the shower to toss the wrapper in a waste receptacle. It took a while to notice, but he was kind of fastidious. He was different here than he was in YouTube videos where he'd been drinking in bars and red-carpet parties. "You know what the amazing part of sex is?" He brought her mind back to the scene in front of her.

She couldn't help but giggle. "I've done this a time or two. The fact that I'm going to make you feel good, maybe?"

"Nah." He came close enough to box her in with his hands flat at the wall beside her head. Between the intensity of his gaze and the way his strong arms framed her and the steaminess of the shower, she was overwhelmed. Completely wrapped up in him.

She ignored the way her stomach dropped at that. And she kept her hands where they were too, stacked behind her ass. "What is it, then?"

His head bent close enough that his mouth hovered over her ear. She could feel his breath, and it left tingles in its wake. She bit her tongue lightly, then harder. Just trying to hold on to her sense. But he was snatching every bit of it. Everything she had to give.

"The amazing thing is that you're never going to forget me, Annie." He framed her face first, then his hands split and stroked down her throat. His thumbs rubbed over her collarbone. Over her shoulders. Separately, he cupped her breasts, but he didn't linger. Instead, he moved on to her ribs and her waist and her hips. Her thighs next.

She felt possessed by him. Completely enveloped. He could touch any inch of her that he wanted and she'd let him. She didn't know what to do with that. She didn't know how to make it normal, to make it only about sex.

Except that was the part of this that was different to begin with, wasn't it? It wasn't only about sex. She'd had sex in the last few years. This was about epic sex, about finding a new part of her. And she couldn't do that if she didn't give up the ties she'd wrapped around herself.

She let herself melt, let her boundaries drop. Her eyes shut first, and her neck bent until her head came to rest against the cool wall. Every touch became more, echoed deeper. He dipped his head and took her nipple into his mouth and she almost exploded. The pleasure jerked her up onto her toes.

There was no heavy-handed fumbling with Sean. She should have known better than to expect such, even on a subconscious level. He took her mouth, sweeping over her with a rhythm that made her want to beg. Made every phrase in her thick head change into words so basic as *please* and *yes* and his simple name. He held that big cock in one hand and zeroed in on her open, needy pussy in one stroke.

He didn't tease. Didn't ease his way in. Once the thick head was already notched in her body, he scooped up her knee high enough to hook over his hip.

And then he fucked her. Straight up, deep into her body, and overwhelmingly sure.

She cried out. Her voice was loud, even under the patter of the shower, and it made her jump. Sean's hands steadied her. Sean's *body* steadied her.

He nuzzled her hair, his mouth slipping over her cheek to her ear. "Deep breath. I'm sorry if I went too fast."

Except he hadn't. He'd gone just right. Tears stung the corners of her eyes. He was inside her, and her body clenched and pulled at his length. She was so full; she hadn't ever felt like this before. The delicious burn was something she'd remember forever. He was right about that much.

Still she wanted more.

Deliberately, she dropped off the tiptoes of the foot still on the floor. Kept dropping until her heel was flat. It drew him deeper into her. She gave another little cry, but this one turned into a desperate moan as soon as he pushed up. A slow, grinding move that dragged his pelvis over the front of her pussy. Her clit sang out with the unrelenting pressure.

She gulped back precious oxygen, but it wasn't enough to drag her back to earth. They were in another world. He'd created a launch sequence that she didn't know how to stop.

Her intentions to let things go, to embrace release, went flying out the window. He was moving in a way that made her spin. That made her crazy. She opened her eyes, but all she could see was tile ceiling and the drip of water and—

Sean grasped her chin between fingers and

thumb. He dragged her facedown until she was looking him in the eyes. "Right here, sweetheart. I'm right here."

"I know," she breathed. "You're everywhere."

"Is that a bad thing?" He stopped moving inside her.

She whimpered. Her hands flattened across his back. The muscles there were hard from restraining himself. "No. Please. Fuck me, Sean. Fuck me. I want it."

He started again. Little thrusts at first, as if he'd make her beg for it all over again. Then deeper. Deeper. "You do, don't you? You want it so bad. You need me to fuck you."

His words were coming harder and faster, mimicking the way he was working against her body. Even the way his chest rubbed over hers, the water from the shower evaporating between them, made more pleasure rock her. She would give anything to make sure he kept going.

She was winding tight. So tight inside. Her clit throbbed with the beat of her heart, which was clattering with rapid, desperate speed. Her nails sank into his back. He hissed in her ear and she was glad to hear it, because she was making needy, animal sorts of sounds. Things that sounded like quiet screams.

She buried her mouth against his shoulder. She was going to lose it, and she'd cry out so loudly when she did. Hiding it against his skin would help. But he wedged his grip under her chin again. "No," he growled. His eyes were burning, and those lean cheeks looked like they'd been carved out of glass. "You'll scream. I'm going to make you scream. And when you do, I want to hear it."

She shook her head. She didn't have the words to protest. His mouth looked like something sculpted by an Italian artist.

"Please, Annie," he said, but it was more an order than a request. "Let me hear you. Let me hear your screams. I'm earning them, aren't I? So you'll give me what I'm working for."

That did it. Oh, that did it so hard. She exploded, shards of sensation working out from her pussy to her stomach. Her legs clenched on his hips and her nails sank into his back. She came hard, and she came well, and it had been everything she'd hoped for.

And she screamed. She screamed his name.

Chapter 21

Sean had gotten what he wanted and victory was sweet. Damn sweet. He couldn't remember a better one, for that matter. His perfect-ten score his first year on the 'CT had been pretty good, but this . . . fuck yeah. He was clasped in Annie's wet heat, her interior muscles clenching and grasping his cock as if she'd never let him go. The room still echoed with her scream.

Her orgasm face was beautiful too. Her cheeks went slack as her mouth opened, and her eyes turned so hazy. She looked like she'd found nirvana.

It was all he could do to hold back his own come. He flattened a hand against the wall. It had sucked up the heat from the shower water. His hand slipped over the slick tile.

She was pinned between him and the wall, almost completely helpless. Her hands had frozen across his back, but her hips still shifted toward him again and again, in progressively smaller movements.

She came back to earth slowly. Her cries softened and by the time she shut her mouth, she was gasping for breath. Her gaze finally came back to his. She licked her lip, swallowing so hard that her throat worked up and down. The pulse at the base of her neck fluttered into overdrive. She lifted a hand to the side of his face, and the fact that her slender fingers shook was a win in his book. "You're not done."

"Nope." She felt so fucking good, though. It was a close call. He moved slowly, his thrusts kept to the bare minimum to extend her pleasure. "Can you handle more?"

She laughed, breathy and free. Her foot hooked behind his thigh. She was strong. Wiry. He liked knowing that he couldn't hurt her. He couldn't offend her either, it seemed. Because she grinned as wide as could be and shook her head. "I'm a woman. We get multiple orgasms. It's payment for all our monthly bullshit. So if you want to try to keep it up, be my guest."

He punctuated his words with a thrust of his hips that made her gasp. "It won't require much trying, sweetheart."

He reached past her to thumb off the shower control. The water stopped immediately, and Annie made a soft little noise of disappointment. "I rather liked that."

"You'll like this better."

He locked his hands around her small ass. It wasn't hard to lift her, and she obliged by locking her legs tightly around his waist. They were dripping wet, which ought to have made his walk across the bathroom difficult, but he barely noticed. He had a goal, and a man with a goal couldn't be swayed.

"Bed?" she asked, nuzzling the top of his shoulder. Her hair traced spiderweb patterns across his skin, and in contrast her mouth was a hot furnace. She added in teeth and he hissed with pleasure. His cock rubbed up and down, over the tender flesh of her mound. His head nudged the little bead of her clit, wrenching occasional sighs from her.

"You gonna object?"

He felt her smile against his skin. She was something different, someone he'd never known. Guileless, it seemed. He didn't see any part of her that was fake, or that she presented as someone different than she was. If she didn't want to give up a part of herself, she kept it hidden. She was nothing like everyone he'd dealt with, all his life.

Maybe it was a good thing that she'd left the surfing world. She wouldn't have made it on the pro circuit for more than a month. They were fierce competitors. She didn't have it in her to go for blood.

"I dunno," she was saying. "Bed seems kinda pedestrian."

"As in boring?" He poured teasing affront into his voice.

She leaned back, then back farther, even though she was still curled in his arms. She was intentionally testing his grip, first by leaning forward, enough so that her hands were barely looped around the back of his neck. Then she pushed farther away, actually letting go of him. He had her like a rock because, fucking hell, she wasn't exactly heavy. Tiny, in fact.

But she was a vicious tease. She dug her nails through her hair, leaving tracks in the damp strands. Her elbows rose, and with them her small breasts as well. Her smile was an imp's, every bit the temptress. "Boring. Completely." She faked a yawn, patting her mouth with the back of her fingertips.

"I could drop you."

The impish tilt of her smile eased into something serene. Her eyes darkened. The stark lines of her abs smoothed out. "You wouldn't."

"How do you know?"

"I know you, Sean."

He dropped her.

She bounced on the bed with a squeal. Her knees drew up tight, and she slammed her hands down fast to save herself. A little extra bounce flipped her up onto her knees. "You ass!"

"You asked for it," he purred. He loomed over her, and her mouth was almost equal with his waist. "You don't know me, Annie. You think you do, but you're paddling out in dangerous waters if you pretend otherwise."

She lifted a single eyebrow, leaning back until her ass made contact with her heels. She was a lean, extended comma of muscle and curves and so beautiful, it almost hurt him to look at her. Because she still didn't believe him. "Tell me one thing you think I don't know."

"Only if you promise to come to Fiji with me next week." He had no idea where that had come from. Impulse. He'd planned most of his life, but occasionally brilliance came to him in sharp blasts. A trip was what they needed. He liked fucking her, but he wanted her near him when he went back to competition. She felt like the opposite of a lucky charm, since the doping rumors had begun to swirl once she'd entered his life, but he wanted her to see him jump back into the circuit.

He wanted her to see him being the best.

She shook her head slowly. "I don't know. . . . Cloudbreak is such a huge wave. Watching you surf it . . . I don't know if I can."

"Sure you can." He put one knee on the bed, easing over her. She slipped flat against the mattress. They were still soaked, leaving handprints and smears from random body parts all over the expensive blanket. Sean didn't give a shit. He was using any weapon in his arsenal. "Come with me. I'll introduce you to everyone I know. If you don't find new funding for your center, I'll still pay cash out of my own pocket, even though you let me go as a client."

She bit her bottom lip. "You know this isn't about money anymore."

So he laid siege to her, though keeping it ostensibly innocent. Petting her hip, her thigh. The skin behind her knee was thin and fragile as crystal. Soft as silk, though. He wedged one forearm along her shoulder and head, and lowered his body to hers.

They both gasped. The air had cooled the water on their skin, but beneath that was a searing layer of heat. Her breasts fit against him perfectly, cushioning him. There was something better about the two of them together. "Besides," he whispered in her ear, "it's a first-class trip to Fiji. I'll get you drunk on good wine and feed you fresh pineapple."

She was breathy. Her lungs were working harder and harder. He framed her skull with his hand, holding her close.

"You know how to entice a girl," she said, half teasing.

His cock found the heat between her legs as easily as Sean dropped into a layback on the front of a wave. Pushing into her was like coming home. Like practicing something until it became as easy as keeping the heart beating. Unconscious. Except this wasn't practiced for them. This was still the first time, the only time.

The magic of that realization hit Sean like a fist in the chest. His stomach flipped, and his hand closed on the back of Annie's head. He pulled her up for a kiss because he had no idea what would show in his eyes. Her mouth gave in to his kiss as if they'd done it a thousand times.

"Yes," she whispered once he'd pulled his lips from hers. Her gaze darted over his features, and he wondered if he'd been too slow on the whole hiding gig. "I'll go to Fiji."

He knew he should have been grinning. Smiling, at the very least. He'd just won. He'd gotten her to agree. But there was a very real part of him that felt about as feral as a wild tiger. He could shred meat with his bare teeth. It was more than agreement; it was victory, and one didn't do something so tacky as *smile* over victory. The victorious were proud. Fierce.

He increased his strokes, lifting her hips with his one free hand. His fingers were long enough to graze the cleft of her ass, stretch around to where she was so wet and plump and accepting. She cushioned every pump of his hips. More. She welcomed them.

Her body strove toward his. Her mouth parted on

quiet gasps that rapidly became less so. "Oh God. Sean, you are . . . Oh, you're good. So deep."

"I can go deeper." Except he balanced his threat with the opposite, drawing out until shallow thrusts barely kept the head of his cock within the opening of her body. She didn't reach for him. Her heel found purchase in the sheets, knee locking as her hips sought him. But she stretched her hands up, up over her head until she was a lean line. An exclamation point of want and need.

He put a hand flat over her upper stomach. Beneath his palm, her heartbeat pounded. Runaway train kinds of speed. She was just as affected as he was. There wasn't a moment of this that didn't seem scripted from his deepest fantasies. The ones he hadn't even realized existed until she came around.

He kept fucking her, because what else was there to do? He wanted. He needed.

He never got what he needed. Not really. His surfing career was the only thing he kept balanced, and even in that arena, he still hadn't reached his ultimate goals. Everything faded or waned over time. He wasn't surprised by it, considering his basic lack of training to act like a human being.

But knowing he was fucked-up in the head didn't make him magically stop wishing for better.

He wanted Annie. At least he had her now. He had her hard and long, and deep, and that would be enough. The way he made her scream again would be enough.

Her hands rose from the way they'd twisted in the soft blankets and wrapped around his shoulders. Her wrists rubbed over his ribs, her fingertips dug into his lats, and she writhed hard enough that the middle of her back came up off the bed.

He braced himself with one hand and framed her face with the other. "Tell me you're coming."

"I am. God, I am. Sean, it's so much." She shook her head, hard enough that her dark hair spread in a fan. "Too much."

"No," he growled. "Just right. Come on me, Annie. Come all over my cock. You know you want to."

"Yes," she breathed, except the soft breath turned harder and she drew it out into a sibilant promise. She went off like a firecracker, all explosions and gasping. Her body held him so closely that he thought the pleasure would turn him inside out.

He took it. Threw caution to the wind and pressed his face to the bed beside her head. He didn't want her to see him when he broke apart. The pleasure started at the base of his spine and worked its way out from there. Pure jolts made his cock twitch, and he buried himself as deep in her as possible. But that wasn't all of it. He was . . . found.

He'd simply fucked girls before. This wasn't that; he was still panting as he tried to get his breath back. His blood rushed hard in his ears, leaving only a wave of sound. He didn't have the brains to figure it out, not now.

So when the doorbell rang, everything in him went swimming-in-the-Arctic kinds of cold.

No one came to his house unannounced. No one invited, at least.

Chapter 22

If Annie hadn't known better, her feelings would've gotten all bundled up in a knot of hurt in an instant. Sean levered off her about as quickly as if she'd said she had a communicable disease. "Shit, sorry," he muttered. He swept in for one more mind-blowing kiss, but then he pulled away again.

He stripped the condom off in one fast gesture and wrapped it in a tissue before tossing it in the wastebasket next to his dresser. He pulled a pair of boxers from the top drawer while she stayed sprawled out in the middle of the bed, resting on her elbows.

Then he checked his phone, pulling up something she couldn't quite see. But she thought it might have been a view of his front door. She hadn't noticed cameras, but she wasn't surprised that they'd been there.

Sean clenched his jaw, cursed, and started laying out his clothes. His movements were slow and precise as he went in and out of his deep closet, starting with his trousers, and finally choosing a button-down shirt. No tossing on a pair of shorts just to open the door.

The doorbell rang again.

"I'm coming," Sean muttered. It was jarring how the word had such a different implication moments ago. Annie now noticed the way Sean's jaw was hidden behind a layer of dark scruffiness, since he hadn't shaved in days—even though its strength was still obvious. It seemed to harden with his annoyance.

"Expecting someone?" She folded up so that she could sit at the edge of the bed. She pressed her knees together and tucked her ankles to one side. It was one thing to be completely, lewdly open when in the middle of a heated, explosive moment. Now, she felt so exposed that goose bumps skittered across her entire back. She wrapped her arms around her chest, tucking one hand into her elbow and nibbling on the thumb of her other hand.

He selected a gorgeous, expensive-as-hell pair of onyx-and-gold cuff links. Evidently he was more concerned about his image. "I knew they would come eventually, but I didn't know it would be today."

She lifted her eyebrows, prompting him to explain more. "Words, Westin. You know how to use them better than that."

He sighed, drawing an expensive pair of sunglasses from a box on top of his dresser. "It's Paul Ackerman. Odds are really, really high he's the documentary maker."

Alarm drew her to her feet, and she scrambled for her clothing. "Jesus, Westin! Are you going to tell him to go away?"

He shrugged, holding both her shoulders. "He

can't break into my house or anything. He'll just wait outside until there's a sign of me, or . . . not."

"What does he want?"

He cracked a smile, but it looked tight on his cheeks, a dull approximation of his usual charm. "There's no real telling. He just scents blood in the water."

She shuddered, and only half of it was the cold creeping through her. "It's kind of distasteful. All this. I mean . . . Why wouldn't he have come to you first?"

"Because obviously he seems to have something that he deems a big deal."

"What could it be? You haven't done anything worth this." Except . . . had he? She didn't know him, not *really*. He had a little bit of a reputation for liking expensive women and the good life, and a little more for being Jack Crews's buddy. But then again, if she hadn't thought that she knew him on at least some level, she wouldn't have painted her toes sparkly black and come over to do dirty things with him.

She knew he liked surfing and loved the water, and he'd worked incredibly hard to make enormous recovery gains. But none of that added up to *knowing* him.

"I see that look," Sean said dryly. He'd turned to the mirror to finger comb his hair. His gaze caught hers through the glass.

Her stomach stilled even as her heart fluttered. "What look?"

"The one that says you're wondering what I've done to earn a situation like this."

She swallowed as she shook her head, and she could feel herself trying to keep her eyes wide. She stopped midshake and sighed. Her gaze dropped to her toes. "If it makes it any better, I don't *want* to doubt you."

He took so long answering that she had to pull her head up and look at him. He wasn't returning the look. He'd braced his hands wide on the edge of the pale wood dresser. His shoulders were a study in a well-muscled, perfectly formed man. The caps were curved and thick with muscle, but the span between was a smooth V. His neck had thick tendons, and his short, cropped hair showed off the place where they met the heavy sweep of his skull. She could put her thumbs there and dig in, and he'd probably only thank her for it.

He turned back to her, but not before grabbing his slacks and pulling them on. "C'mon. I think I'm going to answer the door after all. If you want to be naked, you can, but you don't seem like the type." He was teasing, but his heart didn't seem to be in it.

She had to put on her damp bikini bottoms after shaking them out over the tile floor of the bathroom. Her board shorts went over them, and they were wet too, since it wasn't as if they'd strategically draped their clothing in places where they'd dry. She had to scoop them up from the floor where she'd dropped them so shamelessly an hour and a half ago. She and Sean had been way too impatient.

Her cheeks and the back of her neck flamed, but Sean was so preoccupied with his troubles that she didn't have to worry about him noticing.

He stood, tossing on and buttoning up his shirt.

Every inch of skin that disappeared turned him into a different person. As his abs and that tan were hidden, he became more put together.

He'd seated himself in a chair next to a window and was brushing off his black shoes with a soft cloth. Between his eyebrows was a deep divot of worry. She wanted to go to him and give him a giant hug. See if he'd allow himself to rest on her shoulder a minute. It wasn't like her at all. She'd always found it easiest to comfort those who were . . . God, who were less powerful than she was. That wasn't a particularly pleasant thing to notice. She gave the kids who came to her center plenty of sympathy and love and compassion. She ought to be able to find a little for the man whose penis had just been in her.

Maybe she should stick to the idea of buying him a beer afterward. He'd been off the painkillers for several days, or his new physical therapist wouldn't have given him the go-ahead to surf today. If anyone needed a break from healthy living strictures, it was Sean.

At least the T-shirt he'd given her was warm and soft, the cotton broken-in by probably hundreds of washings. Since she was fairly small chested, she pulled it on over her bare skin, figuring that a wet swimsuit to create damp triangles was probably more distracting than going without. Emblazoned across her chest was TRESTLES, the legendary California break. She tugged her hem down. "Trestles, that's where you grew up, right?"

His mouth twisted, but he leaned back in his chair. His wrists rested on the lightly padded arms, and he stretched his legs out in front of him. "Kind of. Six miles inland."

Her brow wrinkled and her head tilted. "That far in? The story from the magazines is that you were practically a beach bum. Lived there when you weren't in school."

He gave a smile that was all bare teeth and wicked intentions. "That's true enough. But it's not the whole story."

"Then what is?"

"That'd be what Paul is after, it would seem. You promised me Fiji, remember? I'll tell you on the plane." He seemed to be holding on by a thread as he slowly stood. He was a man at the top of his game; he shouldn't ever look creaky or like his bones were hurting him. Hell, he hadn't been affected even when they were.

"First class?" she asked, injecting a teasing tone into her voice. It was hard. Fucking hell, it was hard when her throat felt so tight that she thought she might cry any second. It went along with the burn at the back of her eyes. And wasn't that absolutely absurd?

The problem had to be that she was out of her depth. She wasn't the crying type, but then she hadn't ever felt so completely at sea before. She didn't understand what Sean was hiding that had to be this desperate. It was some publicity, right? No big deal. Except that the story involving his childhood seemed to be freaking him out. And in turn, his tension was leaching into her.

Annie didn't want this. She didn't want to *care* for him so much. She wanted all of it to go away . . . and she felt absolutely helpless and unable to fix it. "Ready?"

He gave a solemn nod. "If you want to leave, I get it. You're not in any way involved with the situation."

"I'll stay." The words came out much steadier than she'd expected them to.

Ten minutes later, she wasn't entirely sure she'd made the right call.

Paul Ackerman was a plain-looking man for being in filmmaking. He had carefully parted brown hair and a short-sleeved white shirt. At least he hadn't worn a black tie.

Sitting in the corner of the living room, Annie tucked her toes under her butt in a sleek black leather chair. "You look more like a Mormon missionary than the man who can make or break Sean's career."

Sean shoved back a smile and turned away from Mr. Ackerman. He shot Annie a *Behave* kind of look. She wrinkled her nose and stuck her tongue out at him. Better she be there to make him smile and laugh than he should have to go through this alone.

The guy blinked at her. His mouth folded into a wry smile and his gently rounded cheeks lifted. "Ma'am, I have no power to break Mr. Westin's career. I only have a few questions."

"Then you should have come to me *first*," Sean growled. "I don't have any problem with shooting footage."

"That's great! Then you won't mind answering my questions? I'd like to start early in your life for this project." He spread his hands wide. "I want to start with Trestles, then pan inland. To . . . Mission Viejo, right?"

"I don't talk about my past," Sean said.

"Where you went to high school is a matter of public record," Ackerman replied blandly. But he was studying Sean with such intensity, Annie knew something was wrong. There was more loaded under those words that she didn't understand.

Surprisingly Sean backed down. His eyes narrowed, and the muscle in front of his ear jumped harshly in the hollow of his cheek. "Fine. We'll talk."

Surprise parted her lips. After all this, he was just going to sit down with the man and give an interview? Except he hadn't said that, not exactly, had he? He'd said they'd talk. That wasn't the same thing as agreeing to answer a whole mess of questions.

Though what did he have to hide, anyway?

She pushed up from her seat and twined her fingers through Sean's. "Hey. It's your choice. Do you want me to be here? If you want space, I could totally make myself scarce by heading home."

"Actually . . ." Something dark flitted across his expression. His mouth almost disappeared when it flattened. He shook his head. "It's probably too big a favor."

She squeezed his fingers. "What is it?"

He sighed. "I'm afraid this will come out wrong."

Ackerman was tracking every word of their conversation with an avid, predatory gleam. Sean spotted it. He gave the slightest, faintest sneer she'd ever seen and folded his hand around her elbow to tug her away toward the kitchen, next to the lanai. "Is it okay if I ask you to take a walk?"

"I can't just go upstairs?"

"I . . ." Sean swallowed his words, then shrugged. "Look. I dunno how polite I'm going to manage to stay with this guy. It depends what he asks me. And . . . all things considered . . ."

All things considered, they'd only fooled around a few times. That wasn't the same thing as a serious relationship, and she wasn't looking for one of those anyway. Not with Sean. She folded her mouth into a smile. "I'll take a walk on the beach."

Relief lightened his face, made his mouth ease into something that was almost a smile. Whatever else could be said, there was no doubt that this whole situation had him on edge. "I appreciate it."

Leaning up on her toes, Annie kissed him. Because it was either that, or find another way to admit how damn happy it made her to be able to give him something. Even if that meant something so stupid as being able to give him distance when he needed it. She'd always thought of herself as independent, but maybe that was another way to say she was lonely. And she didn't want to feel lonely anymore.

Chapter 23

Annie had dashed upstairs again to put her bikini top back on, but she'd been incredibly fast about it. Prompt in a way that felt intentional. She was clearing the way for Sean to do whatever he needed to do. Annie was a hella cool girl.

Unfortunately, as soon as the back door shut behind her, Sean felt as closed in as if a barreled wave had slammed down on his head.

His hands curled into fists as he watched her walk down the back steps to the water. She perched a pair of sunglasses on her nose. Knockoffs. He wondered if he could switch them out without her noticing for a pair of the Heuers that had shown up on his doorstep a few weeks ago. Or more particularly, without her protesting too vehemently.

Probably not. She'd look good in the expensive frames, though.

Sean sighed and turned his gaze back toward the living room. He should get this over with.

Ackerman had seated himself on the couch and was waiting patiently with his elbows balanced on his knees. He hopped up with a smile as Sean re-entered. "I appreciate this. I have to admit, I didn't think you were going to give me an interview at all." He withdrew a slender silver recorder from his pocket. "Do you mind if I use this?"

"I mind." Sean dropped into a chair and waved toward the sofa. "But you can sit again if you like. Make yourself at home. Comfortable, even."

Ackerman sat, but he'd apparently realized this wasn't going to be as easy a conversation as he'd momentarily convinced himself. "I see."

Sean should have offered the guy a drink, even just a glass of water. That would have been polite. The thing a normal person would do.

Sean wasn't normal. "Why are you here, Paul?"

"First off, let me say I'm really stoked that you seem to know who I am." Paul had a nice, anonymous smile. "I've followed your career for a long time. You're not getting half the points you should. It's practically robbery."

Flattery wasn't going to get this guy anywhere. "That's not an answer."

"I want to do a sixty-minute feature on you."

"Out of the goodness of your heart?" Sean lifted his eyebrows. "Out of nowhere? I'm middle of the pack. I do well enough, and I make enough, but a feature on me isn't going to have any traction." Not unless they knew too much.

Not unless it could get juicy.

If Ackerman had figured out what had really happened when Sean's mother died, things could ratchet way past *juicy* to *scandalous*. Nothing sold better than a scandal. Sean's fingertips tingled. This . . . This was not going to end well.

Ackerman tried changing the topic. "I was really surprised to find you at home in the middle of the afternoon. Thought I'd have to camp out on your doorstep until you came in from the beach. Surf must not be up!" he said with a laugh.

Sean hooked his thumbs in his pockets and stretched his legs out. "Actually, it's kicking out there. A storm off Hawaii will be pushing in six-footers in about an hour."

"Have you been out yet today?"

This part, Sean had absolutely zero problem talking about. He put on one of his best smiles. "Yeah. Had my first postinjury surf this morning. Took a lot of warming up, but it's been great."

"I'm glad to hear that." Ackerman leaned forward. Brown hair fell across his forehead. "It'd be a real shame if you got knocked off the 'CT for something like this."

"I'd agree."

"I know this wasn't the first time you were injured, but the damage seemed to be longer lasting. Was this time scarier?"

Sean took a long, slow breath. There wasn't anything to it. He really was just doing his job, and for that alone, Sean should drink a big glass of shut-the-fuck-up. Except he knew where this conversation would finish eventually.

And yeah, it got there. Once Ackerman had exhausted his surfing and recovery questions, he eventually leaned back to rest against the soft couch. His gaze dropped, but then he looked back at Sean. Assessing.

Sean braced himself. The hard stuff was coming.

Impatience rode him like a grom trying his first real trick. The faster they got this over with, the faster Sean could shut him down.

"So," Paul said, drawing the word out slowly, "I've done some preliminary research on you."

"I expected as much."

"I couldn't find any proof that you'd graduated from your high school."

"I'd rather not talk about that."

Ackerman slipped a small black notebook from his back pocket and flipped it open. "We're still talking a matter of record here, Sean."

"Then check records. I'm not talking about it." He was made of ice. Except ice would melt in the parts of the ocean he liked. "Look, I think I've proven over the last forty-five minutes that I'm amenable to giving interviews. That's fine. But there's no reason you need my past history. It's just that. Past and history. Agree to leave them there and you can come back with a recorder. With a camera. Fucking hell, with *five* cameras if you want. I'll let you tag me around." Sean pushed to his feet. "But it's all stuff of the here and now. I'm not going back."

"Mr. Westin, I'm not trying to fuck you over. This isn't going to be some hack-job piece."

Sean plastered a smile on his face. "Then you won't have any problem agreeing to my parameters."

Ackerman stood to match Sean. His pleasant face pinched. "Look . . ." He sighed. "You're not the only source I can go to. I mean, you're the best, of course. I'd *like* to get it right from you. But if you're not willing to talk, I—I'll do what I need to."

"You've already got a source, don't you?" Sean's eyes narrowed at the same time something painful pulsed in his temple. "Who is it?"

Ackerman's head shook. "Sorry. I can't tell you."

Immediately, Sean went mentally careening through the very, very short list of people who might know enough to give any sort of interview. His uncle Theo had been the one to clear up the arson charges and pay off the fire department for its outlay. But Theo was family, and he was pretty well-off too. There was no paycheck large enough to sway him. He'd never gotten married or had kids, so there was nothing in that direction. Sean's mother had isolated herself because of the very nature of her disease. Nothing there. And Sean had never told a soul.

After all, when a person burned down his child-hood home at age eighteen, it wasn't something he went around bragging about.

"What you have is innuendo at best. Maybe some speculation."

"I know you finished out school in a private insti-tution, under your uncle's custody."

Sean flashed hot, then completely cold. His stom-ach lurched. That was supposed to be completely expunged, along with the record he had never quite gotten. It was all supposed to be cleared up. "Get out of my house. Now."

"Talk with me, Sean. Let me have access and this doesn't have to go painfully."

"If you're not gone in ten seconds, I'll have to call the cops."

Ackerman looked back at him steadily and for probably longer than five seconds, Sean wondered if the other man would try to call his bluff. Ackerman gave a small nod and let himself out.

Sean puked in the downstairs bathroom.

No dwelling. No looking back. His stomach was more settled after he managed to brush his teeth, so that was all that counted.

Doing what he had to do didn't make him a bad person.

The litany was all that had gotten him through at first. When he'd been so damn young, and so damn scared.

Before he'd had the pro circuit and the World Championship Tour.

He wasn't sure whether Annie would still be waiting for him. She could have gone around the outside of the house to her car, since her keys had been shoved in her pocket.

He stepped out the back door, trying to keep it cool. He scooped his sunglasses out of a pocket and popped them on against the arrowing glare of the setting sun.

"Over here." Annie was sitting on the hot, powdery sand. "Did he bleed you dry?"

"Not this time." And Jesus, when he spoke to her, his chest filled with that light feeling of relief. He hadn't actually believed she'd still be there. Not when it came down to it. "Tried to."

People weren't there for him. Maybe they said they would be, or maybe they intended to be, but when the shit hit the fan, Sean had learned that a man usually had to make his own way in the world and only rely on himself. He'd been damn good at it, at least.

He sank to the beach beside her. The waves really had started to kick, as the reports had said to expect. He couldn't surf the current conditions, not yet. But he would, and soon. And he'd be back on top of his game.

He'd move forward. Not back.

"What's a pretty girl like you doing in a shady place like this?" He flashed a grin at Annie. It was a lie of a smile, but maybe she didn't know that, because she cocked a grin at him with enough fire that it could have been used to light a seashore bonfire.

Her smile was the kind of thing used to call rescue ships to stranded boaters. She laughed at him. "Shady? Did you just call beachside at San Sebastian shady? This is probably the safest place in the world. Or close. Besides, I'm *always* protected."

He chuckled. "Right. Could you take down a carjacker?"

"I've had some self-defense courses," she said with such serene understatement that he suddenly wondered.

He cocked an eyebrow. "Martial arts?"

"I'm a black belt in judo." She leaned back on her hands. "What do you think about that?"

"Hot as fuck. Come here." He scooped a hand around the back of her neck and pulled her toward him. Closer and closer, but he stopped when his mouth was only an inch from hers. "Thanks for staying. That really sucked." It was an understatement, but it was all he could manage to say. At least for now, when his heart was still slamming with such sickly force.

"You know what doesn't suck?" She'd twisted

most of her hair up in a knot at the back of her head, but heavy tresses had broken free to frame her eyes and cheeks. Because making sure he had the space he needed had been more important than making herself look pretty. Even now, she was giving him that space by not asking him unanswerable questions.

It didn't hurt that she was already gorgeous. And Sean couldn't wrap his head around what she was willing to do for him. "What doesn't suck?"

"Kissing me. You should do that. Often." She lifted her mouth the full distance to his, and the kiss she placed on his lips was like a gift. Soft. Tender. Something they hadn't shared before.

He returned it, making as many silent promises as he knew how to word.

It wasn't much. He was too ruined to keep going long. But in the time between here and loss, she'd get everything he had to give.

Chapter 24

"If I asked you to take care of things around here for about a week, would you ask me a hundred questions about why, or would you just do it?" Annie blurted out the question in one breath. Her stomach was taking flips an X-Gamer would be proud of.

Her mom paused while plaiting a length of safety rope. She tilted her head to the side. Her hair was long enough that it slipped off her shoulder in a dark stream and onto the tabletop where she was working. "Hmm. Let me think about that." She tapped a finger across her lips, but then rolled her eyes at Annie. "Ask a hundred questions, of course. What kind of mother do you think I am?"

"A loving, sweet mother who wants the best for her child, but who understands that sometimes an adult woman needs to be autonomous and trusted in her choices?"

Denise opened her mouth as if she'd respond, but then slumped. Her hands fell into her lap. "Well, fuck."

"Great!" Annie chirruped. "I'll give you all the keys and we'll go over the basics tomorrow."

With that, she tried her best to slip right back out the kitchen door, but Denise was having none of it. "Wait just a minute, young lady."

She paused with one hand on the doorjamb. "Yes, my loving and supportive mother?"

"Get your ass back in here." She pushed aside the safety rope from the tabletop. "And bring us tea."

"I don't drink tea."

Denise grinned. "Fine. Bring me tea and you can have some of that awful-for-you diet soda. When you get cancer long before your time, I'll cry at your grave."

"No one has definitively tied aspartame to cancer deaths." Still, she felt a little twinge as she cracked open the cap of her soda. Her mom was certainly good at putting the maternal guilt trip on a girl.

Lucky for Annie, Denise had been a fairly balanced mother. She'd given support the best she could, and her best was often amazing. So when she finally had a cup of tea curled in her hands and looked at Annie in that particular way, Annie melted. She didn't really have a choice.

"It's that Sean Westin, isn't it?" Denise didn't accuse, didn't say it any way that felt negative. Just words. Just a question.

So why did Annie cringe inside? Her stomach twisted. "Yeah, Mom."

"Do I get to know if you'll be in town or farther afield?"

Annie folded her hands in her lap. Her index finger found a soft spot in the jeans material stretched across her knees. She picked, worrying at the worn spot until she could feel the sharp edge of her nail on her own skin. "I'll be in Fiji."

"Jesus, Annie." Her mom said it softly. "You weren't going to tell me that you were going to another country? That's not like you. I'd expected you to say something like San Diego."

"San Diego's nice," she said weakly.

Her mother made a show of dipping her head and angling her ear toward Annie. "It's nice, but . . ."

She sighed. "But Fiji is where the next ASP World Championship Tour event is being held."

"You're following that man to an island in the middle of the ocean."

She felt her mouth turn mulish. Practically sullen. "You say that as if I'm planning to stay there. It's just a vacation, Mom. When was the last time I took one of those?"

"Don't look at me, missy. I've been telling you to take some time off for about four years now." She curled her hands around the white-and-blue tea mug and leaned forward. "But I meant San Diego!"

"What's with you and San Diego, anyway?"

"Your dad won't go with me to this little bungalow that we could rent, and it's perfect. I've even been planning to sign him up for a sailing lesson, and you know he's always wanted that. But he won't agree." Denise's mouth twisted into a little pout that looked about as familiar as it felt.

At least Annie always knew she came by her stubbornness honestly. She was just like her mom. Besides, Dad wouldn't agree to Denise's newest trip idea because he'd already planned, picked, and paid for a really freaking similar vacation to Santa Barbara for their thirtieth anniversary. He and Denise were bound together for life, in that way little girls dreamed of. Annie had had those same sorts of dreams when she'd been young. She'd played with a piece of lace over her hair as a veil.

She wasn't sure when those dreams had faded away. The first chunk had disappeared when she faced the world of pro surfing. There was no way to be with someone who meant something to you when you were on the 'CT. But then another chunk had faded when she'd dealt with Terry and the aftermath of that night.

"I like him. I like Sean." Even as she said the words, she was qualifying them in her mind. She liked him, but they weren't going to last. She liked him, but he had issues. She liked him, but *she* had issues.

There was no *forever* for them.

"Are you considering surfing Cloudbreak?"

"Oh God, no," Annie exclaimed, jerking backward. "What in the name of God? Why would you think that?"

Cloudbreak was a beautiful wave a mile away from Tavarua, Fiji. Surfers had to take a boat ride to get out there, but they were rewarded with heavy barrels and clean swells if they made it. Except there was a stretch known as the shish kebabs because it was that easy to get skewered on the reefs. The ASP competition would be at that wave and at another break off the mainland of Fiji. It was going to be difficult enough to watch Sean surf it with the full extent of his injury and recovery as plain as his MRI reports. Cloudbreak could kill men, much less rein-jure their shoulders.

Not only would it be incredibly packed, and most likely officially roped off for pro surfers only, but there was the overwhelming fact that Annie wasn't ready. Even though she'd once been an excellent surfer who could have handled it ten years ago. That was then. This was now. She wasn't dumb enough to think otherwise. "Jeez, Mom. No way. I'll surf some-thing on my terms, probably a beach break. Not *Cloudbreak*. Sheesh."

Denise put both hands up. "I worry. I'm sorry if that was a dumb question. It's bad enough to think of you breaking an arm on your backyard ramps. Throw in a thirty-foot wave on the other side of the globe and I get a little irrational."

As if speaking of the ramps made them awaken, a familiar sound came from the backyard. The swoop-ing, steady whirr of wheels on wood. Annie and her mother exchanged a look, then glanced at the door in tandem.

Denise stood, her hands flat on the kitchen table. "Were you . . . ?"

"Waiting on anyone?" Annie shook her head and took half a second to scoop her hair into a ponytail. She had the sudden impulse to have it out of her eyes.

She thought about grabbing the Taser she had locked in a cabinet next to the stove, but she realized that would be ridiculous. Someone who was out to cause trouble would be either pounding on doors or sneaking around, not stopping for a late-evening skating session.

She didn't tell her mom to put down the cell phone she clutched, however. Annie only unbolted the back door and stepped onto her tiny patio. She folded her arms and leaned on the fence that blocked off the pool. "Hey, Tim."

He paused at the table, his wheels balanced in the air over the vert. "Hey, Miss Annie."

"Dude, haven't I talked to you about calling before you come by so late?"

He shrugged and squinted across the street. Unless he was examining the cars lining the street, he was avoiding her gaze. They'd had this conversation a hundred times.

It wasn't as if she'd ever put consequences on breaking the rule. Tim came only when he needed somewhere safe to go. The red hoodie he wore was too thin for the night air, but no one had told him to put on something thicker. No one had stopped him from going out at ten p.m. on a Tuesday either.

Annie wasn't stupid about her kids. She knew some of them were confrontational, and even if a parent had told them to keep their ass in the house, they'd have stormed out to do exactly what they wanted. Not Tim. He was a different kind of kid.

He was bruised at the edges. Sometimes literally, sometimes not. "Me and the stepasshole got in a fight."

Annie's hands clenched on the wood fence. "Physical fight? Because he's got seventy pounds on you. I really think we could make assault charges stick."

"And have Mom kick me out?" Tim shook his

head. He had shockingly red hair in the daylight, but under the orange-tinted floodlights, it looked almost blond. "It's cool. Just a lotta shouting this time, anyway."

"What set it off?"

He shrugged. "The cable went out. He said I was fucking around with it—but I wasn't, Miss Annie. I swear it." He scrubbed his fingers through his hair and tugged. "And that made him throw my backpack across the room. Which was fine, except my report card fell out and I have a C minus in English comp."

"Aw, Tim," she said. "You know I'll help you with that. Bring in any assignments you've got uncompleted this weekend—" Except she had to cut herself off. She'd be in Fiji by this weekend. Living a life of luxury and doing really inappropriate and naughty things with Sean. Hopefully. "When's the quarter end?"

"Not for three more weeks."

"So bring some work by tomorrow and we'll do what we can. The rest of it'll be when I get back from a trip."

Tim gave her a smile she recognized. From him, it meant thank you—and a pretty hefty shot of resentment too. He didn't like how much help he needed in writing, which was probably why he'd willingly fallen behind rather than come to her for help. She'd had a mental note to ask about his English courses, but she'd forgotten.

She'd forgotten because of Sean. Because of the obsession she was developing for him. This couldn't go on. She wasn't going to be able to balance her life between the regular stuff and the places where she took off an afternoon to surf. Where she disappeared to foreign countries because a handsome man with blue eyes asked her to.

It had been four years since she'd gone to sleep without wondering if a teenager would turn up in her backyard. There was that factor. She loved being there for them, being a safe place, but there had to be a limit. That was why she was seeking funding for the new center. Funding for a director who could take care of the two a.m. phone calls too.

She drummed her fingers on the fence. "How long you gonna skate?"

"I dunno. I'm trying to nail a hardflip." He bit his upper lip, since he was asking a lot of her, considering how late it was.

"Lemme go change. I'll be back out in a minute." She was wearing lightweight pajama pants with a drawstring waist. They were inappropriate and too thin for skating, since they'd give her no protection.

Her mom stopped her just inside the back door. "Is he okay?"

"Okay enough for tonight."

"His mom ought to be strung up." Denise's mouth tightened into something flatter than displeasure but not quite as down-turned as when she was about to cry. "She tossed over a good kid for that butthead!"

"She's doing the best that she can. You should hear Tim talk about his grandfather. He's lucky his mom isn't a total heroin addict, really." Impulsively, she squeezed her mom in a giant hug. "Thanks for worrying about me, Mom. But I'm going to be fine.

I'm going to Fiji with Sean, but then I'll be back and everything will be back to normal. This is . . . just mess-around time. Understand?"

Denise leveled a steady stare at Annie. "I understand. But I'm not sure you mean it."

Chapter 25

"This is a ten-hour flight?" Annie was folded in the seat of an airline waiting area, her feet tucked under her butt.

"Ten and a half," Sean said with intentionally lazy inflection. He turned the page in his magazine. Keeping his gaze trained on the glossy pages was difficult.

Annie looked absurdly cute. Sean wasn't even sure what it was about the outfit that was doing it for him, because it was more than obvious she had dressed for comfort. Her striped pajama pants had a natural cotton drawstring. She'd layered two tank tops that had a stylized spaceship that Sean couldn't identify with an open zip-up hoodie.

Her tablet was stacked with movies for the flight, but even though she had it balanced across her knees, the headphones dangled to the side. She had the side of her thumb between her teeth. "I'm surprised you don't charter a jet or something."

"It's Fiji. I'm rich, not made of gold." He coiled his hand around the back of her neck. Soft tendrils fell loose from her ponytail and trailed over his knuckles. "Stuff it and enjoy the first-class lounge."

She wrinkled her nose at him, which was really fucking cute, so he kissed her briefly. She tasted like sugar and coffee from the iced drink at her side.

When she ended the kiss, she left her fingers framing his cheek as she gave him a teasing smile. "It's kinda swank."

"Good." He liked being able to give her good things. He didn't know what had prompted him to ask her along on this trip to Fiji, but he felt better with her at his side. The results of his drug testing would come in before the event started, but since he knew he was going to pass it, he might as well get there early.

Having time to assess the waves and the conditions before a competition was vital. Even though there'd been an event in Fiji for the past several years, that didn't mean the waves would automatically be the same. The ocean was a living, breathing beast. Storms and earthquakes and even the tides themselves could affect the caliber of a break. If a chunk of reef broke away, there could be an entire shift in quality.

He'd been following reports out of Fiji pretty closely, so he didn't expect any big changes, but that didn't mean he would go in unprepared. He wanted his toes in the water and his boards wet. As soon as possible. He also needed to spend time working his shoulder out. Annie wasn't his therapist anymore, but that didn't mean he was off scott free. His new team had given him a list of daily stretches and parameters he had to work within.

It could be the difference between placing well and winning. And a win would do enormous good for Sean's ranking.

Having Annie at his side was a distraction. Something to keep the edge off so that he didn't wind too damn tight. He liked having her under his hand, having her at his side. She'd worn flip-flops, but they were on the floor and she had her bare feet folded into the cushioned chair. She was . . . different. He liked that about her.

"Hi, Sean," said a soft voice. Gloria stood in front of their seats, a bright yellow tote bag over her shoulder. "You headed out tonight?"

Gloria was a beautiful woman in the classic surfer-girl mold. She had long, tousled blond hair pulled into a low ponytail behind her left ear. Her snug leggings showed off a body that most women would envy, and she had on an oversized T-shirt that hung off one bare shoulder.

Sean and Gloria's breakup had gone fairly easily, especially since she immediately replaced him with Nate Coker. She was a constant fixture on Nate's Instagram account. So long as Nate wasn't on a surfboard, the two were always seen together.

"Yup," Sean agreed. "This is Annie Baxter."

Annie slid him a sideways glance, one that obviously noted his lack of descriptor for her. But then again, he wasn't exactly about to call her *the best lay I've ever had* or *coolest chick I know*. Both seemed unbearably tacky. She stuck her hand out to Gloria, who took it briefly. "We met at a party a couple weeks ago. Nice to see you again."

"Same," Gloria said with the briefest display of a smile that Sean would have thought possible.

"Where's Nate?" he asked.

She answered Sean, but her gaze was stuck on Annie. "He went yesterday. But I had some business to take care of."

Sean hoped his surprise didn't show on his face. Gloria hadn't had any ambition for her own career when they'd been dating. Now she lived off Nate, pretty much. Not that there was anything wrong with that. She kept Nate energized and focused. Without Gloria encouraging him, Nate would be staked out in a hammock, ready to blow his prize money on mai tais. Then there wouldn't be much more prize money. Ambitious, the man was not. "What are you into lately?"

She flashed a slightly vacant smile. "Stuff. Some producing, and I had a casting call for a commercial."

"I didn't know you wanted into acting."

"I don't, really. But it was for a gear company I was kind of hoping Nate could get in with. So I went, because maybe I'd get a chance to talk to marketing or PR about Nate."

Sean blinked slowly. He hadn't exactly heard of the industry working like that before, though it was true that it was more about who you knew than how you knew them. "Hope it worked for you, then."

"Yeah." She got a little shark-eating-a-salmon sort of smile going. "I think it may go somewhere. Ta-ta," she said with a twiddle of her fingers over her shoulder. "I'll catch you in Nadi."

"She looks like the sort who'd be in commercials," Annie said with a slightly wistful sigh as Gloria walked away. "What was the accent? It wasn't quite Australian."

"Kiwi. She's from New Zealand." Sean flipped his magazine closed as first-class boarding was announced. "I was the one who introduced her to Nate, actually. He's classic Californian. Knew him when I was growing up."

Annie let that one go until they were tucked in their comfortable leather seats and the flight attendant had offered them complimentary drinks. Annie accepted a fuzzy blanket and tucked it over her lap. "Posh seats," she said.

"They do all right. It's the only nonstop from California to Fiji, so I've been on it a few times."

"All right." She scoffed a little, but then blew it by bouncing in her seat. She wedged up on her knees and clasped the back of the seat, peering down the aisle. "This is supercool."

He laughed along with her. "Yeah, okay. You win. It's pretty awesome."

She twisted in her seat, wedging her back against the bulkhead, which was painted pale purple in keeping with a faintly tropical theme. "How can you be so blasé about this? Look at this seat! I fit in it sideways, for God's sake."

"You'd fit in a shoe box sideways." He slipped his fingers behind her firm calf. "So I'm not sure that counts."

"Did you grow up rich?"

"Fuck no, don't be ridiculous," he blurted. His grip on her leg tightened, but he forced himself to release, finger by finger. He drew in a slow, deep breath. "No, not rich."

The flight attendant interrupted with the safety briefing at the front of the cabin. Sean took the easy way out, facing her and pretending to listen with rapt attention to her lilting speech. Really, he'd heard a thousand variations of the same gig. Traveling the world for a living meant the downsides too. He could recite the emergency exit location for half a dozen different planes.

He wasn't sure how much he wanted to tell Annie. Maybe now would be a good time, while the airline supplied her with free wine and he had a captive audience. Still, that didn't mean she had to hear all of it. No one needed that kind of sob story, and he didn't want her pity. He only wanted her to stop thinking of him as spoiled.

He liked the results of his hard work. He'd never thought of that as a bad thing. He'd put a metric fuckton of effort into his surfing, and taken on gigs that a few of his compatriots looked down on. He'd caught shit from Tanner Wright for years over pulling the occasional modeling gig for a nonsurf company. Sean had never understood that. It wasn't as if Tanner hadn't posed for magazine pictures. He'd just done it holding a surfboard and wearing something that was self-described as "for surfers." Make it a fancy watch and supposedly it was all different.

Whatever. Sean had worked hard for what he had. Living to suit his means didn't seem inappropriate.

They'd been in the air a half hour when he leaned over her shoulder. "What are you watching?"

She pulled her headphones out. "The *Dexter* finale. I'm so behind, I know."

He twisted the end of her ponytail around his fingertip. "I hated it. You'll have to tell me what you think."

"Look, I'm sorry if I overstepped some boundary by asking if you'd grown up rich." She pushed up the armrest between them and gently bumped his shoulder with hers. "It's just I feel like an idiot, jumping around in my seat while you're so cool."

"It's hard to explain how I grew up," he found himself saying. But he pulled her closer. Shoulder to shoulder wasn't enough for him.

She let him too. She unsnapped her seat belt and nestled closer so that he could put his arm around her. Between the comfortable size of the first-class seats and how small she was, she was able to comfortably lean on him with her feet on the armrest next to the bulkhead. "Start with where you were born."

"I was a home birth." He rubbed up and down Annie's arm, but the sweatshirt numbed out their contact. His fingers delved through her zipper, finding bare skin at her waist where her tank tops twisted up. "Mom didn't tell anyone in her family that she was pregnant, actually. Just moved out to a little place on her own. She had a little family money, mostly through my granddad, who was a tool and die maker."

Annie twisted around in his arms, craning her neck to look at him. "How did she keep that secret?"

"Mom was . . ." He sighed, rolling through so many descriptors in his head. *Messed up. Strange. Unbalanced.* "Damaged. She had a whole series of little shitty things happen to her when she was growing up, and when her mom died, it was like she never came back. No one knew how to cope with her."

"Sounds rough."

"Fuck yeah," he agreed. "It was worse than that. It was my whole life."

Annie tried to twist again, but he didn't let her. He kept his forearm across her upper chest, clasping her shoulder and holding her close. Not mean, or hard, but firmly enough that she settled again. The view out the window was a velvety canvas of stars on dark. He focused on it rather than letting the memories of his childhood rise up again.

"She was a hoarder."

"Like . . ." She paused, and he could practically hear her measuring her words and deliberating exactly how to phrase her question. "Was she just a messy person, or are we talking clinically diagnosed here?"

"Clinical. Her thing was clothing. We had a three-bedroom house, but by the end we were both sleeping in the living room because all the rest of the space was . . . gone." The words were easier to say than he'd expected, and a hell of a lot harder at the same time. Annie made a soft noise that he didn't want to hear, so he squeezed her shoulder and kept talking so he wouldn't get a chance to absorb her sympathy. Sympathy led to pity. "So there was family money, but we didn't exactly live large or anything. Flying like this was new when I first started doing well on the circuit, but the shine wears off when you fly every single month. Sometimes I'd rather be home."

She didn't answer for a long, long time. Her head dipped and one hand looped over the arm he had across her. She brushed a soft kiss over his skin, but then patted his wrist. "Well duh. I've seen your house. It's like having first class permanently."

He sucked in a cool, deep breath, though it was of stale airline air-conditioning. At least he'd said something. That was enough for now.

Maybe enough for forever.

Chapter 26

Sean was even more fucked-up than Annie had assumed he was. She'd realized that he'd been hiding secrets, but she'd kind of figured they were the everyday bullshit kind of secrets that most people dealt with. Maybe his mom and dad divorced when he was six. Maybe he'd fucked around in high school or experimented with pot. Maybe . . .

Well, maybe he'd been squeezed out of his bedroom by the physical manifestation of his mother's emotional disorder. There ya go.

And he seemed to think it was the end of the story there. For the next three hours, she half expected him to bring it up again . . . but he didn't. They watched the last two episodes of *Dexter* together, and he proved himself an excellent rewatching companion. Even though he'd seen the episodes before, he didn't prewince or ooh or tease that she was going to like some scene that was coming up. Annie considered that the height of manners in television viewing. Afterward, they argued about whether the ending was feasible or even justifiable, considering the entire eight-season show was about a serial killer.

Eventually Annie fell asleep with her head on Sean's shoulder and his arm around her. The unbearably fluffy blanket she'd been provided by the aircrew was tucked around her knees, but she'd let the pillow fall to the floor. There was nothing better than the firm resilience of Sean's muscles.

She slept like a rock.

So hard, in fact, that they were landing before she knew it.

Sean woke her, pushing her hair back out of her eyes. "Hey. You still in there?"

"What?" Her eyes were bleary and her nose was both itchy and stuffy. Completely ugh.

"You sleep like the dead. I held a mirror up over your nose and mouth at one point to see if you were actually breathing."

"You did not." She clapped her hand over her mouth. She'd brushed her teeth before settling in, but that whole lasts-twelve-hours claim of her toothpaste was a pack of lies. "Christ, I must smell awful. Back away. Ten feet at a minimum until I can get some hygiene going."

"All I can give you is two feet." He tugged on her seat belt. "We're in the remain-seated part of the flight."

"We should have flown a private jet or something," she muttered, keeping her head down. "What's the point of being rich if you can't fly privately?"

"They still make you buckle up on approach." Sean was in an annoyingly good mood. His smile flashed at her. "You're pissy as hell in the morning, aren't you?"

"I want coffee," she grumbled. Her mouth pursed into something that felt surprisingly like a pout. "I don't work right without coffee."

"You slept through morning service. Missed a nice baked soufflé, though it could have done with more bacon."

"Ah, jeez, I missed bacon?" She flopped back in her seat, resting her head against the plastic window. Out there were miles and miles of blue. Above in the sky and below in the water. A tiny streak of island made of sand and green approached fast. But it was fun teasing Sean. "Worst morning ever."

"Next time I'll wake you for coffee and bacon at any cost. Noted." He took her hand, lacing their fingers together. "But if you keep complaining about the details of a free trip to Fiji, I might have to throw you out the hatch."

"Commercial airplanes don't have hatches." She yawned, turning her face away from him and covering her mouth with the back of her free hand. No way was she making him smell what she could taste. "They have doors. Or something. Another reason to fly private: easy body disposal. Besides, we'll be landing soon, right?"

"Already on the descent." He leaned in behind her, his chest pressing against her back as they looked out the window. "That's Fiji there. One of my favorite places on earth."

"How old were you when you first went?"

"Nineteen. I flew economy," he said, and without looking, she knew he wore a smirk. "It was my first year on the tour."

"And how did you place in the event?" She wasn't

sure why she asked. Half impulse, half curiosity, because there was no way someone could remember those sorts of details.

Except he did. He reeled off numbers like a computer program. "I came in fifteenth overall. Scored a sixteen point three in my first heat. Fifteen point six in round two, but only a fourteen point two in third round."

"You're a freak of nature. You remember all those numbers from nine years ago?"

"It's my career. Of course I do."

"Most nineteen-year-olds are barely making it through English 202."

He grinned against her neck, this time adding in a soft kiss. "Sucks to be them. And we need to get coffee and bacon in you as soon as we land. This grumpy routine is unlike you."

"It's perfectly like me," she huffed, but half for play. " 'Feed me, Seymour.' And this whole thing is off if you don't get that reference."

"*Little Shop of Horrors.* We're good."

Except they weren't.

Landing was fine. The plane touched down smoothly if they didn't count the bounce at initial touchdown. It was stepping up to the chest-high customs desk that didn't go as smoothly as they'd have expected.

Sean went first, presenting his much-stamped passport. He had a small wheeled suitcase, the type of high-end leather thing that made Annie feel like her backpack marked her out as a twelve-year-old. She flipped over the customs sheet, reviewing her answers. She hoped she'd filled out the little boxes properly. Even though she knew how to handle herself for the most part, she always got nervous with stupid little forms. She'd only gotten her passport for her trip to Cabo in college, and she hadn't even needed to have it for a trip to Mexico at the time. She'd figured she'd be less likely to be abducted for ransom if she had the official document. Or something like that.

But now she had a Fiji stamp on her passport. That certainly dressed the thing up.

As soon as they stepped through the gate toward baggage claim, Annie knew something was wrong. Sean's hand clenched on her waist. He pulled them to the side of the short corridor, muttering curses.

"What is it?" she asked, trying to peer around his wide shoulders.

"Ackerman's out there." Sean lifted his fingers to his temple and rubbed as if he'd caught an instantaneous headache. "He's got a camera with him."

Annie's stomach took a sickly lurch. "Can he do that? Just ambush you?"

Sean lifted a single eyebrow. "Really? What country do you live in? Because I live in the one where Angelina Jolie can't go to the grocery store without three tabloids reporting on what type of bread she buys."

"Good point," she agreed, rolling her eyes at herself. Surprise had made stupid shit fall out of her mouth. "But I doubt Angelina Jolie buys bread anyway."

"Then it'd be six tabloids. And the cover shot too."

Annie chuckled, then bit her bottom lip. It didn't feel right to laugh when Sean was obviously completely wound up. At least he'd been the one to make the quip. That meant it was fine, right?

Except one glance in his crisply blue eyes said maybe no. Humor could be a defense mechanism, and it seemed like Sean was deep in defense territory. Worry lurked in his gaze.

She cupped the side of his face, fingers tracing over his short-cropped hair. "Hey. It can't be that bad, right?"

He was slightly pale despite his tan. "I don't know."

"Are you worried they'll know?" She swallowed against the thick lump in her throat. Nerves. Pure nerves. He'd only trusted her enough to tell her about his upbringing a matter of hours ago, and now it might become something that blew up in his face. "About your mom?"

He gave a tight nod. "There was something Ackerman said . . . and he's known for getting the dirt. You shoulda seen the feature he did on Michael Adama."

Annie winced. "I did." It hadn't been a good thing. Not in the long run. Michael Adama had been a surfer . . . and then he wasn't. The picture about him was so unflattering, that even though it didn't analyze his surfing technique, he couldn't get any more endorsements.

Frankly, Annie didn't need any extra attention either. She'd severed her professional relationship with Sean before they'd begun their relationship in earnest, but there would still be people who frowned on it. The best she could do was keep things on the quiet side.

Her throat clenched again as she tried to swallow

away her worries. They weren't going anywhere. She had to put effort into lifting her chin. "I'll be by your side."

Sean's smile was wistful. "It's nice of you to offer, but I'm not dragging you into the middle of this."

Annie wavered. There was no other word for it. Her heart was pounding too quickly, and she had those hot shots of fear running down the back of her thighs as her palms turned sweaty. "I shouldn't abandon you."

Sean winced. It wasn't a no.

So he comforted her. He held her face between both of his hands and kissed her hard. She held on to his wrists in return, letting her eyes close and the moment fade away to only their mouths. Only the way they were together.

If she tried hard enough, maybe that would be enough.

"Here's what's going to happen." Sean took two more short, swift kisses. "I'm going to walk out there and do my not-quite-famous duty. You slip out when it looks like Ackerman is focused on me. I'll meet you at our *bure*. There's a driver waiting to take you to our main resort. Then they'll get you out there."

"Are you sure?" She rubbed her thumb over the inside of his wrist.

"Completely."

She'd expected him to kiss her again. He did, but not on her mouth. Instead, he pressed a soft kiss to her forehead. It felt like happiness. It felt like belonging.

And as he walked away, she wrapped her arms around her stomach.

He looked so put together. So stylish and polished. He slipped on a pair of dark sunglasses, then slung his carry-on bag under his good arm.

"Westin!" Ackerman pounced like a cat on a mouse. "You haven't been returning my calls."

"There's a reason for that," Sean drawled. But as he strode toward the baggage carousel, distance swallowed his words.

Just like Ackerman was trying to swallow him up completely. The other man enunciated clearly and loudly enough for his camera crew to catch every word. "Westin, don't you want to talk about how far you've come? Considering your mom?"

Sean's steps faltered. For a moment, Annie thought that maybe he'd punch the shorter man, and then it would all be on film. It was probably what Ackerman was hoping for. If he couldn't get any confirmation from Sean, then a nonverbal, violent response would be just as good.

"My mom's none of your business," Sean bit out.

"That's fine." Ackerman held up both hands. "But growing up in a hoarder's house, how did you cope?"

"No fucking comment."

Chapter 27

Sean wasn't sure what to expect when he drove up to the porch of the isolated *bure* he'd rented for their stay in Fiji. The open air, native-styled cottage was managed and arranged for by the resort on the far end of the property, but it was one of their top-of-the-line, deluxe options. As a result, it was off the beaten path, and the approach required a four-wheel drive vehicle.

That was the case to get to the front door, at least. The back door fronted a private beach, with a regular left break.

He threw the rented SUV into park, then jumped out. The porch was empty, as was the front room. He stood in the middle of the polished bamboo floor and put both fists in the center of his spine, right above his ass. He leaned back and sighed with satisfaction when a series of pops released through his system, joined by something just short of endorphins.

"I'm surprised it took you this long to get rid of Ackerman." Annie stood in the open doorway to the right.

"I had to shake him. I didn't want him following me back here." He held out a hand, but when she came right to him, he couldn't have been any more surprised. "The resort will do its best to keep him out, but this place is kind of isolated. He could find a way in."

She laced her fingers through his. "I got here two hours ago."

"I know," he said with a sigh. He folded her in his arms and rested his chin on her head. She twisted the sides of his shirt in her fists, on either side of his waist. "The driver told me. He also told me that you wouldn't leave the airport until they'd already brought a second staff member to wait for me. That is *not* what I told you to do."

She kept her face pressed into his chest. "I didn't want to take your ride, and then have you come out and have to wait. You had to string that ass along just so he wouldn't see me!"

"This is a fucking mess." He spread one hand across the back of her head. Her hair was silk.

Back at the airport, he'd watched her walk past from behind the shelter of his sunglasses. He'd answered a couple of Ackerman's more innocuous questions about Sean's shoulder and what his recovery was like. The whole time, Sean had been able to hear Ackerman's first two questions echoing over and over in his mind. In his ears.

In his fears.

Everything he'd worried about. Maybe he'd picked the wrong fucking career for maintaining his privacy, but the ocean was the only thing that had ever called to him. The only thing that gave him an escape.

He didn't know what to make of his muddled internal twists. He'd expected Annie to be pissed too. She wouldn't have been totally off track to blame him for the hassle.

"I heard what he asked. About your mom."

He sighed heavily enough that his shoulders bounced. "Yeah. Jesus, you should have heard him asking the same things over and over again. I think I'd have rather bent over and let customs officers stick a finger up my ass than listen to him anymore."

She gave a startled, awkward laugh. "Oh God, you would *not*. Don't lie."

"Okay, I wouldn't. A million questions are way better than inappropriate touching."

"Glad we've cleared that up." She snorted, shaking her head against his chest. Her grip let go of his shirt and she stroked over his waist, up his back. "I thought you were going to be in trouble."

"I haven't done anything wrong," he said, and it had to be growled, because fear had him locking his hands down on her shoulders hard enough that she winced. No one had any idea of the rest of it. He still had his secrets.

"I meant for snapping his neck. What's wrong with you?"

"Worst nightmares are a bitch." It said everything and nothing at the same time. This was his worst nightmare, but it was still developing.

Ackerman said point-blank that he'd started with a source. Sean had no idea who it could have been and, despite a bit of verbal fencing, Ackerman had been cagey enough to keep it to himself. Sean kept running through the possibilities, but no one should have known. No one should have been able to tell. Even his fellow high school students hadn't known. There was only his uncle, and Theo felt so guilty over the situation that he wouldn't have breathed a word.

She pressed her face to his neck, dropping kisses over his skin. Her mouth was soft and delicate enough that it was a whisper of sensation rather than the roughness that buffeted him from the inside. He didn't know if he could match her.

"Annie," he said to warn her. "I've been so pissed for the last two hours. . . . I'm still pissed, actually."

"You have a funny way of showing it." She wriggled her shoulders, pressing against his grip on her. "You're holding me quite nicely."

"I don't know how long I can keep up nice." He kissed her mouth, dragging out the warning further. He'd ramp them up hard, and fast, and he'd like it. It would remain to be seen whether she would as well.

"Here's the thing about sex." She kissed him again, almost as hard as he'd kissed her. They were a new thing together. More dangerous than a great white. "It doesn't have to be nice. Sometimes mean is exactly what the doctor ordered."

"I didn't bring you to Fiji so you could act as my personal stress relief," he snarled.

She didn't know what she was suggesting, not really. His hands ached with the intentions of being good. He wasn't a nice guy, not when it came down to it. She deserved something better than him. Someone cleaner.

"Good. Because I came along on this trip so I can

jump your bones at every opportunity." Her nails scraped over the back of his neck, then down his front. She systematically began opening the buttons of his shirt. "Me. My wants. I could have just as easily stayed home if this was about you. But I want you."

"Why?" He didn't intend to ask such a bullshit, wimpy question. It was all but inviting trouble. Even with what he'd told her on the plane last night, she didn't know the half of it. She didn't know how the story had ended. The fire.

She spread his shirt wide. "Isn't that obvious? I'm using you for the prime digs, of course. Have you seen this place? It's fucking gorgeous."

He laughed abruptly, and the sound came out raw, because he hadn't seen that one coming. "It's not bad."

"'Not bad,' he says," she muttered. Her gaze latched onto his chest, and she was tracing patterns between his abs with the tip of one index finger. "You're fucking spoiled, Sean Westin. This place is amazing. And we have it all to ourselves."

"Yeah? Then I need a tour." He felt like a damn caveman. A smash-and-grab kind of guy. So he might as well fit action to the rough and exploding way he felt. Dipping his knees a few inches, he wrapped one arm low around Annie's pert ass and hitched her. Up. All the way, until her hip was even with his face and she was off the ground.

"Holy shit!" she squealed. Her hands went to his shoulders, trying to hold herself straight upright, but he wasn't having any of that. He put one hand flat on her ass and pushed.

She folded over his shoulder. Her hands slipped down his back to his ass, where she grabbed on tight. He grunted. "That's better."

"You're a Neanderthal."

"Meh," he said, with intentional dryness. "I want a tour, and I want to take you with me. Seemed like the best of both worlds."

"How am I supposed to give you a tour from down here?" she said. Her face was pressed against his midback.

"Not my problem."

She pinched him. "Put me down."

"Just a minute. You said I need to see this place." He strolled toward the open archway she'd been standing in. "Nice bedroom."

It was pretty nice too, though it was hard to notice details when he had a squirming bundle of womanhood hitched over one shoulder. The huge bed was spread with pure white sheets and a coverlet that looked like the bare-minimum thickness. As well it should be. The air was warm and sultry, scented with palm fronds and the thick scent of the jungle that peeked through plantation shutters. They'd be grateful for the wide-bladed fan slowly spinning above the bed once he'd fucked her silly and they were both sticky and exhausted.

"I liked the back porch better," she offered.

"Yeah?" He veered left, through the open archway, toward sand and ocean. "It does have a nice view."

"I'm totally sticking my tongue out at you," she said. "You just can't see it."

"I don't believe you. From the angle you're at,

you'd get a mouthful of my shirt if you stuck your tongue out."

"You suck."

"I know." He hitched her back over his shoulder, though, locking his arms around her and letting her do a slow slide down his front. Her hips, her waist, her breasts. "It's nice out here."

Her lips parted on a quiet gasp. "I know."

The whole place was a matter of understated elegance. Occasional touches of tribal design accented pale wood, but mostly it was simple. Underdecorated. A long, wide bench upholstered in pale cream fabric marked the far edge of the porch. Beyond that, a couple tiki torches sketched the line between porch and sand.

He put her down on the bench, so that she was standing on it. Her ribs were parallel with his mouth, and he pushed her shirt up in order to open his mouth across that flesh. She was made of strength and delicacy all at once. He palmed her hips.

Her hands rested across the back of his head. When he looked up at her, her face was turned toward the sky. She didn't know what she did to him.

It had been a sock to the stomach to see her waiting at the *bure*. She fit in his life. He squeezed her tight. "I'm sorry you had to deal with that bullshit."

She shrugged, her nails tracing patterns that made him want to do dirty things. But even that was half of what he liked so much about her. That it was no big deal to her, and she didn't expect any giant parade of accolades. This was just what she did for people in her life. Steadiness and snarky humor when they needed to come down from tension.

"You'll owe me later. I think there should be champagne involved when you get rid of Ackerman."

"I'll buy you a hundred bottles." He'd buy her anything, anytime. No amount was too good for her. He'd asked her along on this trip on impulse, but he was rapidly coming to think it was one of the best things he'd ever done. He slipped his fingers under the band of her shorts. The flesh where she curved was delicious. He wanted to bite. "Thanks for coming."

She grinned, a smile that kept getting wider and wider as she looked at him and tipped her head. "Did you . . . ? That was an accidental pun, right?"

He choked on a sudden burst of laughter. "Okay, yeah. Completely accidental. But . . ."

He drew the cord of her shorts free. The loose linen fell to her hips and stopped at the swell of her ass. She had on a tiny thong made of lace and prayers. He kissed the soft skin beneath her navel.

Her hands spread across the back of his head, dipping into the shallow at the base of his skull. She twitched as she gave a quiet gasp. His tongue darted out, tracing the top band of her panties. "By all means," she breathed. "If this is the way you give thank-yous, I think I can cope with that."

"You're talking too much," he said against her belly. He pushed her shorts all the way down. She vibrated under his touch, and he fucking loved it. He loved knowing what he could do to her. Anticipation was the best drug in the world.

It was a big portion of why he put so much *work* into surfing. He knew guys who threw a board out, and flopped on it and got what they got and were happy for it. Not Sean. He liked tasting the anticipation and knowing before he even went out on the water that he was going to kill it. He liked the planning.

He was beginning to plan how to keep Annie around in his life. If he kept Ackerman's investigation buried, Sean could keep Annie from figuring out what a bad bargain he was. For a long, long time.

Chapter 28

Occasional moments struck where Annie couldn't believe the good fortune of her life. Times when she had to step back and look around and thank God for having been given what she had. This should have been one of those moments. But if she stood back, she might have had to sacrifice a moment where she didn't feel Sean's touch with every molecule of her being. She might have not been able to pay attention to the way his hands held her close. The way his mouth was open over the arch of her hip, and his tongue did wicked things. The way she wished that he would, holy crap, just take down her panties already.

She spread her feet wider, trying to brace against the weakness shaking down her knees. She wobbled forward an inch, but he had her there too. His grip curled around her hip, propping her up from underneath. His fingertips slipped into the delicate flesh between her thigh and the crease of her body.

She wanted him so bad it hurt. Physically and literally. Her body throbbed. The warmth that built in her stomach and swept up through her chest was so powerful that she hadn't felt anything like it before.

She would go crazy if he left her too long. This was exactly what she'd wanted . . . and what she feared at the same time.

He drew her thong down one bare inch at a time. His fingertips dragged over her skin, adding in a layer of sensation that made promises he had better freaking keep.

She wanted him. But she wanted to be sure of him too. He was something she didn't know how to handle.

She bent, curving down enough that she could take his mouth with her own. She wanted to kiss him more than she wanted to breathe, and that was frightening. There was no other word for it. "You'll make me feel good, right?"

"Of course," he breathed, a low grumble of voice and promise—the promise of those manly things that she didn't know how to touch. Didn't know how to accept.

She'd never had a man like him in her life. When Sean had stomped out of the SUV and up the porch steps, he'd looked . . . intense. More than that.

His white shirt had been wrinkled and casual. His gray trousers were still smooth, but he'd had a line to his back and shoulders that was canted forward with intent. His cheeks had been deathly hollow. His blue eyes were nearly black with their dark intensity.

She'd been shaking, yeah.

But she'd also been turned on.

It was one thing to jump into a summer fling sort of setup. To try Sean out in terms of reclaiming her sexual side. But these feelings were more than she'd expected.

He looked at her in ways she didn't know how to quantify or understand. He said thank you with the power of benediction.

She was a shitty person to recoil under the force of that attention and still let him bury his face at her stomach. But he opened his lips over the divot above her hip bone and she gasped. The wet heat of his tongue made her clench deep inside. "You're a tease."

"Nope." He spoke against her skin, creating a little vibration that made the larger vibrations in her chest rock into overdrive. "This isn't teasing. This is anticipation."

"Anticipation sucks, then."

"No, I love it." He licked the skin at the crease of her legs.

She shook. Her knees dropped out from underneath her, because, holy shit, was she an idiot. She'd been holding her breath and didn't realize it. Her lungs burned as she sucked in a giant gasp and panted. "Please," she breathed.

"Please, what?" He looked up at her with a wicked glint in his eyes.

"Lick me. Please. Make me feel good. I want to come on your mouth. I want you to taste me like I tasted you. It'll be so good. I want it." She slapped her hand across her mouth, eyes going wide. Biggest. Idiot. Ever.

Except he didn't seem to mind. His tiny smile deepened enough that she could see the sharp line of his teeth. She even wanted to feel those on her. "You beg very nicely. I think I want to hear more of that."

"Please. Please, Sean." The words slipped from her like more promises she couldn't keep.

He kept them for her.

His first lick was across the seam of her pussy, where she was wet and achy. She jolted so hard that even his grip on her ass couldn't keep her up. But that didn't even seem to faze him. He lowered her to the bench. The cushions were thin, but they were enough. He arranged her limb by limb, as if she were a doll. Stripping her tank top off over her head, he laid her back. He spread her thighs, his hands big and strong on the insides of her knees, so that she was open across the bench.

He sat at her feet, sideways so that he leaned down on one elbow. His breath was humid over her flesh, even in the thick heat of the tropics. She turned her head briefly, only to see the perfectly curling line of a beautiful wave.

He cupped her breast in one hand, circling her nipple again and again with first the tips of his fingers, and then his nails. Her body curled up into his every touch, almost as if she had little control over herself. She lifted her hands above her head and dragged them into fists under her neck.

"You don't regret coming here, do you?" He pinched her nipple between his thumb and forefinger and dipped his mouth to tongue that bit of flesh. Flares of tingles washed through her. She was electric and magic all in one. Because of him. "Long flight, bullshit questions?"

"And then this." She managed to squeak the words out. "This makes it all better."

"Does it?" He spanned her stomach with one hand, his elegant fingers stretching from her ribs to her pelvic bone. "Then I'll have to make this worth it."

He lowered his head slowly, keeping her gaze until the last moment. His eyes were a wicked blue, one that almost matched the ocean to her left.

But nothing matched the power of his mouth. He left fire in his wake. A single laving path up from her core to the tight furl of her clit. He was bold in the way that he touched her, the way that he held her open under his attentions.

She craned her gaze to the sky and it was no escape. She was overwhelmed. He was breath and action all wrapped up together. There was nothing to her beyond the attention that he paid to her pussy. This was . . . bliss.

She could sink away on it forever. Her hips lifted toward the swirling of his tongue. She was barely in control of herself, and she sure as hell wasn't in control of the little noises pouring out of her mouth. She made them in the back of her throat, gasping mewls that made her feel both dirty and wicked at the same time. He made it so good.

He probably made it so good for anyone he was with, but she couldn't think about it. He'd always have the attention of women like Gloria. Even though she was perma-girlfriend to that guy Nate, Gloria had looked at Sean in the particular way women always did. The way Annie felt from the inside out.

He was a compulsion. He was something she didn't know how to absorb.

Maybe it shouldn't be about absorption. Instead, she should let it all go. She'd gotten into this because she wanted to have a piece of herself back. Complaining because she'd gotten the wrong piece was just crazy pants and absurd.

Sean was like a roller coaster. She should just go along for the ride.

He found a spot that made her shudder with pleasure, so naturally he attacked it with gusto. His tongue circled her clit again and again, patient as a wave rolling into shore. The sand only moved in increments, being washed away by the tide, and Sean was willing to follow the same pattern. He kept at her as steadily as the ocean.

She wanted him. She cupped her own breast. Balance and counterpoint. She scraped her skin, because she wanted more and wanted harder, and she moaned when he rubbed around and beside her opening. He gently pinched her lower lips together, then squeezed. His mouth found her clit again.

But it was the teeth that did her in. He locked his lips around her flesh and sucked her between the sharp edge of his teeth to work her softly against the pressure.

Her hips twitched hard enough that she might have come off the bench except for his locking, latching hold on her hip. There was no getting free of him. The sun stroked down on them both, adding in another layer of caress. Sweat sprang up at the hollows of her shoulder first, then the arch of her ribs. He moved his hand from her hip to her waist, slipping through a soft sheen of dampness.

The patterns his thumb wrung continued echoes of the fantasies he made happen all the time. All around him. This was sex in paradise; it was drinks-on-the-moon level of amazing.

She exploded. Her hands latched around the back of his head. Even that was another layer of sensation, his prickly hair rubbing against her palms and sending a thrill up her skin. It matched the roaring shards of pleasure that spread out through her. Her toes curled. Her nipples were so tight, it almost felt as if someone were playing with them as well.

No one was there but Sean, though. Sean and Annie, twined together in the moment. She panted, staring up at the sky. It was safer to look at than Sean, who stared at her with something sharp in his eyes, expressing intent for more than orgasms. "I like the way you come," he said.

She gave a helpless laugh. "I like the way I come too. Probably feels better from the inside."

"I am inside you," he purred, curling two fingers against her front wall as a reminder. She gave a cry at the surge of regained pleasure. "And you feel good from here. The way you clench on me . . . I want to feel that on my cock."

She nodded, probably a little too frantically for grace or classiness. There was sex involved. She didn't *want* to be a classy kind of girl. She wanted to be the kind of girl who got what she wanted. "Yes, sir, sign me up for that one."

God, she loved making him laugh. It was probably absurd how much she liked it, but he was so suave most of the time. Except when she got under his skin. There was something there if she cared to look at it. Something about the way they fit together. But she didn't want to go there. That would mean opening herself up to someone as damaged as he was. There was nothing wrong with that on the surface, except that she was probably equally damaged. The very fact that she overanalyzed orgasms like this was proof. She couldn't afford to be with him, not for a forever kind of thing.

Not if she had any sort of sense. That didn't mean she couldn't do it now. He probably had no idea she'd lost her mind. There was no point in dragging out feelings when she'd be the only one who'd have them.

Not when there was another choice: more sex with Sean.

Chapter 29

Sean could tell when Annie's mind went from blissed-out come brain to thought processor in overdrive. It was there in the muscles under his hands, the way her stomach clenched. Fucking hell, his fingers were *inside* her, twisting gently in the wet heat of her channel.

He pulled free and touched his tongue to his fingertips. She tasted so good. Slightly salty, but sweet underneath that. She was a woman who took care of herself, and that care was reflected in every inch of her.

Even the way her skin gleamed porcelain white under the yellow stream of Fiji's sun was proof. He couldn't imagine her as a regular surfer. She was too pale and soft. She'd have had to bathe in sunscreen.

There were freckles across the tops of her shoulders that hadn't been there the last time she'd been surfing. They were probably the proof of what the sun could do to her. He bent to kiss them, one at a time. It was close and absorbing work, despite the way his cock throbbed and the intensity with which he wanted her.

She sighed, wrapping her arms around his upper chest. Her hands curled over his shoulders from behind. "Oh, that's nice. Keep going."

He smiled against another freckle. "I didn't plan to stop."

"That's lovely." She sighed again. "You know, this is usually the point where I wake up."

"You often dream about me going down on you?"

She laughed softly, her chest bouncing under his. He wound his grip around her wrist, stretching her arm above her head. She let him. That was the mysterious part, the thing that he couldn't seem to get a handle on.

It felt as if she would slip away at any moment. He got good things in his life; that wasn't the difficult part. The good things were always the hard things, the things that he had to work for. He earned his career, and with it his house and money and the finer things those brought. He had earned respect in the pro surfing world.

Annie was easy. Easy to be around, but also easy to be *himself* around. There were few games. She wasn't invested in the way that he presented himself, or in those fine things that his lifestyle brought. She was appreciative, sure. But she didn't want to make him jump through hoops.

He didn't trust things that came easily. His mother had always taken the easy way out. The one time he'd tried the easy way, the result had been disastrous.

He didn't want to make that kind of mistake again.

Annie wasn't a mistake, though. That wasn't what

he meant. More like he was still waiting for the strings, the later payment. Good things didn't come without complications in one way or another.

That was all down the line, though. It wasn't now, stretched out in paradise with a beautiful woman. She was naked and he wasn't. He liked that faint imbalance, but not as much as he liked the feel of her skin. He pushed off the shirt that she'd unbuttoned earlier, and it dropped to the sand on the far edge of the deck. He'd have to reclaim that later. Or not. It might go down as a casualty to really fucking excellent sex.

Annie pushed to a sitting position, one foot dropping to the deck. She was a siren. A fiery package of gorgeous energy. She petted his arms, his chest, leaning forward to curl against his side. He unbuckled his slacks and pushed them off, and she made a happy cooing sound. He couldn't help but laugh. "What was that?"

Her hand was hot as a brand when it wrapped around his cock. "I like your body. Is that a bad thing?"

"Fuck no," he said on a groan. She worked him with a twist of her wrist at the top when she got to his swollen head.

She squeezed in tighter, her body pressing against his. They created heat in addition to the way the air swirled around them, but he'd be damned if he cared. Some things were worth being too hot for. Her touch was absolutely one of them.

He sucked in a heavy breath when she squeezed him tight. "You'll regret that when I can only fuck you for a half second."

She giggled, burying her mouth against his pecs.

"I doubt that. Your pride would be wounded if you didn't make me come."

Was that what she thought of him? That it was only a matter of pride? She was more than that. Her orgasms were about giving her something good. Not about making her a receptacle.

He held her firmly with one arm while he reached toward the pants he'd dropped to the floor. Without looking, he found a condom in a pocket. "Come sit in my lap and we'll talk about my pride."

"Is that what you call it?" Her hands worked deftly to slip the condom over his length, then she scrambled across him. He shifted back so that she had enough room to balance on her knees.

He helped that balancing act with a grip on her ribs. His thumbs stroked over and over the undercrease of her breasts, which made her give a breathy, soft moan before her pussy even touched him. He could measure how much she liked what he did to her breasts with every clench of her hand on his latex-covered cock. She liked best the way he took her wholly into his mouth. It was enough to make her squeeze as well as moan. He pressed the tight bud of her nipple against the top of his palate and rubbed over and over with his tongue.

Her thighs melted. She dipped, the heat of her pussy caressing his cock. He grunted at the contact. "Tell me, Annie. Tell me what you want."

"I want to fuck you."

He traced the tops of her breasts with his tongue, then pushed them together so he could go from nipple to nipple and back again. "Do you want to fuck me, or do you want me to fuck you?"

Her voice was breathy and shaky. "Is there a difference?"

Locking a hand around the back of her neck and holding her hip, he pulled her down over him. She was fucking tight, even though she was gorgeously wet. Her lips clung to him and her eyes went dark and hazy. Her mouth parted on tumbling, frantic breaths that turned into gasps and moans and breathy sounds. But he knew what she could do, the way she could scream for him.

He meant to hear that again.

"Move," he ordered her.

She balanced her wrists on his shoulders, her hands lifted and fingers curled. Her hips moved slowly at first, but she soon fell into a rhythm that threatened to snatch Sean's breath away. Her stomach tightened and released on every brain-shaking grind. She went shallow at first, only engulfing the head of his cock. Then lower and lower by increments, until she had wedged her pussy so far down that he could feel the wet kiss of her clit at his pelvis. He held her there, not letting her up again, and his fingers dug into her slender hips.

"There." He let her up, but then pulled her hips back down again, this time fast, at the speed he chose. "At first it was you fucking me. Now this is me, fucking you." He bared his teeth in an attempt to hold back the waves of pleasure.

He had a mission here, and he meant to make it happen. There was a tight balance between letting her have what she wanted and throwing all of himself over for her. He'd have her, not the other way around.

Except she didn't just take it. He should have known better. She twisted until she'd come up free of his cock. A lick of breeze squeezed through the narrow inches between them, chilling the sweat across his flesh. She touched his jaw, two fingers across his lips. He was breathing too hard. Almost panting, rough and raspy.

He squeezed her waist, the back of her neck. "Where are you going?"

"What we do . . ." She took a deep breath, kissed him softly. Left her lips hovering millimeters from his, so that they traded air back and forth. They sustained each other and hovered in an in-between world where everything else went away. "There's no winning. No one's going to lose. If you fuck me or I fuck you . . . we both win."

Shit. He didn't want to love her. Didn't want to feel like this, lighter than air and twisted tight in knots at the same time. But she was fucking magic. Unfair and unreal magic, because the illusion always went away.

At least when he was surfing he always *knew* the ocean wanted to eat him and drag him down to the depths. It was the ocean's job to drown common men. And his job to float above it.

He had no job when it came to Annie. No place where he felt like he knew where he was going.

He kissed her. There were no words for her, nothing he could say in return. With softer, gentler hands, he nudged her hips down, twisting them around so that her shoulders lay flat against the cushions of the bench. He held both her ankles in one hand. "Bend your knees."

"Sean?" Her voice was nervous, and her brows knit together with confusion and obvious worry.

She didn't have anything to fear. He'd never hurt her or ask her for more than she could give. It would only push her away faster. He'd keep her near as long as he could. "You can do it, Annie. Make me happy. We'll make each other feel good. You're right."

She gave a small nod, letting him bend her knees. From that angle, he could see the pretty pout of her pussy, her lower lips pressed together. Her flesh was slick and swollen. The tip of him barely fit there, but he thrust slowly to enter her. Luscious pink enveloped him inch by inch.

She gasped. Her hands found his where he held her thighs. "Oh, Sean. My God, you feel so big."

"And you're tight." He held back his growls. It was everything he could do to keep his pace slow as he plumbed the tightness of her body. She was everything resisting and accepting. He rubbed her own wetness over his length and over her flesh. Around and around the small bit of flesh that made her moan and gasp and made her voice start working upward. She wasn't screaming, not yet. But damn, she was close.

He loved this. Loved the way they were together. That was all it could be. Getting his heart caught up would only lead to problems. Heartbreak was the kind of thing that could cost a guy his career. He wanted both, Annie and wins in his tallies. But there was no way his luck would hold out that long, and not enough hard work in the world to get him both.

He wouldn't let that matter for now. He had her,

and he had what they made together. There was electricity in the way she moved. He fucked her deep, then deeper, until she snatched his upper arm and hauled him close. He was bending her in half, but she didn't seem to care. Her nails sank into the back of his neck, and he welcomed the pain as proof of how much he affected her. Her mouth took his, even as he fucked her hard. She moaned. He kept fucking, except he was pretty sure that she was fucking him in return.

Because she wrenched from him the biggest, most uncontrollably explosive orgasm of his life. He hadn't meant to come before her. It wasn't what he did; it wasn't how he worked. But she was tight and wet and responsive and so fucking greedy. He took it. Took her. The feelings rocked through him so violently, he had to bite the edge of his tongue to try to come down. To try to hold back stupid words.

He was able to keep thrusting a few strokes more, and, thank God, they were enough. Her eyes flashed wide. "Sean, there. I'm coming."

She said his name again, then again. Pride and satisfaction made him suck in a hissing breath, as well as the way her body clenched down on his. The sun and sand were close enough to touch, and they'd carved out some section of the world for themselves.

This was paradise. For as long as it lasted.

Chapter 30

Saying that Cloudbreak was a heavy wave was like saying that a bird had wings. It was *yeah, duh, bro* territory. Annie sat cross-legged on a vinyl-upholstered bench of the resort boat used to take them the full mile offshore to the wave. Beneath the boat, fading out to the left, was the shallow reef that broke the ocean's power to create Cloudbreak. The curl was a left break, coming straight at the boat's anchor.

Annie's stomach was tight. A hard little knot, as if she'd eaten something rotten. Her heartbeat thumped in her throat, where it didn't belong. "You're going out there."

It wasn't even a question. Of course Sean was. He was good at what he did. More than that, he was up there with the best of them. He paused in the act of streaking sunscreen over his upper arms and peered out at the wave. "Yeah. It's kind of small, I know. But it's worth trying out."

She rolled her eyes and gave a slightly hysterical giggle. "That was kind of the opposite of what I meant. It's fucking huge."

"It's only ten feet. Not that big. On a good day,

Cloudbreak can double that." He pulled on a white-and-blue rash guard, hiding the damp sheen of his already tanned skin.

"Ten feet on the *back*." She was totally preaching to the choir, but she couldn't help it. "That means twenty on the front."

"It should make for some mean barrels." He flashed a grin at her, but something in her face must have finally given away her worry. "Oh wait. You're not okay."

She swallowed against the sickly feeling in the top of her chest. Rubbing her knuckles over her sternum didn't ease the burn. "Jesus, no wonder Mom asked if I was going to surf it. I mean, I've seen pictures of Cloudbreak, and I've seen video stream, but this is totally different."

He sat down on the bench beside her. The arm he folded around her shoulders was warm, even under the pounding tropical sun. She'd practically dipped herself in sunscreen, and she'd reapply a hundred times before the end of the trip. It made their skin both slip together and sticky. "If you want to head in, the boat can run you back. You don't have to watch."

"But you have to do this."

His jaw tightened, and she knew by the glint in his eyes that he was trying to hold back a smile. "It's more than that."

She sighed. "You love to do this."

He held her close, and she could feel his nod against the top of her head. "It's what I've been dying to get back to. Even six weeks out has been too much."

"You're good."

"I'm the fucking best."

She giggled, because there was only so much ego that she could take with a straight face. But it was more than being good. It was dedication. She'd seen his office and the work he put into the competition. He'd been doing it last night too. After mind-blowing sex on the porch, they'd made their way toward the heart of the resort for an incredibly slow dinner served by staff who seemed to be training Annie to go with the flow rather than actually serve her in a timely manner. When she'd asked Sean if the speed of their meal was usual, he'd just shrugged and said it was island time. So she'd gone with it.

But when they'd gotten back to their lush *bure*, Sean's bags had been delivered post–customs inspection. He'd pulled out reams of printouts and his laptop, then consulted a tide chart for the best times for practice. He'd been on websites, aggregating information that she didn't even understand the name of. All for something that seemed like intuition to her. If this was what pro-land was like, maybe it was better that she'd walked away. To her, surfing was feeling the water under her and trusting the board between her and the ocean.

Except maybe not when it was compared to a wave like this. Cloudbreak could snap necks. Period.

It could snap necks of the unprepared, maybe. Sean most certainly was not.

He rubbed her shoulder briskly to bring her back to the moment. "Your call. You don't have to stay with me."

She swallowed and took a long, deep breath. He

wasn't the only one who was good at his job. She'd been on her iPad and her computer last night and this morning, making sure things ran smoothly at home. "Make it good, yeah?"

"I'll give you a killer show." His mouth tasted like the freshly cracked coconut milk he'd been drinking moments ago. The kiss he gave her was swift, but no less powerful for the way he swept her over. Her lips clung to his, her fingers digging into his back, but she wanted to think that was just the kiss and just his mouth and what he could do to her.

Not doubt. She didn't want to doubt him.

"I'll be back before you know it."

Then he was gone, diving off the side of the boat with his board. His legs were so strong, she wanted to wrap her own around him. The arch of his thighs said he could do wicked things with those legs.

"It's hard to watch the first time, but then you'll get used to it." Gloria had been sitting in the bow, where there was a set of captain's-style chairs set just before the driver's portion. She had on a killer bikini that made Annie drool with envy. The floral pattern should have seemed too old-fashioned, plastic-covered-couch for words, but instead, Gloria's curves filled it out in a way that would make a *Playboy* model proud. Her blond hair was completely casual, pulled back in a low ponytail at the nape of her neck, and she'd gone without makeup.

Annie remembered the dichotomous surfer look. She'd never managed it, instead defaulting to Speedo sports tops and honing her physicality until it meant she could cut killer rips. Her hair got skinned back into athletic ponytails. She didn't think she could stomach regularly watching Sean surf. "I don't know if I'll come out again."

"No?" Gloria shot Annie a sidelong glance. Maybe Annie was reading too much into it, but to her, it totally said *amateur*. "I always try to give Nate my full support. Hell, I did when Sean and I dated too. Some of the girls spend their time lounging on the beach, drinking fizzy things, but I always wonder what the point of that is. You could do the same thing back home."

Annie froze a little bit. Gloria and Sean. Yeah, that made perfect, crystal sense all of a sudden, in a way it hadn't before. The heartbeat that had been too fast minutes ago took a sluggish, ice-laden thump. "Ah. Yeah."

Jesus, she didn't want to get into the business of professional girlfriend. She had her own life. She couldn't match up to chicks like Gloria anyway. A vacation was nice, yeah, but that didn't mean she could sign off the rest of her commitments and do this full-time. She had a center to get up and running, and considering that she'd turned down Sean's financing, she was going to have to return to her previous long-term plans, especially since the WavePro rep had yet to return her phone calls. Which meant returning to grant writing and shilling herself out at charity events.

Not sitting on the beach drinking fruity boozy things. No matter how good they had been the night before. "Anyway, it's totally funny that we keep running into each other."

"Not really," Gloria replied. She had her gaze trained on the bobbing surfers. From this distance, they were mostly wet heads bobbing. At least they wore different-colored rash guards, which helped in telling them apart. "The guys always come out early. Get to know the waves. I was kind of surprised to see Sean. With everything that's going on . . ." She dashed another sidelong glance at Annie. "I bet it's been hard."

"What do you mean?"

"I heard you got blitzed by the paparazzi." Gloria's eyes were wide with sympathy. "I've heard how creepy that can be. All those guys pressing in on you." She gave an artificial shiver.

"It was a little annoying, but it was fine. I lived."

The surfing community was so tiny. Annie hadn't said anything to anyone at dinner last night, but they'd seen Kelly Slater and Mick Fanning at the bar when they'd passed by afterward. And then the Internet had been completely lit up this morning with photos and video of Sean leaving the airport. Word didn't just get around; it flew.

That was yet another thing that Annie had been happy to leave behind when she left the surfing world. There wasn't anything like that when you lived in Orange County but *didn't* live in the insular world of pro sports. She'd been happy to keep secrets. Particularly of how things had ended for her. There was no reason for that to get around.

She hitched her elbows on the rail of the boat and watched the swell build. Sean was out there, in the lineup and ready to go soon. She could tell by his position in the water, the way he was angling his board and starting to paddle. The wave surged, picking him up.

Annie gasped and sat up straight. He stood on the wave's lip, then his board dropped three feet off the edge. For a second, she thought he'd blown it. But he dug into the front. His knees loose, he cut into the wave as if he'd been born to do this. He pumped, bouncing with his full body weight to gain speed.

The wave swallowed him. The barrel curled over his head, minimal white at the lip. There was mostly smooth, blue perfection, and Sean owned it. He owned it.

Annie clapped, even though he couldn't possibly have heard her. Her palms stung with it, and then she cupped her hands around her mouth and cheered. A couple of the resort employees hooted, giving their own happy energy to the moment. Even Gloria grinned.

"It's so admirable, where he's come from. How far he's come." Gloria gave an artful sigh. "Pity no one knows. He'd get a lot of fan support behind him."

"Excuse me?" Annie hadn't been around the pros for a while, but she sure as hell knew mental sabotage when she heard it. "Sean's life isn't something to be mined for fan attention."

"No harm meant," Gloria said, but her beautiful, perfect, orthodontist-endorsed smile didn't go anywhere near her pretty blue eyes. "Nate's mine, of course. He's got my loyalty."

"Doesn't mean others should get you being a bitch, though." Annie gave a perfect smile of her own. "But then, I get it. Nate's nice, but that's the problem, right? He's lacking that cutting edge, the little oomph that gets him to the top."

Gloria dropped all manner of pretense. Her eyes were cold and the sun-kissed bronze of her cheeks went white underneath. "That's why he's got me."

"I don't see you out there pushing him into the lineup to get the waves he needs." She kept the smile, even as she waved the porter down. She needed a drink. Some kind of fruit juice with a shot of rum if she was going to have to listen to this bitch for the next four hours of surfing. "Honey, you seem to have an inflated idea of what you do for Nate's career."

"I do whatever I need to," Gloria said, with what approached a snarl. She pulled her ponytail forward over her shoulder, twirling her fingers through the end. Her nails were blunt but carefully polished.

Annie just nodded along with her, looking back toward the guys out surfing. Unless Gloria was willing to blow judges to guarantee Nate perfect tens, she had no idea what the other woman could possibly be doing for the guy's career. After all, even oral sex wouldn't help much. There were three judges per heat, and that would be a lot of inappropriate contact to guarantee a boost in scores. A lot.

Annie ordered a drink from a porter with a gleaming white polo to match his smile. She wasn't sure if the guy really liked his job, or if he was just a really cheery person, but either way she enjoyed chatting with him for a few minutes about the local fruit and which would go best with rum. He was a nice balance to Gloria's hard-to-navigate personality.

But as soon as Annie turned back to watch the surfing, Gloria was chattering away again. She knew a lot about the surfers, both the few pros who'd turned up to try out the waves a few days early, and the local guys. She pointed out the guy who'd won a wild card by placing first in a local event, just as he nailed a barrel and bounced out as smooth as butter. "But then, at least these aren't tow-in waves today. Must seem small to him."

"Tow-in?" Annie shuddered. She figured that if the waves were so big that surfers had to be pulled by a Jet Ski to get enough speed, maybe humans should stay out of the water temporarily. "Yeah, I don't think I'd even be here on the boat on a day like that."

"Why?" Gloria looked at Annie and did something suspiciously like fluttering her lashes. A faux-innocent blinking thing that Annie wanted to ask her to rewind and do again because did women really *do* things like that and mean it? "At least on tow-in days they wear safety rigs. Today, Sean could get slammed on the reef just as easy as anything. Be a shame if he wrecked that pretty face."

Chapter 31

Sean's first barrel of the morning was the best wave he caught all day.

The wave closed over him, the perfect glass of the blue water closing over his head and then his right side. He put his left hand out and trailed his fingers through the water. The move regulated his speed, so that he didn't pick up too much and shoot out before the perfection was used up, but there was something heady in the act. He was one with the wave. The heavy slab owned him, but he was part of it too. If the opening closed, he could be slammed by thousands of pounds of water, pushed with the weight of an entire ocean behind it.

He leaned forward, increasing his speed so that he shot out through the contracting eye of the barrel. He could have kept carving the front, maybe add a switchback, but there was nothing better than getting barreled, so he cut up the front and dropped down the back. Let the rest of the wave go by him.

He was in paradise. He was somewhere more perfect than he'd imagined. Knowing Annie sat on the white-sided boat that floated in the middle distance only made it more perfect. He wondered if she'd spotted him on that wave.

The photographers had. One of them waved to him from her position in the water. He paddled over to the only female photographer with a lens trained on the lineup. "Hey, Avvie. Where ya been?"

Her nose wrinkled, and she gently sculled through the water to maintain her position with one hand. Her other hand had a firm grip on a camera in a waterproof casing with a safety strap attached by Velcro to her wrist. "You know Tanner hates it when people call me that. Jack never should have started it."

"I don't see Tanner out here."

"I hate it too."

"Well that's different, then." He flicked water at her, but she was already soaking wet. "How you doing, Avalon?"

"So damn awesome." She beamed at him, and he got the feeling that she'd have levitated out of the water if only happiness counted. "Things are going really well."

"I guessed. Never seen you out here before."

It was difficult for female photographers to get assignments to Fiji. They could go on their own, in the hope that maybe they'd sell photos to a magazine and make their investment back, but the outlay was high. Economy tickets started close to two thousand bucks, and that wasn't even counting accommodations. Sharing bunk style with communal bathrooms didn't work as easily for women, and it really didn't work for photographers with thousands of dollars of equipment to protect.

"I'm on assignment." Three simple words, but

Sean knew the weight they carried. And Avalon did too, because she was ecstatically happy.

"Proud of you, chickie." He'd give her a hug, but he was still floating on his board and there was no reason to drown them in the middle of a hard-core wave. "I'll stand you a pint later."

"You've been hanging out with the Aussies too much. Pint?" she teased.

"Eh. Beer. Drink. Whatever you want." He reached out quickly and scrubbed his knuckles across the top of her head. "Not every day a chick gets a deal so big."

She stuck her tongue out at him. "Tanner would kick your ass if he heard you say that."

She and Tanner had been dating for five months now, since about the period when Tanner had nailed his championship with the San Sebastian Pro. Word was that they were happy, even with Tanner home most of the time while Avalon traveled the globe. They went together occasionally, but often Tanner was too busy painting and otherwise improving the school he planned to launch. "Still don't see him. Besides . . . I've got a girl with me."

Avalon's eyes went wide. She pushed wet bangs off her face, sinking a little in the water as she did so. Then she popped back up again. "No, I didn't hear that right. You brought a girl? To a competition?"

He shifted on the board, but that made him bob. His toes dangled in the water, which had felt warm initially. Now the chill was getting to him. His stomach pulled tight. "I brought her to Fiji. Major seduction points."

"You brought her to a competition, dude. Don't be

dense." Avalon was one of those girls who said things exactly how she saw them. No bullshit between her brains and her mouth.

A lot like Annie, as a matter of fact, but Sean had never wanted to pin Avalon against a wall and kiss the hell out of her. "Don't be jealous. You've got the love of your life."

She laughed, and, kicking to keep herself floating, started to push herself away from him. He paddled closer. "Do you mean she's the love of your life? Because I really think that's what you just implied."

"Oh, c'mon," he muttered. "You're acting like you're twelve."

"Nah, I already asked my boy to go steady." She stroked to keep herself even on a slightly larger-than-normal swell. "You're the one who swore since Gloria that you'd have no steady chicks during the season."

"The season is eleven fucking months long. Maybe I got a little tired of that rule," he muttered.

"What's that?" She hadn't been able to hear him over the constant roar of the breaking wave. At this distance, Cloudbreak was so big that it became a constant sweeping engine of sound in the background that had to be shouted over.

"Nothing," he said in the necessary louder tone. "Drinks. Later. Promise me?"

"You got it, hot stuff. I can't wait to meet the girl."

"She'll probably get pissed as hell if you call her a girl."

Avalon's smile went wide. Her round cheeks were pink with the amount of sun she was getting. She had on a racerback bikini top of some sort, because he could see the straps wrapping around her shoulders and behind her neck. "Then she's my kind of woman, and I double can't wait. Now go surf something that I can take a picture of."

"Aye-aye, girlie," he said with a sardonic tip of two fingers to his eyebrow in a lazy salute.

Avalon flipped him the bird. Of course she did. That was what happened when you teased little-sister types, after all.

And little-sister types were also prone to pointing out things that you didn't want to look at. Like his blithely having brought Annie along when he had Ackerman to shut down. Then they'd spent most of yesterday afternoon in bed. Well, on the back patio, and then in bed, coming until he'd been so tired that his knees had been wobbly as he walked across the room to the bathroom.

What kind of training was that? What kind of concentration?

The kind that would lose him the world championship before he even got a crack at it.

He wouldn't allow that. He couldn't.

The last fifteen years of his life had built to this. Every time he'd hidden a board from his mom at a friend's house, so that he'd actually know where it was when it came time to surf. Every time he'd washed off in the locker room at the high school rather than go home. Every time he'd ridden his bike to the beach and stayed. Occasionally, he'd stayed for more than one day. Once he'd even hidden out underneath the San Sebastian pier, just to be able to surf the next day, because he'd known if he went home, his mom would have him. Would trap him.

He'd have to go with her to thrift shops and yard sales, standing there while she bought more shit they didn't need.

More shit there wasn't anywhere in their house to keep.

He had fought hard for his career. He *believed* in his career. Hard work got gains. Got the things worth having in life.

He didn't trust things that came easily.

It was time to get his head in the game.

He paddled out toward the break, watching the sun glimmer off the bright blue ripples of the water. There was bright and then there was bright as diamonds. The water was the latter. It sluiced over his hips and thighs as he lay on his board. Each stroke brought him closer to the lineup. A half dozen men were out there. Fewer than any given day at San Sebastian or anywhere in Santa Barbara. But more than there'd be for the competition.

Then, it would be four men at a time to make up a heat. Round by round. Wave by wave. The weak would be cut.

Which meant he had to work it.

He threw himself into practice. Snatching every wave he lined up for, because when it came down to the semifinals, he would have only thirty minutes to surf. Only his two highest scores would be counted, so there were two schools of thought. Wait for the perfect wave, and hope he got two prime specimens, or take everything he could catch and trust that two of them would be good.

At Cloudbreak, everything was heavy. For most of them, he concentrated on cutbacks and did a pretty decent layback snap. There was too much power behind the waves to gain the speed necessary to catch air at the top. But he wanted another barrel. He was chasing it. The need rode on the back of his heels and pushed him out into the water again and again, even after a hydration break.

Near four o'clock, he thought he had it. He had a perfect drop-in on an eleven-foot wave. He slipped down the front, digging his back rail into the heavy water. Nothing blocked him ahead. The barrel closed in from behind and he shouldn't have fucked it up.

But he did. He threw one hip into the switchback, trying to squeeze just a little more speed out.

Instead, he dug the nose of his board right into the wave. It jerked out from under him. He flew free. He sucked in air as quickly as he could. The air and the wave and the moment froze around him. Everything went into second-by-split-second breakdown. He wasn't leashed to his board. The wave was coming up behind him.

He could see the fucking reef beneath his feet, under the too-clear water.

Screwed.

The wave smashed him in the back first. Heavy-handed. A crushing blow took him down, then down farther. His shoulder screamed. He let the water flip him. Waves worked in a circle. If he let it do what it needed to, the pounding would be the worst of it. He'd get tossed out the back. Air then. Not now. Holding on. He fought for calm.

He only knew he hit bottom by the slight sting across the elbow of his bad arm. Then he was being sucked back up.

He ignored the burn in his lungs. This was pure adrenaline. When he broke the surface, he gasped for air. He tossed his head back. Water flicked out of his eyes.

Adrenaline had his blood surging. The air he sucked down his throat was damp with spray and burned him. Salt stung his eyes. He was better than this. He *surfed* better than this.

There was getting pounded by a big wave because sometimes shit happened, and then there was getting pounded by fucking Cloudbreak because he'd been a jackass and done something stupid. This was stupid. He'd earned the beating. That his elbow hurt and leaked a faint cloud of pink into the water was only exactly what he deserved. His shoulder ached in a sharp, painful way.

He'd fucked up. Not just on the wave. By not keeping his mind where it needed to be. He was on the World Championship Circuit. It wasn't the same thing as being a kid on the Prime circuit and thinking he could have anything. Look how that had turned out. His mom had gone into the hospital for mold-borne respiratory issues, but that hadn't been enough for her. She'd gone back to that shitty house.

Nothing easy was worthwhile. He had to remember that.

Chapter 32

Annie knew something was wrong with Sean. That was the easy part. The hard part was figuring out what it was.

The restaurant at the resort was beautiful. Floral-patterned linens covered the small tables. Black china offset the woven-palm place settings. The stemware was all pure crystal. Annie held her wineglass in one hand, the bowl against her palm. Swirling the rich red wine, she watched the sheen cling to the sides of the glass.

Sean looked amazing. Leaning over the sink earlier in the evening, he'd buzzed his own head with a set of clippers so that his hair was the same length as when she'd met him six weeks ago. It made her want to rub her hands and wrists and cheek over him so she could feel the prickle. His long-sleeved button-down shirt should have been too fancy for their casual beach surroundings, but the way he'd negligently buttoned it and rolled the sleeves back to show off tanned forearms made it work.

Of course, it also showed off the gleaming white bandage covering his elbow. It had nearly killed her to keep her hands to herself. She'd cut their official, business ties, and unfortunately that meant no going back. But she'd completely hovered as the Coyote team doctor checked out Sean's range of motion and pain. Plus she'd kind of nudged for a precautionary X-ray, convincing herself she made the suggestion on a concerned-lover basis, not a former-doctor basis.

She took a sip of the wine. It was fine, so rich that it rolled over her tongue and had none of the bitterness that she'd often disliked about reds. Sean had picked it, naturally. He'd had a smile when he ordered, and he had a smile now, something little that tucked the finely carved planes of his cheeks tight.

But she didn't think he meant it.

"That wipeout today must have sucked," she said.

His lips parted and his gaze dropped to the plate of fish he'd already decimated. All that remained were a few shreds of palm fronds that had once been wrapped around the flaky white fish. Sean burned hot when he surfed; she'd realized that. She was half-tempted to push the uneaten portion of her food across the table toward him, but he was a grown man. He'd figure out how to obtain more food for himself.

"It wasn't great," he said, picking up his glass of ice water. He downed half of it in one swill, giving lie to his casual words.

Watching him wipe out on a wave like Cloud-break had been intense. She'd been on her feet and at the rail in moments, willing him to come up. To pop out of the water. But when it came down to it, she'd had absolutely zero power to make him survive, to make him do better than just survive. Her heartbeat had been trilling like a bird's call, it was so fast.

For the second time since she'd known Sean, she'd wished she'd renewed her Ativan prescription. She'd had to talk herself down from the edge as he'd swum up to the boat and clambered up the dive platform. "It was pretty intense, the way you were dripping blood."

He glanced at the white bandage on his arm, but then shrugged. "Not a break, at least. That one hurt worse. This is nothing."

Her teeth snapped together. He was being so casual about something that could have easily meant a new rupture of his previous injury. Or worse. He could have died out there. It wasn't that she wanted him to stop, but she wanted him to at least give a fucking damn. She pressed her lips into a smile. "Maybe next time you'll attract a shark. That'd be something, yeah?"

"I'm mostly pissed I broke my board. It was a good gun. I've taken that one around the world half a dozen times."

"Can you order another?" The words were right. He was talking. But something . . . Something was wrong. Maybe the way he looked at her. She wasn't used to his gaze feeling that . . . flat.

"Yeah, totally. Sage Wright made it for me, and she keeps the stats on all her customers. The boards she makes for them. Won't be here in time for the competition, but it'll be waiting for me when I get back home." He was being so casual. The pitch of his voice said he might as well be giving an interview. She could have been anyone.

"What's wrong?"

He flashed her a smile and sipped his wine. "Nothing's wrong."

She put her glass down but left a finger on the base. She turned it around and around. "So what's your plan for next week?"

"Surf well and hit it hard," he replied, and she sat upright.

Her hands drawn into her lap, she squeezed her fingers together. "Okay, that's it. What's wrong?"

He shook his head, just as innocent as could be. "Nothing's wrong, Annie. Why do you keep insisting something is? It's a bullshit chick move, and totally not like you."

She lifted an eyebrow, easing back in her seat. The chair was low, but the curving back arched into arms that held her and supported her when it felt like everything inside her was shaking. "No. It's not like me. You're right." She measured her words carefully. "If you're pissed, you can say it. Even if it has nothing to do with me. Or especially if it has something to do with me. If this is just about you being upset with your fall, tell me. But I won't put up with you saying nothing."

"Why do you keep insisting something's wrong?" He injected exactly the right kind of exasperation into his voice, but paired it with good humor to imply that he was willing to tolerate her antics.

"'Surf well and hit it hard,' you said." She wrinkled her nose. "Come on, Sean. Who do you think you're talking to? You have a thousand more plans than that. I've seen the surf charts, for Christ's sake. I've seen your *office*. Nothing's just chance to you."

She couldn't believe that he thought she'd buy his bullshit. It was completely unfair. Her fingers twisted together hard enough that her nails caught skin, and she felt the muscles of her arms and chest working in tight harmony. This was . . . more. This was more than she'd thought.

Watching him surf had been part of it. Out there, he'd been a god, same as he'd been with the way he'd carved and floated through the smaller surf at San Sebastian. He was . . . everything amazing. She was getting to have him for the moment, and that meant she wanted everything she could get.

He wrenched open new parts of her every time they made love.

Her chest squeezed tight enough that she could feel each pounding of her heart against her breastbone. She was a mess. Such a mess, and it was because of him. If she could hand over so much of herself, so blithely, it wasn't too much to ask him to be honest with her.

She leaned across the table. "I don't know this act you're doing. I don't know the shell. I know you, Sean. And I'd like you back. At least for tonight. You don't owe me any more than that, but I'm not having dinner with a stranger. And I'm sure as hell not going back to bed with a stranger."

He stared at her, shock making his eyes stormy and bright. He had one hand on the table, and his fingers spread wide. She wondered what he was thinking. Maybe choking the life out of her?

She wanted to snatch the words back, except not really. She didn't have any right to make demands of him. They weren't anything permanent. She didn't *want* them to be anything permanent, because then what would she turn into? What would he expect her to be? She'd learned damn young that the pro surf world was full of men with big egos who expected devotion from the women around them. Gloria was another demonstration of that.

Sean's smile was perfectly formed, but it was still one she didn't know at all. "Keep pushing, Annie, and you might not like what comes out. You don't know all of me. Not really."

She narrowed her eyes. Her knees pressed together, and she wished she hadn't worn the little halter dress. When she'd put it on, it had seemed like the perfect island sundress, with its flirty hem drifting around her thighs. Now her shoulders and sternum felt too bare. "You're such a poser, Sean."

"Excuse me?"

"This dark and dangerous playboy act . . ." She shook her head. "I don't think I believe it. Scratch that. I *know* I don't believe it. I wouldn't be here otherwise."

For a brief and beautiful second, she'd stunned him. The ocean breeze fluttered around their table, lifting the corner of Sean's discarded napkin. The chatter of other diners hummed along with the clatter of silverware. But from Sean there was nothing. His jaw was as sharp as the edge of a razor clam. His hand clenched so tightly on the edge of the table that his knuckles went white.

Then he broke. His shoulders dropped an inch.

The starch went out of his spine, and both his chin and gaze fell until she couldn't see that blue gleam anymore. He shook his head, kept shaking it until he started laughing. It started as a low chuckle, but then it built. And built.

She shifted in her seat. Her toes were cold, her fingers and palms clammy. Biting the inside of her lip didn't ease any of it, didn't draw her attention away from Sean's inexplicable response. Her stomach twirled oddly. "Sean?"

He leaned back. He'd worn shorts, and his legs stretched alongside hers, under the table. The short hair of his calves brushed hers. At least he wasn't the perfectly constructed, carefully withdrawn man she'd been with moments ago. This Sean might be slightly unbalanced, but hell, at least he was real. "It's not an act. Me. Any of it. I'm just . . . who I need to be."

"Because of your mom." She swallowed, her throat tight. She'd just called him a giant liar moments ago, but now she carefully measured her words in a way she hadn't. "Because of her hoarding."

He nodded. "I was in this weird place. If I told people, it wasn't a bad enough situation to get me removed for more than a few days. Social workers told me to be glad I had food. Shelter." He leaned forward on one elbow. He kept the hand of his injured arm clenching the table, but his knuckles weren't white any longer. "I always thought that one was ironic. I should be glad I had shelter."

"I think I know why." Her hands were still twisting together, but at least she wasn't shaking anymore. She wanted to touch him. But when she leaned forward, across the table to reach between their plates and their used-up glasses and silverware to risk putting her fingertips on the edge of his arm, he flinched. She left them there anyway. His skin was flaring hot. "It was a house, but it wasn't really shelter, right?"

"Exactly." He worried the tablecloth with the edge of his thumbnail, following the petals of a yellow flower. "I definitely had enough clothes to wear," he said with a hefty dose of irony. "And Mom provided me with food. The stove was always obstructed, but we had a path to the fridge and the microwave. Bizarrely, she kept those pristinely clean. Scrubbed them every day, in between trips to the thrift store."

"Maybe it was what she could give you." Pure hypothesis, but it would be what she wanted to hear. She couldn't imagine not having her mother's support. Her parents had been her rock through the shift in her perspective, through everything she'd been through. She wouldn't be who she was without them; that was how the gig worked. "She couldn't control the rest of it, but at least she could make sure there was food and a clean way to have it."

He shrugged. "Maybe. But it didn't help her lungs, when her bathroom sink flooded and mold started growing in her room. That's what killed her. I'm sure of it."

She gasped. He hadn't mentioned this part the other day. "How old were you?"

"I was five weeks shy of eighteen." He caught her with a searing look. His hand turned, snatching hers. "She didn't want to go to the hospital, but I made her. I called the ambulance. Sick as she was, she dragged herself outside to wait for them. Didn't want anyone touching her precious stuff. Maybe stealing things. When she died without ever going home again . . . I went back and burned the place down."

Chapter 33

Sean had never said the words out loud. Not once. Even through the investigation, even the times that his uncle Theo had taken him to the defense attorney. It was "grief" and "immaturity," and people said what a danger the place had been. They talked about how at his age, he shouldn't have been sent home alone to those conditions. They were full of sympathy. They didn't make him say it.

So he'd pushed it away. He'd had to do community service, and the family had paid for the firefighters' response costs. It hadn't been a pittance. Three trucks had been called out to deal with the blaze.

And Jesus, it *had* blazed. Sean could still see the orange flames when he closed his eyes. Hell, even when he opened his eyes and looked through the open window of the island restaurant, he could still see the yellow and orange and the sparks that had blown through the roof. He didn't want to go back there, but it was the memory he needed. The ugly thing he needed to unfold and show Annie. For both their sakes.

She shook her head, disbelief making her mouth a soft pout. "You mean, like . . . there was an accident?"

"No." He felt cold and hard. His bones were made of ice. Telling her this would do what he needed. Push her away. Give him the distance he needed to keep his head on straight for this fucking contest. He couldn't afford to lose. "I mean I burned the house down. On purpose. I'd have used gasoline if I could have found some."

He was so focused on Annie and the way she'd flinched in reaction to his story. After a few beats, she released Sean's gaze. Her mouth bent into something that wasn't a smirk, but it wasn't pity either. Good. He wasn't looking for pity. He was looking for a clear mind, and to gain back the ability to concentrate on what he needed to do. Getting back in the game. Making sure his shoulder didn't hold him back.

"You're an asshole, Sean."

"What the hell?" That certainly hadn't been the response he'd expected. His shoulders flinched as if he'd been smacked by this afternoon's wave all over again.

She crossed her legs. "I'm not an idiot. What is this? Tell the little woman all the deep dark secrets so she'll run away? Pay the check. We have shit we need to deal with."

Sean felt himself smile. A little thing, one he didn't want to give. But sometimes the worst responses were the ones that could be contained the least. "You're a fucking firecracker, aren't you?"

"You're about to find out."

Signing the check to the room, he added a thirty percent gratuity for the speed with which the staff moved them along. Fiji time sometimes meant that things took triple the time they would have in the States. Not tonight, though. Something in either his or Annie's face must have given away that it was a good idea to get them hustled out of the dining area. Annie and Sean walked across the beach to their private *bure*, which had been left open to the evening breeze.

Annie walked ahead of him, then stopped in the middle of the living area. She'd skipped heels, giving in to the island culture of bare feet. Sand clung to her heels and the backs of her ankles. Idly, she brushed it off, one foot rubbing the other.

She reached up to take the pins out of her hair. The silken strands flicked around her neck, and she dropped the pins to the floor. They disappeared in the dark as completely as if they'd been thrown over the side of a boat and into the sea. In the dim light, she was smudges of shadow and dipping curves.

Her hands bent behind her shoulders, releasing the single button that topped her zipper.

His body instantly leaped to awareness. That was all it took with her. He was completely twisted around. "Annie . . ."

"Unzip me."

He repeated her name, and he wasn't sure if he was asking her to stop, or asking her to do it herself. She looked at him. Her eyes were as dark as the night. "I told you to unzip me, Sean."

He moved forward and lifted a single hand as soon as he was within reach. The zipper had a tab that measured only a fraction of an inch. Still, he found it unerringly.

He pulled. The teeth gave way slowly, revealing the shallow curve of her back. At the base of her neck, the delicate bumps of her spine were a chain of islands emerging from the sea. Each separate, but making up a beautiful whole. They called to his mouth. He kissed three in a row.

She shivered.

"What is this, Annie?" He didn't want to ask. But the question was pulled out of him one word at a time by the way she moved. Her shift into each breath. The skin exposed by something so simple as a zipper down her back.

"You tell me, Sean." She turned, and only then did he realize that he'd balanced his hands on her shoulders. His touch stroked across her back, dipping into the opening of her dress. She was softer than the silk. Harder than steel too. "I thought we were fine."

"Fine at what?"

"What we do." Her hands lifted to his shirt. Found one button, then another. "Why should there be any name to it?"

"Because I don't know what to do if I can't quantify it."

She laughed. In the dark, her laugh was music and chimes. He stroked his hand up her shoulder, over the graceful length of her neck. Despite the laugh, she was tense. "You know exactly what to do."

With that, she lifted on her toes and wrapped her arms around the back of his neck. Her mouth was fire and wet, and she swept in and took him as fully as he'd ever taken her. But his hands squeezed tight at her waist. The fabric of her dress shifted and gapped. She was tease and withdrawal, something he'd been seeking out for a long damn time.

Maybe forever.

He took the kiss, flipped it so that it was his and hers. She hadn't run. He'd told her about the arson and she hadn't run. He wasn't sure what that meant yet, not really. But he wasn't good enough to let Annie go. "I had to do it," he muttered against her mouth.

She made a soothing noise, something halfway between agreement and denial. Her hands stroked over the back of his head. She was unknowable to him, but someone he desperately wanted at the same time. "I know. It was hard, right?"

"That house killed her."

Her lips pressed his, slipped away again. "So you killed it?"

He sighed against her mouth. Wrapping his arms around her, he yanked her close. Hard and fast. She tasted like pineapple, the fruit of the island. The tropics would always own a piece of them. A piece of Sean, at least.

He lifted her in his arms, pulling her up so that her chest was even with his. They were balanced that way, even with her feet off the ground. "I didn't mean to. Not at first."

"Tell me," she whispered. "Tell me what happened."

"I shouldn't have." He nuzzled her neck, and his beard growth made her shiver with tickles. "I just wanted some fucking food. But I couldn't get to the stove. There was a stack of newspapers that had spilled from the counter."

"Did you use an accelerant?"

"There was a bottle of dark rum." He gave a helpless laugh. "She always had it. Called it her fucking medicine the last couple years. When the cough wouldn't go away."

Her hands petted and stroked over the back of his head, his neck. She was a wraith in the dark. They were wrapped up together in a way that didn't have anything to do with secrets. Her touch slipped beneath the back of his shirt, so he pushed it off for her, shrugging it down one arm at a time, so he didn't have to put her down.

She made a little noise in the back of her throat when he did it. Pride was a charging beast. It ate him from the inside out. It drove him on, so he could tell this story. Get all this gone and put it behind him, maybe.

He'd thought he would have driven her away. Instead, she was wrapped tight in his arms, one knee lifted to his hip. The dress's skirt was drawn tight between them, more sensation than barrier as the silk rubbed over his stomach.

"What was the cough?"

"Mold. Straight up. The doctors had a series of names for it. Bronchitis. Pneumonia one wet winter." He cupped the back of her head and felt the strands of her hair slip between his fingers. "But it couldn't have been anything else."

"You didn't get sick?" She was peering at him. It was a new sensation, someone who managed to sympathize and draw the story from him without heaping him with pity.

"I had a cough sometimes. My lung power and

resistance training went up once the house was gone."

"Gone because you burned it to the ground."

He sucked in a deep breath of the cool evening breeze. The salt in the air was the ocean, always at his side. His confessor. The only thing that had saved him before. But maybe now things could be different. "I did. I poured the rum on the newspapers, then tried to turn on the gas. But the igniter was broken. I lit it with a Zippo."

He'd finally put her feet back on the ground, but there was still no space between them. They were breathing each other's air, faces pressed so close that they traded it back and forth like promises and vows.

She traced her thumb over the thick arch of his shoulder. He'd been broken so recently. Now he was better. And she was the one he expected to break now. "Did you call the fire department?"

His hands clenched on her hips. He hissed in a breath. "Leave it to you to ask the telling questions, Annie."

"Did you?"

"No." He felt the way she swallowed with his hand on the side of her jaw. His thumb fit in a soft, tender space. His fingers speared into her hair. "Think less of me now?"

"How long had she been dead?"

"My mother?" His teeth were white in the shadows that cut lines across his features. His cheekbones cast more shadows across his jaw. "Hours. Fucking *hours*."

"You weren't even eighteen?" Her voice was sharp. "Who the hell left you alone at that age?"

His laugh was bitter, but his hands spread across her ass, one of them lifting her skirt to the small of her back so the material bunched up. "Don't blame them. Mom and I had been more like roommates than mother and son for so long. There was no controlling me."

"Someone should have tried." She seemed to mean it too. "You were practically a baby. If I'd been responsible for my choices at that age . . ." Her voice trailed off in the darkness.

Sean gathered the hem of her skirt up and up, pulling the whole dress over her head. She wore only panties underneath. As soon as he dropped the dress away, she stood nearly bare. Beautiful. Like something splashed with darkness.

He held his hands out, and she put both of hers in them. Trusting. Her fingertips balanced in his palms, and she flinched the tiniest bit. But he folded his hands closed, then drew her near.

"You're dressed and I'm not again. This isn't fair."

"Lots of things in life aren't fair," he growled. Few things had ever felt truer.

She lifted her hands above her head, then turned. He didn't let her go the whole time. She crossed her wrists behind her back, both holding and yet leading him behind her. Her hips swung. Their fingers were entwined. Her wrists were crossed at the small of her back and maybe he should have let them go, but he liked the way they looked against her scrap of lace panties.

She looked back over her shoulder and caught his gaze fixated on her ass. Usually he'd have expected a saucy smile, but he didn't get it. Instead, there was more of that unreadable expression in her eyes. He wrapped his grip around the bend of her hips and jerked her close enough that her ass and pussy snugged up against his trousers. He was hard. Deliciously so.

His gaze flicked back up to hers. There was more light in here from the moon pouring in through the open windows. Outside, the waves made a constant hum. She was breathing hard, sucking in air through her open mouth and panting again.

She tipped forward and planted her hands flat on the mattress. It was soft enough that it gave, making her position more precarious. "Open your knees," he ordered.

She obeyed. As simple as that. "Touch me?"

"That almost sounded like begging." The things she did to him. The things she did for him. More than he'd ever expected. His palms coasted over her back and her ass and her thighs. Everywhere but where she wanted him.

"Please." She swallowed, licking her lips. "Please touch me. Please *fuck* me, Sean. You know I need it."

"Me," he grunted. "You need me."

"I do."

He planted his hand flat in the middle of her lower back, right above the dimples marking the end of her spine. He pushed. She bent. Bent farther when he wanted more from her, until her cheek was against the soft nap of the sheets. Annie always gave him so much. He brushed over her wet panties when he unzipped his fly and put on a condom, but then he wrapped the flimsy gusset of those panties around his fist.

She whimpered when his knuckles brushed her flesh, then cried out when he yanked. He grunted against the need to be even more brutal. To let everything go. The panties tore away, first digging into her hip bones and then wisping away like a ghost. Gone that quickly.

Then he was inside her. Soaked, she gave way, but she was sweet pressure around him as he filled her pussy. His fingers dug into her hips. Marks would probably show on her skin in the morning, but he couldn't bring himself to care.

Every thrust took him somewhere higher. Somewhere he wanted to be. His hand was firm and hard on her hip, his other still planted in the center of her back. He had her exactly where he wanted. They were working together for the same thing.

His hand in the middle of her back restrained her movement. Her back arched against the confinement and he kept her still. Steady.

Even while he fucked her.

Chapter 34

Sean could become Annie's everything.

Because she loved him.

Her chest worked on a sob, but she held back from making a sound through sheer will. She fisted her hands in the sheet. This was not the time, not the place, not the moment that she'd want to throw herself into an abyss. The trust she'd need . . . She didn't have it. Not really. Real love meant fully giving yourself over, and neither she nor Sean had done that.

The image of him in the restaurant, throwing out words like dares, flashed before her eyes. That wasn't trust. That was pretty much the opposite.

No one had told her body how little Sean trusted her. He fucked her deeply, and the pleasure gathered deep in her belly. Every thrust ground her clit against the slick cotton of his pants. There was more pressure within her. Pushing back and taking more.

She exploded, breaking apart in shards of pleasure that slipped through her body like razors. Quick and painful and amazing all at once. There was little more than pure *feeling*. Her knees gave out, but he held her up. Even while he grunted with his own orgasm and held her near. He carried her weight balanced in his hands.

He carried her heart in his hands. And he didn't trust her.

Annie was panting when she dropped to the mattress. Her thighs were shaky with the force that had just swept through her. She scrunched her eyes closed and pressed her face to the mattress. One hand fisted next to her head.

She was Annie Baxter, and she reached for what she deserved. With or without Sean Westin.

Her brain wouldn't work fast enough to let her pull away, and he'd hooked his arm around her waist and pulled her down so they'd collapsed together. Her head came to rest on the curve of his shoulder into his biceps, a place that normally felt like it had been crafted for her. Now it felt like glass and barbwire.

She'd wound her fingers in the placket of his Armani shirt. This could be the last time she touched him. The tumult inside her was frightening. She didn't know how to put the pieces together.

There was no way to balance the man who'd tried to push her away with the man she'd fallen in love with.

Love. Jesus, it was nearly laughable.

The night air purred with the continuous wash of waves, steps from their bungalow. The open windows and thatched roof only kept out her view of the stars, but that was almost too much. The sparkle would be too much when there were tears in her eyes.

He swallowed, and she could hear the sound from

the way her ear was pressed against his chest. "Teenage arsonists usually become serial killers."

She made a sound halfway between laughter and shock. "You did not just compare yourself to Dexter, did you?"

"It's not unheard of." He chuckled, though the sound was awful to her. "And I don't mean I'm worried that I'm going to reach over and break your neck—"

"Oh, I'm so glad of that," she interrupted dryly.

"But it's just that I've always worried that I was . . . I dunno. A little off. That I could do that. And I sat on the curb and waited for the fire department without crying, or freaking out even a little bit. It was just . . . a thing."

"You're not a closet sociopath, Sean. The fact that you would worry about that proves the very opposite. It was a thing you needed to do. Frankly, I don't think you should have been left alone, for any reason." She pushed up to a seated position. It was easier when he stayed lying down. Her head bowed. She didn't want to see his face when she continued on. This was going to be bad enough. Her throat squeezed tight. "You were a broken little boy and you lashed out. *That* was only a little bit your fault."

"*That* was only a little my fault," he echoed, putting emphasis on the first word as he pushed up on his elbows. "So . . . what *is* my fault?"

She sighed and finally looked at him. He hissed in a sharp breath when their gazes connected. Maybe she wasn't covering everything up as well as she thought. He lifted a hand to the side of her face, trying to cup her jaw.

But she flinched away.

"Annie?" Her name was a question and something more at the same time.

"We should just let this go. You've got a really big few days coming up, and we're here on the far side of the world." She raked her fingers through her hair, trying to convince herself. It didn't have to all explode now, did it? Wrecking their perfect fantasy world? "It'll be fine."

"It'll *be* fine," he repeated. "So it's not fine now."

"Fucking hell, Sean." She snapped, her mouth running away with her. "You really think you can pull bullshit like that and have everything be fine?"

"I knew it," he snarled. He dropped flat to the bed, looking a little like a child avoiding an argument.

"Oh bullshit." The bed shifted as she twisted around. She couldn't hear the rush of the waves past the roar in her ears. She stood and went to her suitcase, pulling on a pair of pajama pants and a tank top. Sean buttoned up the clothing he'd never taken off, and instantly it was as if they'd never been. "I bet a thousand bucks that you're sitting there, assuring yourself that my problem concerns what you did ten years ago. And it does *not*."

"It sure does seem like it. The timing's right." He was flat as a glassy ocean. No waves, no ups, no downs. Everything pulled away in that glossy face he put on for strangers. His rolled-up sleeves displayed his strength when he crossed his arms over his chest. "If it's not what I did after my mom died, then what is it? Say it, Annie."

"Fine." She wrapped her arms around her narrow

stomach. Held herself tight. Her insides felt like they were about to spill over the floor, and it wasn't going to be pretty. "It's the timing. You were pissed at yourself because you wiped out today. So you basically threw a shit fit all over me. You told me your sob story so you wouldn't have to face anything real."

"I did not," he snarled. When she stayed silent, he stalked toward the switch and flipped it on, flooding their room with light. "I didn't, Annie."

"You did." On some odd level she recognized that she was smiling, but her cheeks were tight and her teeth felt like they could grind lava rock into dust. "It was completely on purpose."

"It was not!" Except his protests seemed almost *too* vehement.

"Tell me that you weren't upset this afternoon. I dare you."

"Why wouldn't I be upset? I fucking screwed up a wave that I should have nailed." He threw a hand out to the side, pointing toward the roaring waves at their back door. "I cannot afford to screw up when my qualification for the World Championship Tour is on the line. I've missed two events. I need these points. I need to win. Do you know how many times I've surfed Cloudbreak before?"

She stood ramrod straight, her hands fisting at her side. "You. How many times you've surfed. You need to win." Her chin jerked back. "How many times have *I* been to Fiji before, Sean?"

"Never. You've never been here." His eyes narrowed, and he came a step toward her. "Why didn't you make it to Fiji, Annie? Why did you quit surfing? How *could* you quit?"

Her shoulders went up in a tight shrug. "You know, you've never asked me why before."

"I thought you'd talk about it if you wanted to. Because I didn't want to..." He trailed off. He hadn't meant to say that, it seemed, because his mouth flattened and his cheeks hollowed.

But the pieces were finally falling together. "Because you didn't want to talk about *your* secrets. Exactly."

"Why didn't you go pro, Annie?"

She was tempted to tell him it was too little too late, but there was no real point in that. Her hands tightened in their fists. "I was dating my sponsor rep."

"They're not supposed to do that."

"I know. But I was eighteen and he was twenty-three, and that seemed so damn cool, like he had all his shit together." God, she'd been so very, very wrong. "Two weeks after I graduated high school, the ASP event was in Trestles. So he drove me up for a party."

He shook his head, his expression going dark. "Ten years ago? Things weren't very pretty."

"Nope. Wasn't pretty at all when he made it super clear that if I didn't put out for one of the big stars, then I should at least put out for him. That was 'the way it worked' and I should get on board if I really wanted a career." He'd looked so good and clean and talked so reasonably as they'd sat on the back porch of the party. The waves she'd always relied on had droned on in the background. "I asked him to take me home, but he still didn't get it. He drove down a back road and said he'd give me one more chance. He started . . . He tried to hurt me. I had to take care of myself. I've *always* had to take care of myself."

"You're incredibly strong."

She shook her head, both hands going to her hair. Her fingers twined. "But don't you get it? I shouldn't have to defend myself. This whole fucking world is skewed, and I think you're one of the worst victims, Sean."

He flinched away from her. His shoulders folded as if he'd pull in on himself if he could. "What the hell? I'm no victim. I haven't been for a long fucking time, and I never will be again."

"I get that. I do." The air had been sucked out of her. She could barely breathe anymore, not through the rasping sting that her throat had become.

"I'm sorry I didn't ask why you'd chosen school. That was an oversight."

Her heart withered. The pain spread through her, making her want to be sick. One-way love was a horrible thing. "I want to be something more than an oversight."

"You are, Annie." He crossed the room in a few steps. They had been too far apart, but when he held her shoulders, she could barely feel his touch. Lowering his head, he pressed their foreheads together. "You're important to me. I . . . Jesus, Annie, I love you."

A soft sound wrenched from her. She put her hands on either side of his face. Compared to the chill in her fingertips, his skin was flames. "You want to love me. Maybe you could someday. But I don't think you do now."

"You don't get to say what I feel."

"You don't get to say *I love you* as a weapon."

He kept his eyes closed. She didn't, though. She watched his mouth, waited to see what he'd say. Even though she wanted words to fix all this, she couldn't imagine what possible solution there could be.

"Don't leave," he said softly. And it wasn't enough.

"I can't be near you right now." Her voice shook, after all her talk of strength. She still couldn't stop the tears that welled, though. They fell and caught on his thumbs. He swept moisture over her cheeks. It felt like rubbing the pain into her skin.

"I'll go stay with someone. I know . . ." He gave a helpless noise, something just shy of a laugh. "I know everyone. And no one. No one knows me like you do, Annie."

"I'm sorry for that, Sean."

It didn't take him long to pack a bag. From the bed, Annie watched him go. She sat in a tight little knot, her arms wrapped around her lifted knees. Her cheeks felt heavy, and it probably didn't help the situation that she kept staring at him. She wanted him to be better. She wanted to be better herself. No, that wasn't right. She just wanted them to *fit* better. But it felt like their messed-up parts hit at just the wrong angles.

He stopped in the doorway. "Will you stay in Fiji at least?"

Her nod made his blazing eyes lighten. But then she added, "But you won't see me, Sean. Not if I can help it."

Chapter 35

Annie stayed away from alcohol at the post-Pro party. It was strange enough to be there. Her hands were shaking and her stomach was a twisting mess. Adding alcohol to the mix seemed like a really poor choice.

Especially since she was standing in the middle of a party thrown to celebrate Sean's victory.

He'd won the whole fucking event. First place. Everything he could have dreamed of.

He'd stomped through each round like a man on a mission. Annie had watched from the bar at the resort, since piping a live feed into the big-screen TVs was better than having a half dozen boats out at the break just so people could watch. He'd relied on classic moves and getting perfectly barreled. He'd made the first perfect ten of the event on the second round by dropping into a wave and letting it close into a barrel so large that he'd lifted his hands full length and barely skimmed the water above his head.

He'd been amazing.

The final round had been against Nate, and despite the other man getting his own ten-point wave, Sean had beaten him by three points, which was considered a wide margin when the highest possible score was only twenty.

He must be on top of the world.

And Annie was in hell.

She had her hands clenched around a Coke as she stood near the bar. The resort had set up an open-air party room of sorts. A thatched roof was held up by the occasional wooden beam support. The sides were completely open to the setting sun. At one end, they'd set up a bar manned by three bartenders, and trough-sized buckets were filled with ice and beer at points around the room.

The whole event had been sponsored by Coyote. This was Sean's gig. Any moment, he'd walk in like a triumphant king.

Annie should back away. She should leave. Just like she shouldn't have watched every second of the last five days of competition. She could have gone home instead of giving in to compulsions.

But her other choice was retreating to the *bure* they'd briefly shared. The bungalow was too big for only her, and too fancy. She'd tried surfing on her own too. The resort had a beach break that was a hundred yards of beautiful but not-too-intimidating points. She'd gone out two afternoons in a row with a board she'd rented from the resort; touching the short boards that Sean had left behind in the *bure* would have been like licking poison. The idea made her heart and her stomach clench.

Surfing hadn't been the same without him. Being in the bungalow hadn't been the same without him.

Fucking hell, *breathing* hadn't been the same without him.

That didn't mean she hadn't been right.

Commotion at the other end of the oversized cabana made Annie jump. Her heart took up residence somewhere around her ears, apparently figuring her throat just wasn't dramatic enough. She tried to calm herself with long, slow breaths, but it didn't work. She had no way to ground herself. She floated in a paradise that was more like hell.

Sean had arrived.

He was surrounded by a knot of admirers. The playboy was back in full force. He already had a blonde and a brunette on each side, though they were flanked by managers and event coordinators in turn. Sean lifted one hand in a fist above the shoulder that could have taken him out all together, and the crowd roared. They loved him. He was the hero of the moment.

Her heart was a crumpled, crumbled disaster zone.

She was such a fucking idiot.

Turning away from the triumphant scene at the other end of the room, she pressed her fingertips to her eyes. Her sockets burned. Her neck felt so tight, it ached.

He didn't even miss her, and how fucking juvenile a thought was that? She tugged the hem of her T-shirt. It wasn't that she wished he'd have lost or anything like that. He'd been the best. He'd *deserved* to win. But the tiny, petty, childish part of her wanted him to *miss* her while he won. He hadn't even looked for her across the crowd. He'd just had on his front, the shiny happy kind of look that made it seem like everything was fine.

Well, for all she knew, everything *was* fine with him.

"It's a swizz, ain't it?" Gloria sidled up next to Annie, leaning one arm on the bar. Her gaze was trained over Annie's shoulder, though, toward where the cheers in the room started. "He's not half of what he's cracked up to be."

"What?" Annie rubbed the dip of her temple, where the burn in her eyes had traveled and twisted itself into pain. If she wouldn't let herself cry in public, her body seemed determined to give her a headache instead.

"Sean." Gloria had the stem of a cherry and worried it between thumb and forefinger, making it spin and spin. She nibbled the knot at the end. "He's decent, that's true. But there's no fucking way he's better than my Nate."

"There're five judges. It's not possible to cheat." Annie narrowed her eyes at Gloria.

"Not that way." She was a bundle of cynicism. She lifted her brows and cocked her hip. "You think Sean's perfect? I thought you'd have figured out the truth. Everyone knows he's been staying with the junior Coyote team. The very idea of Sean bunking with nineteen-year-old kids who're practically frat boys . . ." Gloria snickered. "It's been kind of a pick-me-up the last few days."

"Sean and I hit a rough spot." She took a sip of her soda, but it didn't do anything to wash the nasty taste from her mouth. Gloria was quite the piece of work, but Annie hadn't realized exactly how bitter she was. "What's that got to do with his surfing?"

"Apparently nothing." Gloria gave her a faux-innocent smile. "But then, considering where he's come from . . . what he's risen above . . . he's no stranger to adversity."

Annie's spine became something made of wire and blades and knives. "What are you implying?"

Gloria laughed. "Oh, come on. You can tell me. I already know. Or did he not tell you that we dated?"

"He mentioned it." She looked at the taller woman. "But he also said you couldn't take a hint when things were done." He hadn't said anything of the sort, but Gloria didn't have to know that.

"Whatever. He liked me well enough at the time, and Nate's moving up in the rankings." Gloria edged closer, her body language closing them off from the rest of the room. Annie wanted to step back, but there was a chair behind her and she didn't want to make it too obvious that she was freaking out. The air was leaking out of the open room. "Look, everyone knows you've split. And I know there's something going on with Sean. If you give me any kind of information, I can pass it on to the people who need to know."

"What the hell?" Annie shook her head, leaning back as far as she could. She needed air that was scented with the salt of the ocean, not Gloria's light but cloying perfume. "There isn't any information to give."

"Why would you defend him?" Gloria's voice hit a near screech, but she pulled it down again, taking deep breaths to get herself under control. "Look, maybe you just don't know. I've followed this sport for years. Practically my whole life. I know Sean's hiding something major. He was when we dated, and he still is now."

"So you think you have a right to know? You're the one who's been talking to Ackerman, aren't you?"

Gloria's expression turned cagey. She cast a quick look back over her shoulder. "I didn't say that. I haven't done anything."

Annie set her soda down on the bar. The glass didn't make a sound against the roughly polished bamboo, but the condensation immediately drew a circle on the wood. Annie licked her bottom lip and watched a bead of water drip down the side of the glass, past the bubbles and dark liquid. Separate and still connected. "I'm not really sure what's wrong with you, Gloria, but you're way too invested in this sport. It's their job. Not yours."

The other woman laughed. "Oh, you're cute. If you think Nate would have gotten half as far as this without me, you don't belong in this world. They need our devotion. They need us to be there supporting them. They think they're superheroes, but they're not."

"No, they're not. They're human beings." Annie looked up at the other woman. "Humans who make mistakes and who deserve forgiveness."

"What the fuck are you talking about?" Gloria's brow wrinkled with confusion.

"I'm . . . not exactly sure." Except this was a very, very strange conversation to be having revelations in the middle of.

But when a dark, deep voice sounded from behind her, she didn't flinch. "When you figure it out, I'd like to be the first to know."

Part of her had realized that Sean was behind her before he spoke. It felt like every cell in her body was aligned with his. She was focused on him. Couldn't look away from the other half of herself, after all. It would be like ignoring her own legs. They'd get in the way if she tried.

She turned slowly. He looked good. So good. The five days of competition had deepened his tan another fraction. The blades of his cheekbones were tight with tension, and there were little wrinkles that she hadn't seen before, fanned out from his eyes. Maybe she was messed up, because she liked knowing that truth. He'd been affected by their distance.

She breathed his name. He didn't answer, not in words. But the way he looked at her . . .

There was still hope. Maybe. If she could get her brain out of her heart. This stuff didn't have to be all mind over matter. There was something to be said for instinct and only listening to the way she felt.

Nate stood behind him. As the second-place contender in the competition, Nate would have been giving a handful of interviews with Sean. He was taller than Sean, and Annie realized that the only other time she'd seen him had been in the water, on surfboards. She had to crane her neck to look up at him, and Sean had already made her feel short.

"Gloria?" He put a hand on his girlfriend's shoulder. Gloria's entire attitude immediately changed. Her smile turned into something gentle and real. Her eyes softened. She tilted her head slightly. "Everything all right?"

"Sure, sugar." She was everything sweetness. "Annie and I were having a bit of a chat. She let me vent a little. Gonna be sad she won't be coming around on the circuit anymore." She aimed a deliberately saccharine smile at Annie, who knew exactly what the other woman was really saying.

Sucks to be you. Ta-ta and see ya!

Annie snorted. "Sure. If that's what you want to say."

Sean didn't touch her. Not directly. But he came so close, they could have been breathing the same air. He wanted to hold her. She knew that all the way through her, but she didn't know how to start it off. If she touched him first, she'd probably shatter into a million pieces. She was barely being held together by a smash of surf wax. If she was put out into the warmth of Sean's sun, she'd melt. "Is there something you want to tell me, Annie?"

She flashed her own saccharine, faked-out smile at Gloria. "Just that Gloria here is probably the one Ackerman is citing as his source. If I had to lay money on it, I bet she probably dropped a word about your record to the ASP as well." Oh, fuck it. If she was in for a penny, she might as well be in for a pound. "And I love you, Sean. Gloria and I weren't talking about that, not in so many words, but the way she talks about you . . . I couldn't stomach listening to it."

Sean's jaw had been tightening while she talked about Gloria, but as soon as Annie made her awkward segue, his gaze jerked around to her. "What?"

She laughed, because suddenly she felt as light as air. As high as a kite, like she had been the first time he'd taken her surfing last month. "If you'll let me, I want to say I'm sorry. For everything. Because I love you."

Chapter 36

Sean's win that afternoon had been pretty sweet, but he'd had a strangely detached feeling. Like maybe he'd popped into a parallel universe where things had an odd tint. It started with his waking up in a shared bedroom at the Coyote team bungalow, and Matthew Medina snoring. Badly. It hadn't helped that Matty had stumbled in past three in the morning. He'd been knocked out of the competition two days earlier and had been drinking it off.

Even the ten-point tube ride he'd had in the final had been something Sean did. Not something he felt.

Now, though, with Annie's face turned up to him, her dark eyes confused and filling with a gleam of hope at the same time, he had a full grasp of the moment. His blood charged hard. Shocks of sensation rocked down the backs of his legs and through his arms. He was as light as air, and he could bounce on the balls of his feet to get the energy out.

But she'd lobbed two bombs in his lap at the same time, and one of them was about to go off with the sputtering, protesting Gloria. That had to be dealt with. Since it was a woman he was facing, for once he couldn't deal with the problem with his fists.

Sean needed to touch Annie, though. He brushed the backs of his knuckles across her jaw, soft as white-water mist. She didn't pull away. His breathing froze for a second.

He hadn't thought he'd be able to touch her. Not ever again. It had been a literal ache in the pit of his stomach. He'd lain in his borrowed single bed, staring at the ceiling.

She reached up and folded her hand over his, holding it to her face.

A disgusted sigh echoed behind them. "Come on, Nate. I have no idea what that psycho was talking about, but they're obviously being drama queens. Let's go."

"No."

"What?"

Sean couldn't remember the last time Nate had actually said no to Gloria. The dude was so easygoing, he usually didn't get up in the middle of anything. Not even his girlfriend. But she'd turned away, holding Nate's wrist, only to freeze when he issued the simple declaration. She twisted her shoulders toward him. Nate stood with his feet set hip-width apart, steady as a mountain.

Gloria jutted her chin out. "No? What?"

Sean wrapped his arm around Annie's shoulder, halfway expecting her to pull away again. When she didn't, his heart took a strange little leap. They had a pile of shit to deal with, but maybe . . . Maybe there was something worth dealing with. He could work with that. "No, you're not going anywhere. Is Annie right?"

She gaped at Sean. "What the hell, Sean? You're going to take that little bitch's word over that of someone you've known for years? She *dumped* you right before the biggest heat in your competition. You and I have had a positive relationship since we broke up!"

"That's not an answer," he said flatly.

"And why are you trading on how many years you've known him, Gloria?" Nate folded his arms over his chest. "You've never made any secret of thinking Sean's more player than surfer."

"So?" She tossed her hair over her shoulder. "That doesn't mean we aren't friends."

As far as Sean was concerned, once they weren't in a relationship, Gloria could have disappeared. But she'd stayed in his life because of the quick way she'd taken up with Nate. "Answer the question, Gloria. Did you influence that documentary? Are you the one who told Ackerman about—" Sean jerked his words to a halt, before he could drop the truth. They knew part of the story. That was enough. He hated that enough.

"God, *no*," she said, propping her hands on her hips. "Fine? No, I didn't. I shouldn't have to answer that at all, but I didn't."

A dark expression shuttered Nate's eyes. His mouth pressed flat. He had a bold nose, but in his stress, it seemed to get even bolder with strain, making the skin around it go white. "That's a lie," he said in a voice barely more than a rasp. "She always says it three times if she's lying."

Anger whipped through Sean like a monsoon. He squeezed Annie's hand too tight, until she squeezed back in return. "I've never done shit to you, Gloria."

"God, it's not even that big a deal," she squealed. "So you grew up in a shitty place. You ought to be *thanking* me. Between the publicity for all that and your win today, you're on top. You should pull in three new contracts for this!"

"That's not how I want to make a name for myself."

"Then you're an idiot." She crossed her arms over her ample chest, her chin coming down so that she looked like a three-year-old in a full-on pout. "I just don't know how you could have won today after your damn shoulder anyway. Nate should have had it. This should be his year."

"Congratulations," Annie said in a fake-chipper voice that sounded more like Gloria's normal tones. "You've probably screwed up his head game for the rest of the season. How's he supposed to get his confidence together when his girlfriend's a lying harpy?"

"Thanks for that," Nate said dryly.

Annie shrugged. "Sorry, but if I were you, I'd be wondering about myself."

"I want you out, Gloria," Sean said.

"This is a *team* party. You don't get to make those choices." She tossed her blond hair again.

"Try me." Sean lifted a hand in the air and snapped his fingers.

In near moments, two porters and the Coyote team manager were at his side. "Something wrong?" asked Greg Tamiya.

"I need Gloria taken out. Don't make it a big deal as long she doesn't make a fuss."

Greg's gaze jumped from Sean to Nate to Gloria. "Look, if there's some kind of disagreement that needs to be worked out, we can sit down and talk it out. . . ."

Sean held on to his barely leashed temper. His teeth ground together. "Not the time, Greg. I'll tell you about it later. But trust me. It's better for the brand if she goes."

"Come on," said Nate. He latched his grip around Gloria's slender wrist. "We need to talk this out at home anyway."

"I'm not going anywhere," she protested. "He's a bullshit surfer."

"He won fair and square, Gloria. It was legit." Nate didn't give her any more room to protest, only herded her away. He wasn't being mean, but he wasn't brooking any disagreement either.

Greg watched them go. He turned a concerned expression to Sean, his mouth disappearing into a flat line. "Look, if this is going to have blowback, we're going to have to talk about it."

"I think this might actually solve problems." Shit, he needed to get Greg fully up to speed. Sean could call his manager and figure out where things needed to go for cleanup. But he looked back at Annie. Business faded when compared to the other thing she'd said. She loved him. He wanted to hear more about that.

She could have been reading his mind. Her mouth was bent in a soft smile, and she lifted up on her toes to kiss his cheek. "Deal with her. It's a problem."

"But . . ."

"I'll be waiting for you at the bungalow, okay?"

"Promise?"

Her gaze flitted over him, and he could feel the air burning in his lungs as fiercely as it had a week ago, when he'd burned out at Cloudbreak. But her eyes softened. He could get lost in that dark for a long, long time. "I'll promise lots of things, if you'll let me."

It took Sean about an hour to wrap everything up. Greg was brought up to speed, and then they had a conference call with Max in California. Thank Christ for the age of Skype. The higher-ups at Coyote were worried about the tabloid stories, but they'd be pleased to hear that there would be no more. Combined with his win, they were happy with him. The ASP wanted Sean to invest some time in positive press, just to cover their ass, but Sean had no problem with that. He was fine on the press junket so long as they had a shiny new win to ask him about.

By the time he walked into the *bure* he'd shared with Annie, he was exhausted. He'd been sitting in a little room, shouting into a computer screen because the connection was mediocre to crappy, and the stress had ridden him for months.

Despite that, he felt like he could have run full tilt through the door. Only to come to a screeching halt when the living room was empty. The bedroom had no sign of Annie either, beyond her open suitcase. At least she hadn't gone too far. He kicked his shoes off at the back door.

He stepped through the archway to the lanai, and at first he still didn't see her. She'd seated herself at the high-tide line, folded up into a small ball. Her knees were practically at her chin, and she had her arms wrapped around them. Her hair had been skimmed into twin ponytails.

She'd changed clothes since he'd last seen her. Then she'd been wearing a T-shirt with a video game icon on it, along with navy shorts. Now she'd switched out for a bright blue bikini. He liked the splash of color.

"Sorry to keep you waiting."

She gasped and launched to her feet. Her hands flew to her stomach and her throat, and she started panting. "Jesus! Jesus, you shouldn't sneak up on me like that."

He slung his hands in his pockets, rocking back on his bare heels. The sand was hot under his feet and between his toes. He'd always loved that feeling. "Didn't sneak. Not even a little bit."

She shook her head. "Yeah, sorry. You're right. I didn't hear you over the sound of the waves. I was stuck in my own head too."

"Find anything good in there?"

"Depends." She stepped closer to him. The tide was coming up, but even the farthest-reaching waves washed up several feet from them in a shell-thin curve of white foam. "Will you listen to me talk about how much of an idiot I've been?"

He felt his shoulders loosen a fraction, and only then did he realize how tightly he'd been holding himself. Each breath he took worked against unclenching the pressure in his chest. "Only if you stop calling yourself an idiot."

She'd put on makeup for the postevent party, dark

gray shadow over black liner. At some point in the past hour, she must have cried some, because she'd smeared out at the corners in flares like wings. He rubbed his thumb over the proof of her upset. She stopped him by laying her hand over his. "That's what it feels like. I hurt you. For no real reason that I can come up with beyond that I was uncomfortable."

"I didn't mean to make you uncomfortable." His hand tightened on the side of her face, cupping her jaw. "I wish I hadn't said anything."

She shook her head almost frantically. "No. No, it was the best thing. Your delivery kind of sucked, and I stand by my point that you can't throw things like that at someone because you've had a crap day—"

He squeezed her shoulders. "It was unfair of me. I know that. I really did mean to drive you away, and that was one of the stupidest things I've ever tried to do. I'd have been pushing away my own heart."

She gasped. Her lips parted, and tears welled up in those big, dark eyes of hers. Her mouth was a soft pout. "Goddamn it, stop being so sweet when I'm trying to apologize."

He couldn't help but chuckle. A tear welled over her bottom lashes, and he caught it on the edge of his thumb. "Maybe we both need to do some apologizing."

"I'm first," she said, showing her stubborn streak. "I was so mean, Sean. You're the last person in the world I'd want to be awful to, but the words just dropped out of my mouth, and at that moment I was so damn sure I was right. But then . . . since then . . . it's like my heart has been missing from my chest."

He swallowed and traced the curve of her ear. It was easier to tuck a lock of hair away than to look at her eyes. "Then why did you say those things? Jesus, Annie. I told you something I've never told anyone else."

"It felt like manipulation."

He winced. "And that's my fault."

"No, no!" Her hands spread across his chest. "It only felt like that because of how strongly I was affected. How bad I felt for you and the way I wanted to wrap you up and promise to make sure you never hurt again. I didn't understand that I was even capable of feeling that deeply. So I misidentified it. That's all on me. Not on you."

"Fuck, that's harsh." He swallowed. The lightness that had started in the middle of his chest began to sink away. "That's the kind of suckage that I don't know if I can forget."

Her shoulders drooped, and her head did too. The tears that had barely been leaking out suddenly broke in a cascade of searing tracks. Her tiny *oh* was as dejected a sound as he'd ever heard before. "No, okay. I get it. I fucked up. You can't be with someone you can't trust."

Except the last thing in the world that he wanted was to walk away at this moment. He was glued to her. Tied with invisible bonds that might have to learn to stretch or to twist . . . but they'd never break.

He thumbed away her tears and lifted her face. A thin track of mascara marked the path of her tears. "Annie . . . I trust you."

Chapter 37

Annie had never thought she'd hear those words from Sean. Not after what she'd done. How badly she'd freaked out. His head was bent toward her, and his hands on her had more power than she'd ever felt. The tide started to lick their feet with the relative chill of the waves, but she hardly noticed. The water nibbled away at the sand beneath her feet, but she only dug in and held on. And that was exactly what she meant to do for the rest of her life with this man.

"Sean, don't say that if you don't mean it."

He flashed her a smile that was faintly dumbfounded. His eyes were so bright, she almost thought their intensity was caused by a sheen of tears. She couldn't quite tell in the gleam of the setting sun. Her heart wanted to believe it, but the stunned part of her brain said she had finally lost it. Then he followed it up with a harsh laugh. "I tell you that I love you, and you tell me that I'm wrong. But I tell you that I trust you, and that's what does it for you?"

She giggled, even though the response felt a little

hysterical as the sound bubbled up through her throat. "What can I say? I'm a strange girl."

He wrapped his arms tightly around her. She was safe there. She was even safer when she lifted her face to his and he took her with an overwhelming kiss. His lips skated over hers, came back again and again to sip at her. Even the waves coming up around their ankles weren't enough to tear them apart.

Annie wound her arms around his shoulders and laced her fingers together. She'd do whatever it took to hold him close, to keep him wrapped up with her. "I need you, Sean. I thought I was all better, all healed and perfect as I was. So independent that I insisted on doing everything alone." She sobbed. "But I needed your life. I needed you to bring me back to the things I'd once loved."

"You're the one who brought yourself back to life." His strong, broad hand on her face was a source of heat and strength. "You're a surfer, Annie. That's your joy. I didn't do anything but offer you a board. That was all."

"You're so full of it." Her tears and laughter mixed together in a strange hybrid of emotion. Everything smacked into her at once. She hadn't realized how empty she'd been. How much she'd been looking for someone like Sean to stand at her side. "I love you. I think I've loved you for a long time, or I wouldn't have fired you as a client."

"I made it worth it," he said with a ghost of his usual cocky smile.

She let her neck bend enough that her forehead pressed against his chest. He still wore the red rash guard he'd competed in. He'd gone straight to the

winner's podium, to interviews, to what was supposed to be his big party. The celebration of his win.
And she'd thrown a giant monkey wrench into the
process. Still, it was the most casual she'd seen him
other than when he was naked. For Sean, there were
only two speeds—hard and harder. One involved
impressing everyone to make sure they didn't see
behind his image. The fastest way to impress everyone was *winning*. Winning wasn't as easy as breathing for him. It was something he fought for with
every bone in his body and every brain cell he could
fire up. If he could start tapping into that fire, he
could move right up the ranks.

He rested his chin on the top of her head. She was
sheltered in his arms, completely safe from the rest
of the world. "So I suppose this is a good moment to
tell you that I signed off on all the funding for your
center?"

"What?" Her voice approached a screech. No,
scratch that, it was a total screech. She pushed back
in his arms so far that she could see the way his blue
eyes gleamed. "You're lying."

"Never."

"When the hell did you do that?"

He cupped the back of her head, and she wasn't
sure if he was trying to keep her from leaning back
too far, or trying to bring her closer to him. It didn't
really matter, though. The point was that she loved
the curve of his mouth and the way his cheeks had
softened. "About fifteen minutes before I walked
into the Coyote team afterparty."

The sobs welled up like lava from a Hawaiian vol-
cano. They burned her from the inside out. She

pressed her face to the silky fabric of his rash guard. "No. You did not. Why would you do something like that?"

"Because it's the right thing to do." He kissed her cheeks, his lips wiping away the tracks of her tears. "Because the center is a good thing that deserves to happen. Even if it's not your bonus. Even if you and I weren't going to be together . . . I wasn't going to punish the kids who could have benefited from it."

"You're insane," she said, but her sobs were fading away. In the wake of the lava was new land. New territory she'd explore.

"Does that mean you don't want it?" he teased, dipping his knees to look her in the eyes. His smile sparked her all the way from her toes to the tips of her fingers. "I suppose I could figure out a way to take it back."

"Don't you dare!" She hiccuped, she'd been crying so hard. She dashed away her tears with the backs of her hands. The smile on her face threatened to squeeze her cheeks. "If you take it back, I won't be able to hire a director. And if I can't hire a director, I can't visit you on tour."

He froze. "Do you mean that, Annie? I wouldn't ask it of you. I'd come home to Southern California all I could. It could be enough."

"It could be . . . but I don't want it to." She pressed her mouth to his, taking in his growl to herself. His grasp squeezed tight around her waist. She was possessed by him, but that was okay, because she possessed him right back. "I love you, Sean. You're not getting any farther away from me than absolutely necessary."

"Say that again."

"I love you."

He shook his head. "No, the other part."

"That you're not getting away from me?"

"That." He sounded reverent. "I wasn't wanted before, Annie. I've been thrown away many times in my life before this. The thought that you might do it too . . ."

"Never. Never, never. I promise, Sean. We'll be together. And I want you desperately."

"I want you too, Annie. Forever."

Epilogue

Five months later

Annie dropped off the lip, free-floating on her board for a split second that felt more like a year. The back rail caught, and she thought she was going to lose her balance. She dug down, reaching between her bent knees to catch the rail. Her other hand flew out toward the tail of the board for balance. Her heart leaped into her throat, but she swallowed it down.

The wave was chasing her, the barrel throwing down over her head. She leaned back on her board, dropping her balance toward the tail in order to slow down a fraction. Too much speed would cause her to chase out the far end and never get barreled.

It worked. She was surrounded by water. The green room swallowed her. Her instinct was to close her eyes. She fought it. She kept her eyes peeled, even as adrenaline sang in her veins and her vision blurred. A perfect oval of blue loomed in front of her. Something few people ever saw.

She spread her arms wide so it was like flying and

being held tight at the same time. She was surrounded by the ocean. It could swallow her any second, but she wouldn't let it.

Pumping her board, she sped up enough that she spit out the far end. The gleaming sun suddenly reflecting off acres of water stung her eyes. She finally blinked. She stood long enough that all the speed dropped out of her. Her hands fell to her sides and she turned her face up toward the sun.

She was blessed. This was the best life.

Her board sank at the end, until cool water sloshed over her toes. She dove out, the leash attached to her ankle keeping the board behind her. Getting back to shore was a little swim from the reef, but so worth it.

Especially because Sean was waiting for her. He threw his arms around her as soon as she yanked the Velcro leash strap off her ankle. "You did it!"

He spun her in a full circle. Her feet flew up, and her arms were tight around his shoulders. He was bone dry, and she was soaking wet and had to be clammy as hell. He didn't seem to care. He held her as close as possible.

"I did Pipeline." She suddenly realized her heart was thumping a thousand miles an hour. "Oh my God. I did Pipeline. Am I smoking something? I can't believe I did that."

Her knees went weak as soon as he put her down. She wobbled, but he was right there. He always was. Whenever she needed support. "You haven't smoked anything. You're a damn good surfer. I can't believe how fast it's come back to you."

She laughed. "I've been to the best surf spots in the

world over the past five months, thanks to you. There's no better coach." She lifted, her toes digging into the hot, gleaming white sand. His lips were hot compared to her wet ones, and their kiss was flavored with the salt of the ocean. "You're amazing to me."

"Coaching you has been good for my game." He pushed wet hair back off her cheeks. "The Pipeline Pro tomorrow will prove it. If I don't fuck it up."

"Don't say such a thing," she said, and gave him a light swat across the chest. Sean wasn't quite in the lead for the championship, since Jack Crews had that all but tied up. But Sean was doing pretty well in the top ten. At least he wouldn't have to worry about making the tour next year. Coming back from his injury had infused him with so much extra determination, he'd been practically unstoppable. "You'll do great."

He kissed her hard at first, then softly enough that it felt like worship. Tears prickled the backs of her eyes. He was always so good to her. Treated her like she was something special in his life. Living up to the way he looked at her made her a better person. She was something more for having him. And she liked to think that she gave him everything she had in return. "I love you, Sean. You know that, right?"

"I know it." He kissed her deep and fast. "I love you too. And I'll love you double as much in a couple years, when I'm a world champion."

She laughed, hard enough that she went lightheaded on the tail of her Pipeline-fueled adrenaline rush. "Promise?"

"Promise."

Read on for an excerpt from
the first book in
Lorelie Brown's Pacific Blue series,

RIDING THE WAVE

Available everywhere print and
e-books are sold

The past ten years of the waves down under hadn't been home to Tanner Wright, not like the gray-green swells of San Sebastian. He'd been raised on these Californian waves. His father taught him to surf on a long board, carve out what he could from the slush and be the man he was born to be. It hadn't been until they were halfway across the world, in a much brighter blue ocean, that he'd realized his dad wasn't half the man *he* was supposed to be.

Now Tanner was home again.

And Hank Wright was dead. Buried six months ago.

Tanner faced the waves of San Sebastian alone. The weight of the breeze pushed over his bare neck, scraping across his skin. His toes burrowed into the damp, cool sand. The sun rose behind him, over the expensive beach houses and stores that still hadn't turned to chains over the decade he'd been gone. The water was the same.

The surfers bobbing past the swells were the same too. Tanner ought to be with them, but he carried a weight. San Sebastian had become an anchor.

In four weeks he'd have to not only surf here, but he'd have to win. Or he'd lose his shot at this year's pro-surf World Championship. The points were too damn close. Jack Crews, pretty boy and part-time model, didn't fucking deserve the title. Tanner would be damned before he'd hand it over because he couldn't man up enough to surf.

A decent set surged, bringing a surfer cruising in with a deep layback before peeling off to the side again. Tanner hardly noticed. A woman popped up on the second wave, taking it all the way in. She didn't push any tricks, didn't grab for the rails or try to make air on a front that probably could have supported her.

She breathed pure grace. The easy acceptance of the moment she'd been handed and the tiny fraction of the giant ocean she rode. Her face turned up toward the still-rising sun, golden light kissing the rounded apples of her cheeks. A smile curved her generous mouth and she kept her eyes closed, apparently enjoying the feeling of floating into shore. The water soaking her ponytail made it look almost black, but he knew otherwise.

He couldn't help but smile as he eased down toward the edge of the water. Cool, foam-topped minisurf licked at his toes.

The woman glided in as far as she could standing on her board, but finally hopped off into knee-deep water when she wouldn't float anymore. She pushed back damp bangs with one hand as she scooped up her board.

Summer's deep grip meant that even a half hour after dawn it was warm enough for her to be wearing only a bikini top and black shorts. The red halter did good things to a figure entirely more curvy and filled out than he remembered.

"You never could spot a good trick, could you?" He couldn't keep the laugh out of his voice. "All you had to do was shift and you'd have had a nice little cutback swish on the end."

Dark gray-green eyes went wide. The nose of her board dropped to the sand with a soft *thump* and a miniature splash. Her sharp words were in direct contradiction to her stunned look. "Swear to God, if you call me a lazy surfer one more time, I may toss you to the sharks."

Avalon Knox had always been a bit of a smart-ass. There was no denying the truth. "It's not my fault you passed up a pro career," Tanner teased.

She gave a wry smile and looked at him out of the corner of her eye. Lifting a hand to her hair, she skimmed loose strands back toward her ponytail. She hadn't had those pert breasts the last time he'd seen her. But then, she'd been at most fourteen years old and he'd been twenty. Looking at his sister's best friend would have gotten him strung up.

"Not everyone wants to go pro." She picked the board up and hitched it under her arm. "C'mon. I'll walk you back to the house."

"I'm not going to the house." The thought felt like scraping the inside of his skin with broken seashells. Tanner had never been able to separate the shitty memories of his father from his happy memories of his childhood home.

"You're not . . ." But her voice faded off. A light pink flush crept across her sternum. She put her board down again, this time setting the tail in the sand and standing it up. One arm curled around it. "You know, we didn't think you were going to be in town for another week or so. If you even made it at all."

The blow wasn't unexpected. He deserved no better. It had been more than nine years since he'd been home. Seeing his sister and his mother in Hawaii every year or flying them out to Australia for his birthday wasn't the same thing. He'd invited Avalon too, but she'd passed every single time.

"I was injured last year. Pulled hamstring, remember?"

"Uh-huh." She scratched idle fingers across the plane of her stomach as she looked out over the water. Tanner looked too. It was safer out there. Out on the water, he knew who he was. A surfer.

On the shore, he remembered he was a surfer who hadn't won a world championship in nine years. Who got injured more often than not. Who wasn't one of the little kids still scrabbling his way up in the rankings.

She side-eyed him again. That was Avalon, poking at dark corners. Always had been. "And what about the five years before that?"

"That . . ." He looked back at her, away from the deep surf that had claimed his whole life and created his father's golden image. "That's none of your damn business, sweetheart."

She flinched visibly, the tendons at the base of her neck popping. Her tongue flicked out over her pink lips. "I see."

"No offense meant, of course."

"Most of the time when someone says 'no offense,' they mean they wanted to hit the max possible offense."

He shrugged. "Take it how you want. But if I'm not discussing it with my mother, I'm sure as hell not discussing it with you."

Avalon wasn't exactly a member of the family, but she was more than a friend too. She'd been twelve when Tanner's mom took Avalon under her wing for mentoring. He'd been eighteen and striking out to hit the pro tour. Skinny little waifs hadn't held his interest compared to the beach bunnies who bounced their way down the sand. Plus he'd known Avalon a long time.

She wasn't the type to keep her mouth shut very well. He could practically see whitewater churning behind those almost gray eyes.

"The whole world wants to know, Tanner," she finally said. "Not just the family."

"You still work for *Surfer*?"

Her narrow shoulders lifted in a shrug. "I never really worked for them. I've sold them some photographs."

"You'd like to though, wouldn't you?" He tugged a pair of sunglasses that dangled by one arm from the pocket of his cargo shorts.

"Don't be an ass." She flicked her ponytail over her shoulder. "Of course I would. But I'm not going to sell out Sage or Eileen to get there."

That was Avalon too. Honest to a fault. "My mom and sister count, but me you'd sell out in a second, wouldn't you?"

The wide, bright grin she flashed him was everything appealing. He had the sudden, strange urge to taste it. Kiss that smile and see if it tasted as sweet as it looked. He could have shaken off the impulse if he wanted to. The years when he hadn't been in control of his own body were long gone, if you didn't count the times when it inconveniently gave out on him.

Avalon Knox . . . she wasn't off-limits. Not for any real reason beyond longtime ties to the family. From the way her gaze flicked over his shoulders now and then, maybe she wouldn't be averse to spending some time together while he was in California.

But then her smile turned out toward the water again. "You've been gone so long, you hardly count."

He laughed off the sudden sting of that blow. It was the hardest part of it all—that no one knew he'd been doing a good thing by staying away. Keeping his dad's secret meant keeping the family harmony. Who the hell was he to break his mother's heart?

And to be honest, there was a little envy there when it came to his sister. Sage still looked on Hank Wright as a god among men. Tanner remembered that feeling. He'd do anything to make sure Sage got to keep it.

Avalon's shoulder bumped into his arm in a friendly nudge. Her skin was still damp, and slightly chilled, but underneath was warm heat that was all her own. "Come back to the house. It'll be water under the bridge. Eileen'll make breakfast— you know it."

His mom put together an awesome spread when she got it into her head that her brood needed feeding. Regret pooled in his gut with something that felt strangely like fear. Even if his dad was gone, the house was still Hank's territory. "I don't think I can. I have a meeting with some WavePro reps."

"The big bucks," she teased.

He shrugged. He'd been lucky to be sponsored by WavePro when they were a tiny clothing line with only three styles of board shorts. The company had been the backbone of his support when he'd cut ties with Hank. Lately things had been strained because Tanner hadn't produced a major win. The San Sebastian Pro would have to be it. "Gotta keep 'em happy."

"Do you like working for them, though? I've got a meeting there this afternoon. Don't know what they want."

"They're businessmen at heart, but they know surfing too. Can't go too wrong."

Her mouth pulled into a firm line, but that quickly eased again into a kissable shape. "What are you doing out here, if you've got important places to be?"

"I got in so late last night, I didn't get a chance to look at the waves." He smiled down at her, testing. The way he'd like to lick the salt from her skin . . . He let it ease into his gaze. She didn't flinch. Her smile tucked deeper, the apples of her cheeks rounding. "I didn't expect to run into you."

The gentle curve of her chest, even before it swelled into her breasts, was something remarkable. He wanted to trace his tongue over it. "Life's full of weird little twists."

"It is." But she really did have to get going. "I'll be by the house this afternoon." Once he worked up the last bit of guts he'd need, but there was no reason to admit that. He'd have to hand over his balls. "Do me a favor?"

Her smile turned flat-out cheeky. The green in her eyes sparked brighter, washing away the gray. She cocked her hip. "Depends. I don't give away favors lightly."

The changes were definitely enjoyable. "Don't tell Mom you saw me."

"Want to surprise her?"

"Something like that." More like he still needed a little bit of time to gather himself before he could see her. The second his mom knew he'd landed in town, she'd be blowing up his phone. He wasn't a big enough asshole to be able to ignore that. After all, he always did everything he could to make up for the fact that he hadn't been home in years. It was hard enough keeping his dad's secret from miles away. He'd missed his family and the places he used to feel comfortable in his own skin. The pain of balancing everyone else's needs and wants and expectations had been the only thing sharp enough to balance the rest.

Eileen's kitchen had always been magic. As a teenager, sitting down at the counter while she set a glass of fresh-pressed juice and a sandwich in front of him . . . it was like having a switch flipped. Truths spilled out of him as easily as floating on the water on a flat day.

He'd only have to hope that being thirty-one and a full-grown man would provide immunity.

Spilling all the dirty details about Hank Wright's secret family on the other side of the world wouldn't help anyone. Hell, the man was dead. Let the truth die with him.